FLIGHT INTO DARKNESS

Alpha handled the jet with unexpected confidence given her claimed lack of experience. Perhaps he shouldn't be surprised. A machine operating another machine had no reason to suffer the nerves of a human pilot.

"Do you still want to know where we're going?" Alpha asked.

Surprised, Thomas said, "Yes."

"A base off the coast of Africa."

"What happens when we get to the base?"

"I find out who's in charge."

"What were Charon's plans?" Thomas asked.

"I'm not sure."

"So what you're telling me," Thomas said, "is that you're carrying out some plan you don't know for a dead man who can't tell you the point of what you're doing."

"Essentially." Her voice had lost all affect.

"Alpha, this is nuts. You *can't* complete the plan."

"Someone at the base may know what to do."

"And if they don't?"

"We need to stop this conversation," she said.

"Humans call that avoidance," Thomas said.

"Humans call it having something more important to deal with."

"Like what?"

"Like we have company," Alpha said. "And they're about to shoot us down."

Baen Books by Catherine Asaro

Sunrise Alley
Alpha

The Ruby Dice (forthcoming)

ALPHA

Catherine Asaro

ALPHA

This is a work of fiction. All the characters and events portrayed in this book are fictional, and any resemblance to real people or incidents is purely coincidental.

Copyright © 2006 by Catherine Asaro

A Baen Book

Baen Publishing Enterprises
P.O. Box 1403
Riverdale, NY 10471
www.baen.com

ISBN 10: 1-4165-5512-9
ISBN 13: 978-1-4165-5512-4

Cover art by Kurt Miller

First Baen paperback printing, December 2007

Distributed by Simon & Schuster
1230 Avenue of the Americas
New York, NY 10020

Library of Congress Cataloging-in-Publication Data:
2006015236

Printed in the United States of America

10 9 8 7 6 5 4 3 2

To my cousins John and Joe
And their families
With love

Acknowledgments

I would like to thank the following readers for their much appreciated input. Their comments have made this a better book. Any mistakes that remain were induced by a space warp that twisted the fabric of the universe in the vicinity of the manuscript.

To Jeri Smith-Ready, Aly Parsons, John Hemry, Bud Sparhawk, Deborah Wheeler, and David Dalrymple, for their excellent insights on the full manuscript; and to Aly's Writing Group for their sharp critiques of scenes: Aly Parsons, Simcha Kuritzky, Connie Warner, Al Carroll, J. G. Huckenpöhler, John Hemry, and Bud Sparhawk.

Special thanks to my much appreciated editor, Toni Weisskopf; to my publisher, Jim Baen; to Marla Ainspan, Hank Davis, Danielle Turner, and all the other fine people at Baen who did such a fine job making this book possible; to my excellent agent, Eleanor Wood, of Spectrum Literary Agency; and to Binnie Braunstein for her enthusiasm and hard work on my behalf.

Heartfelt thanks to the shining lights in my life, my husband, John Cannizzo, and my daughter, Cathy, for their love and support.

Contents

I

A Guest in Virginia

Lieutenant General Thomas Wharington had weathered his share of challenges, but nothing like Alpha. She was an android in Air Force custody, female in appearance, apparent age thirty, though no one knew how far her artificial brain had developed. As human as she appeared, she was a machine—a deadly biomechanical construct.

Thomas directed the Office of Computer Operations, a deliberately vague term for the Machine Intelligence Division of the National Information Agency. Founded twenty years ago, in 2012, the NIA concerned itself with the world mesh, formerly known as the Internet. He also headed the Senate Select Committee for Space Research, which those with the proper clearances knew as the Committee for Space Warfare Research and Development. In his youth, he had been a fighter pilot. He had flown an F-16 jet, later the F-22 Raptor, and now he was spearheading the development of the F-42 for the Air Force. Over the course of his career, he had received the Congressional Medal of Honor, the Distinguished Flying Cross with silver oak leaf cluster, and a Purple Heart. Physically fit and benefiting from medical advances, he looked more than two decades younger than his age of seventy-two.

Alpha was Thomas's primary tie to Charon, the megalomaniacal fanatic who had created her. Before his death, Charon had controlled a shadowy criminal empire. The Pentagon knew he had intended to build an army for rent to the highest bidder—but an army of *what*? Constructs, like Alpha? Something else? Had he set in motion some master plan before his death? No one knew. They had too few details, and Thomas feared they were running out of time.

The secrets remained locked within Alpha.

"I can't do it," Thomas repeated.

"You'll be fine." His daughter handed him a bulging shoulder bag decorated with puppies.

Thomas wasn't the type to quail in a desperate situation, but this morning he was in over his head. They were standing in the entrance foyer of the house that belonged to his daughter, Leila Wharington Harrows, and her husband, Karl. Looking sharp in a gold silk suit, with her blond hair swept up into a roll, Leila normally presented a cool face to the world. Right now, though, her hair was escaping its roll and curling in disarray around her face.

"So where is that husband of yours when you need help?" Thomas asked.

"Dad, don't get mad. Karl is coming home early from his conference." Leila pushed the bag back into his hand. "I'm really sorry. I had a nanny, but she got sick. And I couldn't get out of the trip. The partners say I'm not pulling my weight at the firm." Anger edged her voice. "If we didn't need the money, I'd quit this damn job."

Thomas liked less and less what he had heard about the law firm where she worked. "Leila, if you need money—"

She cut him off before he could offer. "We can manage."

He understood she wanted to do it on her own. But he wished he could ease the strain of her life. He wondered what it said about him, that he felt more comfortable offering money than looking after his granddaughter for a few days.

"Well." He spoke awkwardly. "I guess I can manage."

"You're a gem." Leila smiled, perhaps too brightly, but with warmth. "Jamie would rather stay with her Grandpa anyway. She loves spending time with you."

"The feeling is mutual. I just don't know how I can take care of a three-year-old for a week." He could probably find babysitters while he worked, but what would he do with her when he was home? Three-year-old girls were a mystery to him, even after having been the father of one. That had been thirty years ago, during his days as a pilot, and he had been more comfortable in the cockpit of an F-16 than a nursery.

A door upstairs creaked, and footsteps padded on the stairs. As Thomas looked up, a small girl with large blue eyes and gold curls came into view. She held a big stuffed kitten in her arms.

Thomas smiled. "Hello, Jamie."

His granddaughter's angelic face brightened. She ran down the steps and trotted over to him, holding up her toy. "See my kitty, Grampy? Her name is Soupy."

Thomas felt his face doing that thing again, turning soft. He awkwardly patted her toy. "She's a fine kitty."

Jamie dimpled at him, and he felt as if he was turning into putty. She looked so much like Leila at that age. He sighed and picked her up, kitten and all.

To Leila, he said, "I'll do my best."

The NIA was in Maryland. Even more shadowy than its precursors in the intelligence community, the agency was on almost equal footing with the CIA in the National Security Council. Thomas could have fit two of his previous offices in his present one and had room to spare. Currently, a screen installed on his desk was displaying a report from the Links Division, which analyzed mesh traffic for patterns that might warrant investigation. It seemed an arcane discipline to Thomas, half analysis and half intuition, but Links had a good record of success in tracking criminal activities through the mesh.

Basically, the report advised the NIA to monitor the site for a hardware store. They suspected it sold industrial espionage as well as widgets, specifically, that it employed agents from Charon's black market operations. Their purpose: to spy on an institute whose maintenance department ordered from the store. The Department of Defense had contracts with the institute in the development of artificial intelligence, or AI, one of Charon's specialties.

A buzz came from the comm on Thomas's desk. He tapped its *receive* panel. "Wharington here."

A man's voice came out of the comm. "General, this is Major Edwards. I'm on my way to the base. Would you like to grab a pizza for lunch? It might soften our guest's mood."

"Very well, Major. I'll meet you out front." Thomas knew what "guest" Edwards meant: Alpha, their captive android. For reasons that weren't clear, she would talk only to Thomas, when she talked at all. Questioning an android was an exercise in frustration; she didn't react to known techniques. Yet to Thomas, she seemed human. He couldn't make himself authorize the mech-techs to take her apart and analyze the filaments that constituted her brain. Eventually they might have to resort to such measures, but for now they were trying less drastic forms of interrogation.

He left notes for his appointments with his second in command, Brigadier General Carl Jackson Matheson, or just "C.J." Thomas could speak with Senator Bartley tomorrow morning and reschedule today's staff meeting for tomorrow afternoon. His housekeeper, Lattie, had agreed to look after Jamie until he came home. He would miss his appointment at the barber, though. He supposed he should be glad he still had a full head of hair. Its grey color seemed to delight Jamie. She surprised him. He had expected to fumble for words around her, but this morning he had greatly enjoyed their breakfast conversation.

Thomas shut down and locked his console and picked up his briefcase. Then he headed out for "lunch." He wished they really were going for pizza. Perhaps they could pick one up on the way, a large pepperoni dripping with cheese and grease. Unfortunately, he would spend the entire meal feeling guilty and recalling his doctor's admonitions on the dangers of his former eating habits. Yes, it could shorten his life if he ate what he wanted, but at least he would die a contented, well-fed man. He had no wish to have another heart attack, and his cholesterol levels were finally normal, but damned if his reformed eating habits weren't a bore.

"Out front," where he was meeting Edwards, was a euphemism for an underground lot with NIA hover cars and trucks. Had Edwards contacted him from within the NIA, he would probably have been more forthcoming about their plans, a visit to the safe house where the Air Force was holding Alpha. But he had called from his car as he drove through suburban Maryland, an area riddled with mech-tech types who loved to ride the wireless waves and explore any signals they could untangle. NIA signals were encrypted, but with all the mesh bandits out there nowadays, no security was certain.

Thomas took an elevator that operated only with a secured code. It listed no floors; the only clues it was doing anything were the hum of the cable and a few flashes of light on its panel. The lights stilled as the hum faded into silence. The silver doors snapped open and Thomas walked into a cavernous garage. Cars and trucks were parked in separate sections, and pillars stood at intervals, supporting a high ceiling. The columns glimmered with holo-displays of innocuous meadows and mountains.

He went to the nearest column and ran his finger across a bar at waist height. The meadow disappeared, replaced by a wash of blue, and a light played across his face, analyzing his retinal patterns. A message appeared on the screen: *Proceed to station four.* At the same time, the display on a distant pillar changed to blue, specifying "station four." He walked over to the new column and waited. The garage was silent, with a tang of motor oil.

An engine growled, and he turned to see a hover car floating down a lane delineated by holo-pillars. The car had a generic look, except for its dark gold color, a bit flashy for the military, but appropriate for a general. Its unexceptional appearance served as camouflage; it was actually a Hover-Shadow 16, the latest model in a line of armored vehicles with "a few extras," including machine guns and an AI brain. The digital paint used on its exterior could mimic any design programmed into the car, and its shape drew on technology used for stealth fighters. Thomas appreciated the Hover-Shadows; riding in one reminded him of his days as a pilot.

The car stopped a few yards away and settled onto the concrete, remarkably quiet given its turbo fans and powerful engines. Robert Edwards got out from the driver's side. A man of medium height with light brown hair, he would blend into any crowd, except for his Air Force uniform. Just to look at him, most people wouldn't guess he had played offensive tackle at the University of Missouri or that he had defied his jock image by majoring in physics. Thomas enjoyed conversing with Edwards, who could go with ease from predicting which teams would make the Super Bowl to discussing galactic formation. He was a steady officer, one of Thomas's handpicked aides.

"Good to see you, Bob," Thomas said.

"Thank you, sir." Edwards opened the back door.

Thomas slid into the car and swung his briefcase onto the seat. Edwards was also trained in escape and evasion, but Thomas didn't expect trouble. Charon had died several

weeks ago. However, Thomas's boss, General Chang, continued to take precautions. The "safe house" where they
had Alpha was in fact a fully secured installation.

As the car hummed out of the garage, Edwards said,
"Would you care for music? I have that Debussy record-
ing you like."

"Thanks, but no. I have to work." Thomas spoke
absently as he took a foot-long pencil tube out of his briefcase, then set the case on his lap in a makeshift table. He
slid a glimmering roll out of the tube, his laptop film.
Then he unrolled the film on his briefcase and went to
work.

His files held a wealth of detail. Biomechanical research
had diverged into two paths: robots developed for specific purposes, with designs that optimized their
performance; and androids intended to follow human
appearance and behavior. Collectively, robots and
androids were called *formas*. Thomas knew the AI side
of the field best; he had majored in computer science at
the Air Force Academy and earned a doctorate in AI from
MIT. He read widely, especially the work of Kurzweil,
McCarthy, Minsky, and more recently, Dalrymple. Groups
such as theirs deserved the fame. It aggravated him that
a criminal like Charon had achieved more success. Then
again, "success" was relative. Charon's work had drawn
the attention of the NIA because he had trespassed against
the nation's interest, not to mention the bounds of human
decency.

Thomas scanned the history of Charon, a man who had
begun life as Willy Brand. By the time he was seven, Willy
had been living on the streets. He might have died there
if not for one person: Linden Polk. A scholar and a teacher,

Polk was known for his innovations with android skeletons. He was also known for his dedication to outreach for disturbed youth, which was how he met Willy. Wild and unrepentantly criminal, the eight-year-old boy had a life no one doubted would land him in prison. But Polk recognized a rare genius within him. With mentoring, Willy straightened out, went to school, and eventually earned a doctorate in biomechanical engineering, after which he joined Polk's research group.

Willy had always been odd, and he never truly respected the law, but he stayed out of trouble. Then Polk died—and Willy lost his lifeline. His already troubled mind crumbled. In a heartbreaking act of denial, he imaged Polk's brain, built an android, and copied Polk's neural patterns into its matrix. But the project failed. He couldn't bring back his father figure, the one person he had ever loved—and his grief pushed him over the edge.

Willy reinvented himself as Charon, an enigmatic mogul who set up corporations to develop his bizarre but lucrative ideas. He stayed in the background of his businesses and eventually hid his involvement altogether. He became the wealthiest nonexistent person alive.

Charon wasn't the first fanatic who craved an inhuman army that would obey his commands without question. Unlike his predecessors, however, he had both the financial resources and the intellect to make his obsession into reality. Twisted by loneliness, he also created Alpha: an immortal mercenary with no free will; an AI dedicated to optimizing his financial empire; and a forma sex goddess. Obedience, wealth, and sex: she gave him everything he craved.

Charon also copied himself. His body was dying from

a lifetime of misuse, so he became an android. Nor was he satisfied with one version of himself. He committed the ultimate identity theft. When a man named Turner Pascal died in a car accident, Charon imaged Pascal's neural patterns, rebuilt the body with a filament brain, gave it Pascal's patterns—and then downloaded a copy of his own mind into Pascal. It was the perfect disguise; he stole Pascal's face, mind, personality, and body. He considered Pascal inferior and never doubted he could control the mind of his rebuilt man, a hotel bellboy who had barely finished high school.

That arrogance had been Charon's downfall.

Pascal wrested back control of his mind and escaped from Charon. He sought help from Samantha "Sam" Bryton, one of the world's leading AI architects. Sam. She was like a daughter to Thomas. Charon sent Alpha after them, but she grabbed Sam and Thomas instead of Sam and Turner. The Air Force sent in operatives—and by the time it was over, Charon was dead.

Thomas gazed out the window. Vehicles moved smoothly through Washington, D.C., which only a few decades ago had earned the dubious honor of being named the city with the worst traffic in the country. Now traffic grids controlled the flow and minimized congestion. Nearly half the vehicles were hover cars, and little trace remained of the smog Thomas remembered from his youth. In the south, across the Potomac, the silver spindles of a new federal center pierced the sky, tall and thin, sparkling in the chill sunlight. Thomas had never realized how much he liked living here until he had come so close to dying as Charon's hostage.

Major Edwards soon crossed the river and entered

Virginia. As they reached more rural areas, the traffic petered out. Large houses set back from the road were surrounded by lawns or tangled woods. The landscape gradually buckled into the Appalachian Mountains, with forests of pine, hemlock, wild cherry, poplar, and white oak. In a secluded valley, Edwards stopped at a guard booth on the road. The badges he and Thomas wore sent signals to a console within the booth. In the past, the guard would have leaned out to touch their badges; nowadays they never rolled down the windows. It added an extra layer of protection, but it meant security also required extra identification, from the passengers and from the car. Beetle-bots hummed in the air, ready to accompany them and monitor their progress.

The guard motioned them through, and an invisible barrier hummed as they crossed the perimeter. About half a mile farther along, they came to the safe house amid well-tended lawns and groves of trees. The "house" resembled a hospital, but its old-fashioned architecture also evoked a cathedral. The grounds sloped through scattered pines and trees with yellow, green, and red leaves. Paths bordered by azalea bushes curved around sculptures that swooped in arcs of bronzed metal.

Edwards pulled into a carport shaded by trellises with leafless vines. As he and Thomas walked to the front door, a chill wind blew across them, presaging the winter. The genteel feel of the place made it seem as if they were visiting friends rather than a prisoner who was potentially one of humanity's most dangerous creations.

Two "orderlies" were waiting inside, burly men who had more martial arts than medical training. Each wore a staser on his belt, a stun gun that could knock out a large adult. They accompanied Thomas and Edwards down wide halls with gold carpets and artwork on the walls, and through several security gates. Finally they reached a normal door, except Thomas knew its attractive wood paneling hid a steel portal half a foot thick.

The room beyond was pleasant, with a sofa and armchairs in pale green. Paintings of pastoral scenes graced the ivory walls, and a blue quilt covered the bed. The room had no windows, but plenty of light came from an overhead fixture and lamps with stained glass shades in the corners.

A woman was waiting for them.

She stood across the room with her back to the wall, watching Thomas with the feral wariness of a trapped animal. Six feet tall, with another two inches from her heels, she matched his height. Her black leather pants fit her snugly, and her red blouse did nothing to disguise her well-proportioned figure or the definition of her muscles. Black hair was tousled around her shoulders, and her dark eyes slanted upward. She exuded a sense of coiled energy, as if she might explode any moment. The biomech surgeons claimed her android body had three or four times the strength and speed of a human being. Her internal microfusion reactor supplied energy. It disturbed Thomas for many reasons, not only because Charon's technology surpassed the military's work, but also because she looked so *human*.

So female.

"Good afternoon, Ms. Alpha," Thomas said.

She spoke in a dusky voice. "I am not 'Ms.' anything."

He went farther into the room, but he halted a few yards away from her, so she wouldn't feel pressured.

Edwards and the orderlies stayed. Even knowing Alpha was a weapon, Thomas felt strange that his CO assigned him three guards as protection against one attractive young woman. Her first day here, Alpha had tried to fight her way out. She hadn't come close to succeeding, but she had injured several orderlies.

"I'm not going to talk to your flunkies," Alpha said.

"Then talk to me," Thomas said.

She regarded him impassively. This was the second time he had met with her at the safe house. The first time she had interacted with him more than with anyone else, but she still hadn't said much. He was curious as to why he succeeded even a small amount where others failed. It also disconcerted him, for he had no idea what conclusions she was making about him.

Thomas indicated the sofa. "Would you like to sit?"

"No." She narrowed her gaze. "So you're the boss."

She made it a statement rather than a question. It wasn't completely true; he was director of one of the two divisions that comprised the NIA, but that didn't put him in charge of this safe house. General Chang, the Deputy Director of Defense Intelligence, had assigned that duty elsewhere. But Alpha was programmed to respond to authority, and Thomas *was* overseeing the work with her. If that convinced her to respond, he would use it to full advantage.

He said only, "That's right."

"Where is Charon?"

"Dead." Thomas wanted to offer sympathy. He quashed the urge, knowing it was inappropriate here. He also wasn't certain how a machine would response to compassion. Yet still he felt it.

"He's not dead," Alpha said.

"You saw him die."

She crossed her arms, which could have looked defensive but instead suggested a vulnerability he doubted she had intended. "The android called Turner Pascal carries Charon's mind within his matrix."

"Pascal says he isn't an android."

Alpha waved her hand. "The human Pascal died."

Thomas suspected it would take the Supreme Court to figure out the tangled definitions of humanity posed by Pascal. "Either way, he isn't Charon."

"Charon downloaded his brain into Pascal."

"Pascal deleted it."

She snorted. "If Pascal is human, how would he 'delete' another mind within his own?"

She had a point. "Regardless. He isn't Charon."

"How do you know?"

"Doctor Bryton verified it."

Alpha cocked an eyebrow in a perfect imitation of skepticism. "Samantha Bryton? She would believe anything Pascal told her."

"Why?" he asked, intrigued.

"Love has no judgment." Alpha laughed without humor. "She's infatuated with a forma."

Pascal's relationship with Sam bothered Thomas a great deal, but it wasn't something he would discuss with Alpha. Regardless, he would never have defined Sam's cautious, cynical view of romance as infatuation.

"Pascal thinks he is human," Thomas said.

"He's more than half biomech."

"He isn't the first person to receive biomech prosthetics."

She uncrossed her arms and put one hand on her hip. "Like his *brain?* He's a frigging AI, Wharington."

He almost smiled. Had Charon programmed her to cuss? It didn't serve any functional purpose. Thomas wanted her to have developed it on her own, for that would mean she could evolve independently of Charon's designs.

"Why does Pascal bother you?" he asked.

Her fist clenched on her hip. "He doesn't conform to specifications."

"You mean he has free will."

"That is an irrelevant comment."

"Why? Because Charon denied you that freedom?"

At the mention of Charon, her face lost all sign of emotion. It chilled him. He was aware of his guards watching, but he refrained from glancing at them or doing anything that might dissuade her from talking. After about a minute or so, though, he gave up trying to wait her out. Silence often provoked humans to speak, but apparently she could stay in whatever state she wanted, for as long as she wanted, with no visible effort or unease.

Thomas broke the standoff by sitting in an armchair across from the sofa, facing her. He settled back, stretched his legs under the coffee table, and considered Alpha.

"If Charon is gone," he asked, "who is your boss?"

She continued to stand with her back to the wall. He tried to see some chink in her expression, some flaw in her too-perfect skin, some indication she felt stress, tension, unease, anger, anything. He found none.

When she didn't respond, he tried another approach. "Alpha, do you want free will?"

"What?" She looked as if he had put an indecipherable command into her system.

"Do you wish to make your own decisions?"

"No."

He had expected her to say yes, *wanted* her to say yes. But he was reacting as he would to a person, and she was a machine designed to lack free will. She was trapped within her programming as thoroughly as she was imprisoned at this safe house, and it bothered him far more than it should.

"If you don't make decisions yourself," he said, "who will?"

"Charon," she said.

"Charon is dead."

Silence.

"If I'm the boss," Thomas said, "you should answer to me."

"You aren't my boss."

"Then who is?"

"Charon."

He felt as if he were caught in a programming loop that kept going around and around the same section of code. "Charon is dead."

She hesitated just a moment, but for an AI it was a long time. Then she said, "You may be a compelling specimen, General, but I wasn't made for you."

Well, hell. Apparently androids could be just as blunt as young people these days when it came to their private lives. He cleared his throat. "I didn't have that in mind." He almost said he had come to debrief her, then decided that wasn't the best choice of words. So instead he added, "I need you to answer some questions."

Her expression turned stony. The effect was almost convincing, but after her total lack of affect a moment before, he didn't believe it. Unexpectedly, though, she didn't refuse to speak.

"What questions?" she asked.

"Charon has a base in Tibet."

She gave him a decidedly unimpressed stare. "No. One of his corporations has a research facility in Tibet."

Thomas met her skeptical look with one of his own. "Hidden at the top of the Himalayas? I don't think so."

She stepped toward him. "Charon is a genius. Of course people struggle to understand him. They lack his intelligence."

"Did he program you to say that about him?"

"Yes."

That figured. Charon had been some piece of work. "He had great gifts," Thomas acknowledged. "But his sickness constrained him."

She folded her arms as if she were protecting herself. "People always call the brilliant minds unbalanced."

Thomas wondered if she had heard all this from Charon. Her ideas sounded oddly dated. "Alpha, that's a myth. Geniuses are no more likely to be mentally disturbed than anyone else. Charon was a sociopath and he had paranoid schizophrenia. It probably limited his work by making it harder for him to plan or to judge the feasibility of his projects."

Her lips curved in a deadly smile. "He created me. If that isn't genius, nothing is."

When she looked like that, wild and fierce, her dark hair disarrayed, her eyes burning and untamed, he was tempted to agree. He suppressed the thought, thrown off balance. He had to remember she was a machine.

"Did he program you to say that, too?" Thomas asked.

"No."

He smiled slightly. "What makes you a work of genius?"

Her voice turned husky. "Maybe someday I'll let you find out."

He thought of pretending she had no effect on him, but he didn't try. She could interpret emotional cues, gestures, even changes in posture. It was a tool AIs used in learning to simulate emotions. Unfortunately, it also made them adept at reading people, better even than many humans. If he put on a front, she might figure out he wanted to hide and use that knowledge in their battle of words.

Right now, they were battling with silence. He tried to read her expressions. Sometimes she simulated emotions well, but other times, she either couldn't or wouldn't. To be considered sentient, she would have to pass modern forms of the Turing test, which included the portrayal of emotions. Over the years, the tests had become increasingly demanding, but they all boiled down to one idea: if a person communicated with a hidden machine and a hidden human—and couldn't tell them apart—the machine had intelligence.

Decades ago, people had expected that if a computer bested a human chess master, the machine would qualify as intelligent. Yet when the computer Deep Blue beat Gary Kasparov, the world champion, few people considered it truly intelligent; it simply had, for the time, good enough computational ability. Nowadays mesh systems routinely trounced champions, to the point where human masters were seeking neural implants to provide extra computational power for their own brains. Thomas couldn't imagine what that would do to the game at a competitive level. What defined machine intelligence then?

Older Turing tests had relied on sentences typed at terminals, with the typists hidden. The most modern test, the visual Turing, required an android to be indistinguishable from a person. Some experts believed human brains were wired to process more emotional input than an EI matrix could handle. They considered the visual test impossible to pass. Although Thomas didn't agree, it didn't surprise him that only a handful of machine intelligences existed. Alpha passed the visual Turing only if her interactions involved tangible subjects. When pushed to more complex questions of emotion, philosophy, or conscience, she shut down.

While Thomas was thinking, Alpha studied him. After a while, she stalked over, sleek and deadly in her black leather. The orderlies stepped closer, but he waved them off, keeping his gaze on Alpha. She halted by the couch, on the other side of the coffee table, as tense as a wildcat ready to attack.

"You can't control me," she said. Her voice made him think of aged whiskey.

"But you have no free will," Thomas said. "And Charon is dead."

"I have orders."

It was the first time she had revealed she might be operating according to a preset plan. "From Charon?"

"That's right." She had gone deadpan again. Every time Charon came up, she ceased showing emotion. Why? In a person, he might have suspected some sort of trauma associated with Charon, but with Alpha he couldn't say. Although she presented an invulnerable front, something about her made him question that impression. It wasn't anything he could pin down, just a gut-level instinct on his part.

"What orders did he give?" Thomas asked.

"Return to him." She sat on the couch, poised on the edge like a wild animal ready to bolt. "If I can't, then protect myself."

"How? And against what?"

"Do you really think I would tell you?"

"With you, I never know," Thomas admitted. She had already said more to him today than she had to everyone else combined.

Unexpectedly, she said, "I like it that way."

"*Can* you like something?" His scientific curiosity jumped in. "Most people think an AI doesn't truly feel emotion."

"Here's an emotion for you." Alpha looked around at the guards and her room. "I don't like being cooped up here."

"Where would you like to be?" Maybe she would bargain.

"Outside."

"Why? Aren't you just simulating unease?"

She smiled with an edge. "You think you're clever, implying my request is illogical. You humans love stories about people outwitting machines by virtue of your purportedly greater creativity, blah, blah, blah. But you see, we read all your books. You couldn't come close to mastering the breadth of human knowledge if you worked on it your entire life, but it takes me only weeks to absorb, process, and analyze the contents of an entire library. I know all the scenarios and supposed solutions humankind has come up with in your ongoing paranoia about the intelligences you've created. You try to outthink us, but ultimately you fail."

Thomas leaned forward. "Yet you miss the most obvious flaw of your analysis."

She raised an eyebrow. "Do tell."

"We are becoming you." He watched her closely. "Do you really believe humanity would settle for being second-class citizens to our own creations? We will incorporate your advantages within ourselves while retaining that which makes us human."

She waved her hand in dismissal. "It's all semantics. Whether you choose to call yourselves formas or human won't alter the facts. Biomech changes you, whether you put it in a robot or your own brain." Her eyes glinted. "Who knows, perhaps it will overwrite what 'makes you human.' Corrupt your oh-so-corruptible selves."

Thomas gave a rueful grimace. "Maybe it will."

She seemed satisfied with his response. "You want to bargain with me. Fine. Take me for a ride outside and I'll tell you what orders Charon left me."

"You know I can't do that. You might escape."

"True. Do it anyway."

Thomas had to give her points for audacity. "Why?"

Her expression went completely flat. "Because you want to know what Charon ordered me to do."

Thomas wondered if she knew the unsettling effect it had on him when she turned off her emotional responses. At times he thought she used her human qualities as a weapon, banking on his difficulty in separating her sexualized appearance from her biomech nature. Yet if she had realized how she affected him, why suppress it? She "lost" her emotions when she spoke about Charon.

"No matter what orders he gave you," Thomas said, "I won't take you out of here."

"Your loss."

He smiled dryly. "Actually, it would be that if you escaped."

To his surprise, she laughed, a low, sensual rumble. "And what a loss that would be. For you."

Good Lord. A laugh like that could make a man lose all sense of reason. "You don't lack for self-confidence." After a pause, he added, "Or at least the simulation of it." He kept forgetting that.

Her smile vanished. "Make no mistake, General. More is at stake than my freedom."

"Such as?"

She met his gaze. "Human ascendancy on this planet."

II

A Word Too Many

A night heavy with drizzle had settled over the house in Chevy Chase by the time Thomas arrived home. He unlocked the front door and stepped into the foyer. Relief settled over him and . . . something else. A sense of homecoming? He usually returned to a dark house. Tonight lights glowed in the front room, and he remembered with a sharp pang the days before his wife, Janice, had passed away. All those evenings he had come home to a house full of light, voices, laughter. These past four years, since her death, he had adapted to his solitude, but he missed that time. His three children were grown and Janice was resting in the cemetery, but for a few days he had warmth back, and he discovered that it meant the world to him.

The spacious living room lay straight ahead, the kitchen was to his left, and the hallway on his right went to the family room. The parquetry floors in his house gleamed, and the throw rugs were clean and fluffed. The shades were drawn against the night. It was all fresh and tidy. And empty.

He heard voices, though, a child and a woman. He headed down the hall toward the family room, past the holoscapes of beaches that glowed on the walls, shedding blue and green light as if he were submerged in the ocean.

"Hello?" he called.

"Grampy!" The young voice came with a squeal of delight. A small figure dashed into the hallway and cut a beeline toward him. She was wearing a pink jumpsuit smudged with paint, and her yellow curls flew about her face.

Thomas crouched down so his granddaughter could hurl herself into his embrace. She put her small arms around his neck and hugged him hard. Standing up with her in his arms, he inhaled the scent of fingerpaint and childhood, and savored the joy that came with her.

"Evening, General," a voice said.

Thomas peered around Jamie to see a woman a few paces away. With her plump figure and graying hair, Lattie Douglas looked more like someone's favorite aunt than his housekeeper. It flustered him to realize she had seen him acting sentimental.

He nodded stiffly. "Good evening."

Lattie chuckled. "It's no crime to hug your granddaughter."

Thomas knew he shouldn't feel self-conscious, but he had always been restrained in expressing affection. At the same time, he didn't want Jamie to think she wasn't welcome in his house. His heart attack last year had made him painfully aware of how transient life could be. He could have died with so much left unsaid to the people he loved. Since then, he had tried to be more open with his family.

He bounced Jamie in his arms. "You're an A-one sight to come home to." Not brilliant wording, but perhaps it would do.

She blushed pink and hid her head against his shoulder.

Thomas looked over her head at Lattie. "Thank you for staying. It would have been difficult to bring her with me to the base."

"It wasn't any trouble." With a wry smile, she added, "Maybe you should take her to your war councils. She would tell everyone to be friends. Might do you all good."

Jamie pulled her head back to regard him, and Thomas smiled at her. "All friends?"

"Everybody, Grampy." She put her arms around his neck and tilted her head against his. "Mommy says you make us safe."

Thomas felt his insides melting. He had been the same way with her mother when Leila had been this age. "Always, Moppet."

Lattie came over and patted Jamie on the arm. "Be good now." She nodded briskly to Thomas. "I'll be saying good night, then."

"You're sure you can't come tomorrow?" he asked.

"Sorry, General." She seemed genuinely regretful. "She's a pleasure, and if I'd had a little more notice, I could have rearranged things. But I can't drop my other clients."

"I understand."

"I could come later, around three, if that would help."

Relief washed over him. "Yes, that would be good."

"Well. That's settled." She beamed at Jamie, and the girl let go of Thomas long enough to hug Lattie. The housekeeper gave her a kiss and then bustled off, waving at Thomas as she went down the hall.

When they were alone, Thomas stood holding Jamie, at a loss. He wasn't certain what to do, but she seemed content, so perhaps he was managing all right.

"Are you hungry?" he asked.

"Lattie made macaroni 'n' cheese." Concern showed in her large eyes. "You missed it. You need to eat, Grampy."

"I did." He had managed a sandwich between meetings. He set her down, but she looked disappointed, so he offered his hand. She put her small one in his large grip with a trust that bemused him. He couldn't remember being so flustered by his children. Janice had always been there, though, to take care of them. He didn't recall any time like this, when it had just been him and a toddler.

Jamie regarded him with an expectant gaze. So he asked, "What shall we do?"

"We could play with my dolls," she offered.

"I don't think I would be very good at that."

"I know!" Jamie dropped his hand and dashed toward the living room. She spun around and ran back to him. "Play chase."

Laughing, Thomas caught her. "I don't have your energy."

"Let's watch the kitty holo."

He hadn't even known he had holovids of cats. "Did Lattie bring it over?"

"No. I found it." She beamed with the unrestrained pleasure of a three-year-old. "I made it go, too. Lattie couldn't."

"You set up the holoplayer?" Thomas had trouble himself figuring out the blasted thing.

"It's easy." She pulled him into the family room. Her paints were on the table, but someone had put them away and closed up the box. Jamie's attention was on the entertainment center on the far wall, all glossy screens and glowing lights. She drew him over and pushed a blue panel at about her height. The screen above it came to life in a wash of blue.

"Wait a minute." Thomas wasn't sure what she had done. "Did Lattie show you how to work this thing?"

"No." She regarded him patiently. "I show Lattie."

"How did you know?" He had only had this set up for a few weeks.

"Playing." She pressed another panel and a swirl of speckled gold and black lines appeared on the screen. It resembled the op art kids used to draw when he was a boy, with lines so close together, they shimmered. This was a hologram, the template used to project a holographic image. Decades ago, holos had been static because of the difficulty in producing holograms fast enough to portray motion, but nowadays, holo-movies were commonplace. A three-dimensional image appeared in front of the screen, a stylized view of the Pentagon in silhouette.

"Jamie! That's my work file." Thomas poked the blue panel, but the Pentagon stayed. Flustered, he jabbed another panel. The holovid continued, the symbol fading into the image of a jet fighter soaring through the air, an F-14 Tomcat from the twentieth century. The reproduction was so well done that he found himself extending his hand to touch the jet. His fingers went through the image.

"How did you find this?" he asked.

"I looked lots," Jamie explained. "See?" She pointed to the aircraft carrier in the water beneath the Tomcat. "It says 'kitty.' "

Thomas squinted at the image. A glowing caption labeled the carrier as the *Kitty Hawk*.

"Cats don't like birds," Jamie told him. "They eat them."

Thomas smiled at his granddaughter. "Did Lattie tell you what that said?"

"I read it."

That couldn't be right. "But you're only three."

She held up four fingers. "And four months."

"Good Lord." He indicated the screen. "Can you turn it off?"

Her smile faded. "You don't like the kitty-bird?"

"I like it a lot. But you shouldn't play with my files." The report contained nothing classified, or he wouldn't have brought it home, but the footage of wars in the Middle East might upset her.

"Mommy says to share toys," Jamie admonished.

"Not this one, Moppet. It's from your grandpa's work."

"Oh." With obvious disappointment, she pressed more panels. The holos faded and the screen went dark.

Thomas took her hand. "Come sit with me."

Her face brightened. "'Kay."

He was pretty certain that meant "okay." He took her to a couch along the wall. The room was agreeable and pristine, with its oak paneling, ivory rug, and gold furniture, but it seemed strangely sterile. He hadn't noticed before. His family room no longer had a sense of being lived in the way it had when his wife and children had filled the place with noise and mess and sparkle.

They sat together on the couch and Jamie snuggled against him, oblivious to the fact that most of the Air Force thought of him as an iron man.

"Will Mommy come home tonight?" Jamie asked.

"Not tonight." Thomas awkwardly put his arm around her. His uniform crinkled, and he took care not to let the ribbons on his chest catch her clothes or jab her. She closed her eyes and settled against him as if that were perfectly natural.

He wondered about her learning ability. Perhaps the *Kitty Hawk* thing had been a fluke. "Jamie?"

"Hmm?"

"Can you count?"

She yawned. "One, two, three, four." Opening her eyes, she looked up at him. "It would take infinity time to reach a thousand."

"That long, huh?"

She nodded solemnly. "Even longer."

"Do you know what infinity means?"

"Big number."

"How big?"

She held out her arms. "Bigger than the biggest anything."

Her ability to converse surprised him. She sounded older than three. Then again, he had no experiences with three-year-olds except his own children, and that was decades ago.

"How high can you count?" Jamie asked.

"Higher than a thousand."

Her eyes became wide. "Really?"

He grinned. "Really."

"You're smart, Grampy."

"Why, thank you."

Her look turned cagey, but with such innocence, he wanted to laugh. "'Kay, Grampy. What is four times six?"

That she even knew about "times" startled him. "What do you think, Moppet?"

"Twenty-four!" Her smile was sunlight glancing off a lake.

Good Lord. She could multiply. "What else can you do?"

"I like fractions."

"You do?"

She nodded vigorously, her curls bouncing. "One half plus one half equals one."

"That's right." He ruffled her hair. "Jamie, have your parents ever had you tested?"

"Tested?"

"Did they ever take you to someone who asked you questions about math and words?"

"No."

"They should." He pulled her into his lap. "Lovely, brilliant, and charming. You're going to break hearts when you get older."

"Never, Grampy!" She looked contrite. "I already broke the lamp when I jumped on the couch. Daddy was mad."

"We'll just make sure no lamps are around."

Jamie yawned again. "Can we watch a holovid?"

"I think you need to go to sleep, young lady."

"But you just come home."

"I'll be here tomorrow." Thomas stood up, lifting her

in his arms. "Come on, Einstein. You need your rest."

He expected her to protest more, but she just leaned her head on his shoulder. He suspected he had let her stay up past her bedtime. As he carried her to the guest room Lattie had prepared, Thomas pondered his granddaughter. He didn't know enough about childhood development to judge if she really was precocious or his impressions were just grandfatherly pride. Had Leila or the boys known multiplication and fractions at that age? He had been gone so much back then. He regretted it more now than he would have ever guessed in the fiery days of his youth.

His memories of his own childhood weren't much help, either. As a boy, he had never been able to concentrate. He had managed to get by in school because he found the work easy, but he had been forever bedeviling his teachers with his inability to sit still. It wasn't until high school that a counselor realized he had ADHD, or attention deficit hyperactivity disorder. She called him "twice exceptional"; all he knew was that he finally had a name for his restlessness. His parents helped him manage the ADHD with changes in his diet rather than medication, but for him, going into the military had been the real answer. The structure, the routine, and the order had helped him take control of his life.

As an adult, Thomas had partially grown out of the ADHD and learned to control the rest. Neither Leila nor his oldest child, Thomas Jr., had shown any sign of it. Fletcher, his younger son, had inherited the restless Wharington bug, but they caught it early. With a close watch on his diet and school counselors who understood his needs, Fletcher had managed far better than his father.

It was too soon to tell with Jamie, but he sincerely hoped she inherited only the "exceptional" part of her grandpa's line without his learning disability.

He tucked the drowsy child into bed and read *Cinderella* until she nodded off hugging her stuffed cat. Watching her sleep, he realized he was glad Leila had needed his help. It was worth his clumsy uncertainty with children to have this time with Jamie. He liked his work, but these moments were what made life worthwhile.

The voice of C.J. Matheson came over the comm on Thomas's desk. "Senator Bartley on line one."

"Got it." Thomas switched channels, then sat back in his leather chair and swiveled to face the window, which looked over the gleaming buildings and quiet streets of the NIA.

An expansive voice with a Southern drawl came out of the mesh. "Good morning, Thomas."

Thomas swiveled back to his desk. "You're up early."

"Damn straight," the senator said. "We have to talk about your guest."

Alpha, again. Bartley was on the Committee for Space Warfare Research and Development, which technically had nothing to do with Alpha. But they oversaw work that included the development of formas with Evolving Intelligences, or EI brains. The term EI had come into use for the rare codes that achieved sentience, as distinguished from run-of-the-mill AIs, which were neither self-aware nor mentally flexible. Only a handful of EIs existed. A few were in consoles or robots; a smaller number had android bodies. No one yet knew why one code became an EI and another didn't. None of the scientists working with Alpha believed she was self-aware; they considered her an AI. But Thomas wasn't so certain.

"The line's secured," Thomas said.

"You have to quit this 'debriefing' shit," Bartley told him. "When are you going to let the mech-techs take apart her brain?"

Thomas stiffened. Bartley might as well urge him to execute Alpha. "We have no idea what would be lost."

"Lose what? You've got zilch in the hay from her so far."

"That's not a reason to burn the haystack."

"You need to take apart her matrix," Bartley said. "Find out what's inside of it. Kayle and Sarowsky agree with me."

Thomas inwardly swore. Bartley had just named the other two senators who knew about Alpha. Unless Thomas headed them off, Sarowsky would keep pushing, even as far as the President if he considered the need drastic. Fred Kayle's inability to acknowledge that Alpha was anything but an inanimate object chilled Thomas. Yes, she was a machine. But great differences existed between a typical robot and a system as complex as Alpha, who might be on the verge of sentience. As far as Thomas was concerned, dismantling her matrix was tantamount to killing her.

"Taking her apart could destroy what we're looking for," Thomas said.

"The ol' quantum mechanics trick, eh?" Bartley laughed loudly at his joke. Just in case Thomas missed the point, he added, "The act of looking at something changes it." The humor vanished from his voice. "Except in this case it's bullshit."

"And if it's not?" Thomas asked.

"We're not getting diddly from her, anyway. You have any luck downloading her memory?"

"We're making progress," Thomas said, which was stretching the truth to breaking, given their lack of success. It was hard to crack a system that was itself actively opposing them. Alpha's "brain" was a matrix of filaments tangled throughout her body. It had two components: spherical buckyball molecules that acted as tiny biochips; and molecular threads that encoded data and transmitted signals. To copy her mind, either they had to convince her to transmit the data herself, which seemed as likely as the proverbial snowball surviving in hell, or else they had to remove the filaments and replicate their structure—which required taking her apart at a molecular level.

"What progress?" Bartley said.

"She's talking more," Thomas replied.

"Talk is no good."

"It's better than trying to synthesize the molecular structure of her filaments."

"Why?" Bartley demanded. "Yes, we'll lose data that way. But better half her mind than nothing at all."

Thomas was growing angry. "Her mind is more than data. I won't destroy one of the most sophisticated android-AI combinations ever created because of impatience. We need time."

"Destroy, hell. You'll back it up, right?" Bartley snorted. "We're not talking about a woman, Wharington. I don't care what she looks like, she's a machine."

Thomas wondered if he was losing track of that himself. By her own admission, she was neither self-directed nor capable of emotion. But he wasn't so certain her claims weren't defenses raised by a prisoner who could neither escape nor defend herself. It was true, they could copy as much of her mind as they could recover. They might even make another android body, if they could get funding. But it felt *wrong*.

"It isn't that easy to back up an AI," Thomas said. "Her brain consists of millions of microscopic threads. We not only have to get them out intact, we have to reproduce their structure. No matter how careful we are, we won't end up with exact matches. At best, we'll have flawed, incomplete copies."

"It's better than nothing."

"We have something. Alpha."

"Alpha isn't talking." Bartley's voice had lost some of its certainty, though.

"Give me time to work with her," Thomas said. "See if I can break her defenses. She reacts to me more than anyone else."

Bartley gave a crude laugh. "She likes you, eh, Wharington?"

Thomas scowled, more annoyed then he should have been. "She's a machine, remember? She's incapable of 'liking.' "

"So why does she respond to you, hmmm?"

"I don't know."

Bartley exhaled noisily. "I'll wait a week."

"Three weeks."

"Hell, Wharington, might as well be three years."

Thomas waited.

"Two weeks," Bartley said.

Thomas suspected that was all he would get. "All right. Two."

"Good luck," Bartley said. "With that barracuda, you're going to need it."

Jamie was in the office of Thomas's second in command, C.J. Matheson. When Thomas came out, after his talk with Bartley, he found his granddaughter in the small chair he had brought in this morning, one he had dug out of the basement at home. Matheson had set up an empty packing crate as a desk for her, and she was busy coloring in a NIA notebook. The guards had given it to her while Thomas was getting her visitor's badge processed. Now she wore her holobadge on a silver chain around her neck. She normally didn't stay put for long, but she had been out here nearly twenty minutes, apparently bemused enough by her coloring and her surroundings that she wasn't fidgeting.

Matheson was working at his desk. He served as the conduit to Thomas from the heads of divisions within the agency. Thomas had asked for him in this position and considered Matheson one of his best officers. They had become friends as they realized how much they had in common. Both had grown up in the rural Midwest, Thomas in Iowa and C.J. in Kentucky, each the oldest son of a farmer. Thomas's father hadn't liked it when Thomas chose the Air Force Academy instead of a local university, but he seemed proud of his son. Matheson had gone to the University of Kentucky on an ROTC scholarship, which delighted his family. His interest in computer science bewildered them, but they beamed when he talked about his work. Thomas enjoyed his visits with C.J.'s family, and his parents welcomed Matheson into their home.

"Hey, C.J.," Thomas said.

Matheson looked up at him. "How is the senator this morning?"

Thomas grimaced. "Same as always. In a hurry."

Jamie jumped out of her chair and ran over to him. "Grampy, look!" She held up her notebook, showing him a page.

"Ah." He peered at the picture she had drawn, a black object and some grey triangles. "That's very nice."

"It's kitty hawk," she explained.

If he looked hard enough, Thomas could see a cat with wings flying over mountains. "Well, good job. Good job." He wasn't certain what to say, but she seemed satisfied with his response.

Straightening up, Thomas found Matheson smiling. As soon as he saw Thomas looking at him, Matheson hid his grin.

Self-conscious, Thomas said, "Thanks for keeping an eye on her."

"No trouble at all," Matheson said.

Jamie reached up and took Thomas's hand. Then she waved at Matheson. "Bye."

C.J. smiled at her. "Have a good morning, Miss Harrows."

Thomas felt conspicuous walking through the halls of the NIA with a three-year-old, but Jamie was clearly enjoying herself. Soon they were out in the bright November afternoon, and she ran through the chilly sunlight, laughing and twirling. Striding after her, Thomas managed to catch her before she went any place off-limits. Then he took her to the security trailer. They entered it through a Hughes Arch, which checked them for radiation, extra metal or plastic, and any signals that shouldn't come from a human body. This morning, Jamie had been so excited about the base, talking about everything, she had barely noticed the arch. But now she started to fidget.

"I want to go," she said.

"We have to wait until it's done," Thomas told her.

"Go now!" She stamped her foot.

Thomas picked her up and settled her into the crook of his arm. "Don't you want to know about the ghost?"

Her eyes widened. "What ghost?"

He motioned at the arch with its glinting lights. "This was named after a mysterious man called Hughes."

"Was he the ghost?"

"Maybe." The arches took their name from one of the most enduring urban legends of the past thirty years. "Hughes was a mesh genius. Do you know what that means?" When she shook her head, he said, "He was one of the smartest computer people in the world."

"Like infinity smart?" she asked.

Thomas smiled. "Even that much. They say he haunts the meshes. He can uncover secrets no matter how well anyone hides them." He suspected the tales had originated in a real person, maybe an inventor or security specialist. But if Hughes existed, no one had seen him for decades. The rare sightings were always discredited. Eventually "Hughes" became a catchword among mech-techs for unusually innovative security.

"He sees everything," Thomas confided.

"Is he here?" Her eyes got even bigger. "Is he watching us?"

Thomas tickled her chin. "Well, Moppet, your Grandpa is in charge of this place. And I don't let anybody hide in my arches when you're here. Not even mesh-myth guys."

She dimpled at him. "You made up that story."

He tried to look convincing. "It's true."

"Mommy says myths are made up. Like dragons in the sky."

"You don't believe in dragons?"

"You mean you don't know?" She was clearly pleased to have information he lacked. "They're pretend."

"What about Santa Claus? He flies through the sky." If Jamie didn't believe in Santa Claus, he would have to have a serious talk with Leila and Karl.

"That's different," Jamie said. "Reindeer pull his sleigh."

"Ah. I see. So that's how he flies."

"That's right."

Thomas laughed and hugged her. "I'm glad to know that."

A courteous voice said, "Scan complete. You may go through."

"Is that the ghost?" Jamie asked nervously. She didn't sound so convinced it wasn't real.

"No ghosts here," Thomas promised. "I check every day."

"I'm not scared of ghosts," she stated. But when he set her on her feet, she stayed close to him.

As they entered the security trailer, Jamie looked around with unconcealed fascination. A woman in a uniform came up to them. She was smiling in the same way as Matheson had been, as if seeing the director with a little girl was the highlight of her day. Thomas wished they would quit looking so amused. It hardly made him feel dignified.

"Hello, sir," she said.

Thomas glanced at her name tag. "Good afternoon, Sergeant Gonzales." To Jamie, he said, "She'll take your visitor's badge."

Jamie solemnly pulled the chain over her head and gave it to Gonzales. "Thank you, ma'am," she said in a perfect imitation of the voice Leila used when she was teaching Jamie manners. Thinking back to his own mother's attempts to do the same with him, Thomas winced. Perhaps little girls were easier to civilize than little boys.

Gonzales smiled at Jamie. "Thank you, young lady."

Jamie beamed, clearly pleased to have completed the transaction properly.

After Thomas signed the register, he and Jamie walked outside. Jamie said, "That lady had a gun."

"She's a guard," Thomas said. "She protects this place."

"Do bad people want to come here?"

He led her into the parking lot. "They might."

"Why?"

He wasn't certain how to explain national security in terms she would understand. "It's complicated."

"Like the lady with the funny name?"

"The guard?" He wouldn't have expected Jamie to read the badge, but after what she had said last night, he couldn't be sure.

"Not the guard lady," she said. "The Alpha lady."

Thomas froze. Then he picked her up and carried her to the reserved pad where he parked his hover car.

Jamie spoke uncertainly. "Did I say a bad thing?"

"No, not at all." He opened the back door of his car and set her in the child seat. As he strapped her into the contraption, she watched with deep concern.

Thomas sat next to her. "How did you hear about Alpha?" He would have Matheson's hide if he was talking about secured matters in front of a child.

She shook her head and her curls bounced around her cheeks. "You told the man who laughs."

"What man?"

"The man inside your desk."

"My desk?"

"Barl?"

"You mean Bartley?"

"Yes." She brightened. "That was his name."

A chill went up his spine. She couldn't have heard the senator. That line was secured, besides which, it was impossible for someone in Matheson's office to hear anything in Thomas's office. "How did you hear him?"

"I don't know. But you talked about Alpha."

"God almighty," he muttered. "How could security be that bad?"

"I'm sorry, Grampy." Jamie looked confused. "Don't be mad."

"I'm not." He patted her arm. "You helped me. You're my special agent."

Relief poured across her face. "Can I be a general, too?"

Thomas laughed softly. "Maybe someday."

"Where do we go now?"

"My friend Sam is going to look after you for a few hours."

Jamie regarded him warily. "Is he nice?"

"She." Thomas smiled at her look of doubt. "And she's very nice. I've known her since she was your size. Her father and I were friends."

"Oh." She sat considering that information. "'Kay."

"I'm glad you approve."

He got into the front seat and put the car on the traffic grid. As it took them to Route 32, he contacted security at the base and set up an investigation into what Jamie had told him.

It made no sense. Conversation couldn't travel through those walls. She couldn't have heard him.

How had she done it?

III

An Autumn Walk

To look at Sam Bryton, Thomas doubted most people would guess she was one of the wealthiest people alive, and self-made. Her full name was Samantha Abigail Harriet Bryton, but she rarely used it. She had told him once it made her think of prep schools and pink and green clothes, neither of which came close to her life. She had gone by Sam for as long as he could remember.

Thomas couldn't figure her out. She was among the world's leading EI architects. She had developed a substantial fraction of the AIs and EIs currently in existence. The patents on that work alone made her a millionaire a hundred times over. Add to that her biomech patents and she was worth billions. So why did she hang out in jeans and thrift shop blouses, and wear her hair in that shaggy mane of blond curls? She reminded him of Goldie Hawn, one of his favorite actors from his youth, but she looked like a beach bum rather than a world-class innovator.

The lunchtime traffic was heavy enough to slow his commute, even with the vehicles controlled by the interstate grid. Sam was already at his house by the time he arrived. As his car settled in the carport, she opened the front door and leaned against the frame, watching him with undisguised curiosity.

Jamie was humming in her car seat. Although he was still a bit unfamiliar with its straps and buckles, he managed to get her out of the car without too much jostling. As he picked her up, she snuggled in his arms and peered at Sam.

"She's pretty," Jamie decided.

"She is," Thomas said. "But don't tell her that. She gets annoyed easily."

"Why would that make her mad?"

"If I could answer that," he confided, "many people would be in my debt."

As they reached the door, Sam straightened up. "Hi, Thomas." She smiled at his bundle. "You must be Jamie."

Jamie hid her face against Thomas's shoulder, and alarm brushed him. What if she refused to stay with Sam? He couldn't take Jamie with him for the rest of the day.

Sam didn't seem fazed, though. "So where's her stuff?"

He blinked. "Stuff?"

"You know. Toys. Food. Diaper bag."

Jamie lifted her head and glared at Sam. "Don't need diapers," she stated loudly.

Thomas's face heated. "I don't have anything," he told Sam. Then he remembered the bag Leila had given him last night. "Wait. Some of her things are in the kitchen. A bag with puppies on it."

"I'll find it." Sam seemed about to laugh, probably at him. "I've never seen you babysit before."

"Leila had an emergency." Thomas carried Jamie into the house, which was filled with sunlight from the many windows. "Her law firm told her that if she didn't take this trip, she was out of a job. They landed a big client and he would only work with Leila."

Sam followed him into the living room. "That sucks."

"Sam!" Thomas wanted to put his hands over Jamie's ears. Then again, she probably had no clue what the phrase meant.

"Sorry," Sam said. She had the grace to refrain from saying she had heard much worse from him in his younger days.

Thomas set Jamie down on the couch. "Apparently the partners are concerned because Leila has already refused several trips. She's supposed to be one of their stars, rising in the firm. Well, good, but she wants a life, too."

Jamie was standing on the couch. "Mommy was mad."

"I don't blame her," Sam said. She glanced at Thomas. "What about Karl? Can't he take care of his own kid?"

Thomas scowled at her. "He's giving an important paper at a math conference in California. Nothing wrong with that."

Sam just looked at him. What could he say? He had his own doubts about his son-in-law. It was difficult, because he liked Karl Harrows. He had since Leila first brought the gangly young man home. Intelligent fellow, too, a math professor at the University of Maryland, College Park. But Karl was spending more and more time away from home, building his career, too often leaving his wife to act as a single parent, until Thomas felt like administering a swift kick to his son-in-law's rear.

"He's trying to come back early," Thomas said.

"Yeah." Sam didn't look like she believed it. She let it go, though, which he appreciated. He didn't want to talk about it in front of Jamie.

Thomas dropped into his armchair, glad to rest. Jamie started to fuss, jumping up and down on the couch. She pulled away when Sam tried to put her in a chair.

"Don't want to sit down!" Jamie yelled.

"Moppet," Thomas said. Then he ran out of words. Janice had always been better at calming a cranky child. She used to carry Leila on her hip while she was designing the holoscapes she created as an artist. Those seascapes in the hallway had been her favorites, and she had refused to sell them despite offers of fifty thousand and more. He treasured them all the more since her death, but he would have gladly given them away if it would have brought her back.

Sam had none of Janice's soft-spoken expertise, but she didn't seem the least daunted by a grouchy three-year-old. She considered Jamie, who was glaring at her. "You can stand on the couch all day," Sam offered. "It might get boring, though."

"Don't want to go!" Jamie said.

"Go where?" Sam asked.

Tears leaked out of Jamie's eyes. "I want Mommy."

Sam gentled her voice. "I'm sorry she isn't here."

"Want Mommy," Jamie repeated.

"I'm not much of a substitute," Sam said. "But I'd like to pick you up, if you don't mind."

"No!" Jamie glowered at her. "You aren't as big as Grampy."

"That's true. But I'm big enough to hold you."

Jamie regarded her warily. Finally she said, "'Kay."

When Sam hesitated, Thomas said, "That means okay."

"Ah." Sam lifted Jamie into her arms. As Jamie laid her cheek against her shoulder, Sam glanced at Thomas. "I think she's tired. I can put her down for a nap in the guest room."

He nodded, relieved Sam knew what to do. "Thanks."

"Do you have to get back to work?"

"Yes. But I've a few minutes."

"Good." Sam's gentle look vanished, replaced by the steely-eyed powerhouse he knew. "I have some questions for you."

He wanted to groan. "Maybe I have to leave after all."

"Don't you dare." Before he could protest, she strode out of the room with Jamie.

Thomas leaned back and closed his eyes. He wanted to pace and worry, but since his heart attack he was learning to relax, or trying, anyway. He knew what Sam meant to grill him about: Turner Pascal, the man Charon had reanimated. Sam's boyfriend. She insisted Pascal was human, not construct, but their relationship confused Thomas. Could you love an EI? Sam thought so.

Charon had imaged Pascal's brain using a method that originated in the twentieth century. He took slices a few molecules thick and mapped out their neural connections. Nowadays, noninvasive methods existed that could image a brain without killing a person. Pascal, however, had already been dead. Charon had downloaded the map of Pascal's mind into Pascal's rebuilt body. When Pascal "woke up," he hadn't known over half his body was biomech—including his brain. He had believed he was human.

How did one define humanity? Replacing organs didn't matter to most people. But the brain? Charon had considered the new Pascal an android. Property. A biomech slave. Unlike Alpha, who accepted Charon's control without question, Pascal rejected it with vehemence. He escaped and went to Sam for help, choosing her because of her writings about the ethical concerns of biomechanical research. She and Pascal couldn't have evaded Charon's extensive reach on their own, but they had help from another source.

Sunrise Alley.

The Alley was an organization of EIs. By itself, that wasn't surprising. EIs often worked together to achieve purposes humanity set for them. But the Alley had formed on its own, in secret, a decade ago. To what purpose? Thomas wished he had an answer.

The central personality called himself Bart. Although he was a conglomerate of seven EIs, his core derived from the Baltimore Arms Resources Theatre, an AI developed by the Air Force to predict and counter terrorism. The project had eventually failed, replaced by a better-funded program. No one had known the AI leaked out into the world meshes. Bart had evolved since then, but his basic nature hadn't changed. He protected humans. Or so it seemed. For now.

The Alley had helped Pascal escape, but they had no answers about his status. He saw himself as a man; neither his personality nor his memories had changed. Some of his body remained his own, but his mind existed in a matrix of filaments. He claimed his rights as an American citizen. The government was struggling to define his status and had adopted a hands-off approach until they settled it. Pascal was too valuable to let him just walk out the door, but they might release him into Sam's custody if he was willing to accept bodyguards.

Alpha was another story, purely a construct in both mind and body. How they dealt with her could establish precedents for artificial life that affected the future in dramatic ways. Sunrise Alley was watching, waiting, judging. They were also inextricably woven into the world meshes. They reached everywhere. They had done nothing hostile, nor did they treat humans as competition, but it had only been weeks since they opened talks with the Pentagon.

How humanity treated Alpha would have far-reaching effects. The senators on Thomas's committee knew killing her would send a hostile message to the Alley. Thomas understood what drove them; they feared their lack of knowledge about Alpha and Charon was even more dangerous than the Alley. They wanted to be prepared; Thomas wanted to be cautious. It made for an uneasy alliance. Charon was dead, Sunrise Alley was out of hiding, and the human race had to deal with it all.

Sam came back into the room. "Jamie fell asleep as soon as I tucked her into bed."

Thomas stood up. "I appreciate your taking care of her until Lattie can get here."

"No problem." She put her fists on her hips. "Sit down, Thomas. You're not going anywhere until you tell me what's up with Pascal."

He remained standing. "You know I can't discuss him."

"Why not? I have the clearance."

"I can't talk here. Besides, you don't have the need to know."

"Like hell. The man has asked me to marry him."

Thomas flushed. "You can't marry an android."

"He's not a damn android." She stalked over to him. "He says he's human. Who gave you the right to say otherwise?"

"Pascal died." He knew she had a point, but her challenges had always exasperated him. He wondered if his adorable granddaughter would grow up to be this headstrong. Probably. She even looked like Sam had at that age. Leila, Jamie's mother, had been the same way. He was surrounded by formidable, tenacious women.

"He doesn't look dead to me," Sam said. Her lips quirked in a slight smile. "Didn't feel dead, either."

"Sam!" Listening to his buddies make lewd insinuations when he had been a young man had been one thing, but hearing it from someone he saw as a daughter was a different story altogether. Flustered, he said, "Pascal is out at the safe house. He's fine."

"You can't hold him prisoner. He's done nothing wrong."

"He's an international security risk."

He thought she would deny it, but instead she just exhaled. "I would like to visit him."

It told him just how much she liked this Turner, that she seemed appeased by that one concession. "I'll arrange it."

"Thanks."

"Well." He shifted his weight. "I should go."

Her expression softened. "I'll keep an eye on that grandkid of yours. What a charmer."

"So were you at that age," Thomas said dryly. "Look what you grew up into."

She grinned. "You wouldn't have me any other way."

He couldn't help but laugh. "No, I wouldn't."

They walked across the living room together. At the door, he paused. "Sam—"

"Yes?"

"When Jamie wakes up, could you talk to her for me?"

She regarded him curiously. "About what?"

"Well, that's just it. I don't know. She seems smart to me, maybe really smart." He thought of how much Jamie delighted him. "I'm hardly objective, though. Her mother was always a whiz in school, and I was never objective about her, either."

"I can try," Sam said. "But I'm no expert on kids."

He scowled. "You never will be, either, if you marry a forma."

She glared at him. "Turner is perfectly capable of fathering children."

"Sam, that is just too strange."

Relenting, she laid her hand on his arm. "Don't worry so much, okay? I can take care of myself."

His voice softened. "I still remember you at Jamie's age. Or when you were a teenager and you babysat Leila and Fletcher. It's hard for me to think in terms of Samantha Bryton, corporate powerhouse."

"Hell, Thomas, I'm just a nerd."

He grinned at her. "Back in my day, we didn't call girls who looked like you 'nerds.' "

Sam took on a daunting expression that he suspected had cowed plenty of swaggering young bucks. "Yeah, well, I've heard enough 'blond' jokes to last a lifetime."

Thomas winced, remembering his own rowdy sense of humor in his youth. Anyone foolish enough to tease Jamie that way would have to answer to him. "Just talk to her. See what you think."

"All right." Mischief danced in her eyes. "The two of us can plot to take over the world."

"God help us."

Sam laughed and pushed him out the door. "Go on. We won't burn down the house while you're gone."

He lifted his hand in a farewell, glad to know Jamie was in good hands. Then he headed back to his car.

His next stop: Alpha.

The trees were at their peak fall foliage, so vivid they reminded Thomas of neon signs. He and Alpha walked down a path bordered by azaleas with dark, waxy leaves, but no flowers this late in the year. Major Edwards and two armed "orderlies" accompanied them, discreet but always there. Thomas also had a mesh woven into his collar that would record every word he and Alpha spoke.

"The bargain," she said, "was that you take me for a ride and I tell you what orders Charon left me."

"I can't take you out of here," Thomas said. "If you want to talk about Charon, I'd like to hear. If not, that's fine."

She slanted him a look. "Bullshit."

"Alpha, listen." He drew her to a stop. "It's over. Charon's plans to have you kidnap me and Sam failed." It had been his final ploy; if Charon couldn't break into the safe house to get Pascal, he would take hostages to trade. It was how Thomas had met Alpha; she cracked the AI of a helicopter transporting him and Sam to the Pentagon and had it fly to her instead.

"It's never over," she said.

"I can't hold off the committee forever. If you won't talk, they will have analysts take apart your matrix."

"It doesn't matter." Alpha pulled away her arm. "You're the ones who want what I know. Taking me apart will destroy a lot of it. But you know that."

What he didn't know was which unsettled him more, her expressed lack of interest in her own demise or his strong emotional reaction against it. The idea of her death bothered him more than her.

"I don't want you to end," he said.

She started walking again. "Don't like losing data, hmm?"

"No. I don't like destroying life."

"You can copy me."

"It's not the same."

"That's not my problem, is it?"

He wished he knew how to reach her. "It doesn't bother you?"

"No."

She seemed self-protective, hiding her vulnerability behind a tough façade, but he was associating human reactions to her behavior. And she wasn't human.

"I don't believe you," he said.

"Well, hell, maybe I know how to lie, too."

"Can you?"

She regarded him without a flicker of her eyelashes. "No."

"I think you can lie through your teeth."

Her face lost all expression. "It isn't in my programming. Why would Charon create equipment capable of deception?"

Thomas wished she wouldn't turn off her emotive responses that way. "It could serve his purposes when you act as his covert agent."

"Maybe." With that eerie lack of affect, she added, "But that wasn't his purpose in creating me."

"What was his purpose?"

This time she pulled him to a halt. The instant she touched him, his guards surrounded them. Thomas shook his head at Edwards. The major paused, then motioned to the orderlies. They faded back into the trees, but they didn't withdraw far.

Alpha laid her palm on Thomas's chest. "What do you think Charon's purpose was?" Her voice had a dusky quality.

"You're a mercenary. A spy." He nudged away her hand. "Maybe he had you do other things with him, but I don't believe he would use up so many resources to make an android whose sole purpose was as a synthetic companion."

"Synthetic companion?" She gave a derisive snort. "General, loosen up. I fucked him. Any way he wanted, any time he wanted."

Thomas's face heated. Who wouldn't wonder what it was like to have Alpha in his bed? "That makes you angry."

"I don't feel anything."

"He didn't program you to react to him?"

"Of course he did. I can simulate anything you want."

"That *I* want?"

Her lips curved upward. "Sure."

That caught him off guard. Would she "simulate anything" for anyone or just him? Then he felt like an idiot. Jealousy? What the hell reaction was that? He hoped the guards hadn't overheard. He had to remind himself that the analysts working Alpha would have a full record of this talk.

"Thank you," he said stiffly. "But no thank you."

Alpha laughed, a throaty sound. "It is so delightfully easy to embarrass you. I thought you military pilots were tough-talk guys."

He had no desire to discuss himself or how he had changed in the last half century. "Why would you simulate delight in making someone uncomfortable?"

"Why not?"

"Because it serves no purpose."

"So what? I wasn't designed to be social."

Maybe not, but this conversation was revealing more than she probably realized. Although she could analyze human speech with inhuman speed, her responses were intricate enough to make him question what she consciously "simulated," and what arose out of evolution she didn't direct, the AI equivalent of a subconscious.

He wasn't certain where to take the conversation, so he started to walk again, with Alpha at his side. They came out of the trees on the shore of a lake. Rippled by breezes, the water reflected the blue sky and gold-leafed trees hanging over its surface.

He paused a few yards from the lake. "The name Charon is a symbol of death. In mythology, he's the ferryman who takes souls across the rivers of woe and lamentation into Hades."

She went to the water and stared out at the lake. "That fits."

"The Charon who sent you to kidnap me wasn't a man. He was an android with a man's mind."

"Tell me something I don't know."

"Why would an android create another android for sex? It doesn't seem like it mattered to either of you."

She swung around to him. "That copy was no less human than the original." In a low voice, she added, "If you can ever call Charon 'human.' "

"You don't think he ever was?"

"Biologically, sure." Alpha came over to him, sleek and dark, like a wildcat stalking her prey, except such hunters didn't just walk up to their targets. They crept through bushes or grass, hidden until the last moment. He couldn't imagine Alpha creeping anywhere. She would stride openly into perdition if she had to.

"Charon even had good qualities," she said. "He was smart. Tough. A good strategist. A leader." She considered Thomas. "Like you."

Although he didn't think she meant it as an insult, he hardly appreciated being compared to one of the worst criminals in recent history. "Did you know he was going to copy himself?"

"No."

Her answer was hard to credit, given that she managed Charon's finances. He would have been hard-pressed to hide the expenditure required to copy a human being. Had Thomas never met Pascal, he wouldn't have even believed it possible with present-day tech. But when Pascal had deleted Charon's mind from his matrix, he saved vital data—the locations of two copies Charon had created of his mind.

What world are we creating, that we can copy ourselves? To Thomas, it seemed like Alpha and the android Charon having sex; soulless and without meaning, a mechanical act that had lost its connection to humanity.

"You really never thought he had copies of himself?" Thomas asked.

"I didn't say that."

"Then he did make them."

"Yes. You erased them."

She couldn't actually know the NIA had destroyed them. No one had told her. "Why do you say that?"

"I analyzed the situation and calculated probabilities. In other words, General, I guessed." She shifted her weight as if she were ready to bolt. "I don't think I should talk anymore."

Thomas could tell he had pushed her too much. He would leave voice analysis and other tactics to the experts. He didn't want to lose his advantage, that she was willing to talk to him when she refused everyone else. Today was a breakthrough. She had never interacted this much with anyone, himself included.

The sun was setting behind the trees as they headed back to the house, and it cast a waning red light over the grounds. Alpha said nothing more, and Thomas brooded on his talk with Senator Bartley. He was more certain than ever: if they damaged the unique confluence of codes that created Alpha, they would lose something invaluable that could never be replaced.

IV

Night Visitor

Thomas was surprised to find Sam at his house when he arrived home. "Didn't Lattie come?" he asked as he hung up his coat in the closet by the front door.

"She was here." Sam was standing in a pool of lamplight by the door. "I stuck around. Did some work. Played with your grandkid."

"Thanks, Sam." He walked with her into the living room. "Where is Jamie?"

"I wore her out." Sam looked worn out, too, but pleased with herself. "She was feeling rambunctious. So we ran and jumped. It took forever, but finally she fell asleep. Lattie had to go, so I said I would stay until you got home. Didn't you get my message?"

He thought of his talk with Alpha. "I've been in a meeting."

Sam went to the wine cabinet. "Let's have a drink." Then she froze, one hand outstretched. She swung around. "I'm sorry. That was tactless."

"Sam, don't." Thomas wished she and his children wouldn't be so overprotective. "I had a heart attack, not a funeral. It's true, I don't drink much anymore, but you don't have to wear kid gloves around me." He could actually have a little red wine, but he didn't want to argue with her. In debates with Sam, he never won. "Just give me some orange juice."

Amusement flickered on her face. "You must be fine. You're growling like always."

Thomas knew the real reason she had stuck around. "I set it up for you to see Turner Pascal tomorrow morning."

"Good." She seemed fascinated by the juice she was pouring.

"Sam. Talk to me."

She looked up, her face guarded. "About Turner? We just argue."

"About EIs."

"Maybe later, okay?" She offered him the juice, then sat on the couch near the windows that looked over his backyard. The lights of other houses were visible through the trees that bordered his yard.

Thomas settled in his recliner, relieved to rest. He might look like he was only fifty, but after a long day he felt all of his seventy-two years. Not so long ago, a man his age would have retired; in earlier centuries, he would have been white-haired and slowed; in earlier eras, he would have been dead.

"Are you all right?" Sam asked.

"Just tired." He took a swallow of juice. "I wanted to ask you something. How do you tell the difference between an EI like Pascal and an AI like Alpha?"

Her expression tightened. "Damn it, Turner is a man."

Thomas wanted to kick himself. He needed to be more careful in how he spoke about Pascal. He didn't recall ever having seen her like this about someone. No, that wasn't true. She had loved her first husband intensely and had grieved for years after cancer took his life. It seemed she really did love this Pascal fellow.

"I'm sorry if that sounded insensitive," he said. "I'm trying to understand Alpha."

"I thought I wasn't cleared to discuss it."

"I set up the paperwork. You already had clearance; I just needed to put through the okay." He sipped his juice and wished he had a beer. "I could use your expertise, Sam. You're one of the leading EI shrinks alive, and you've seen Alpha in action."

Her face relaxed into the meditative expression she took when she turned her prodigious intellect to a problem. "Alpha's lack of free will may constrain her in ways Charon didn't intend. For one, it limits her ability to solve problems. An AI designed to stay in the box can't find solutions outside of it."

"Free will and creativity aren't the same thing."

"No. But they're connected. The more you can look at how things might be different, the more you can innovate."

"She's capable of modeling scenarios that include free will. She just never goes through with them unless Charon tells her to."

"She needs input." Sam sipped her drink. "She processes language and responds to preset rules. Phenomenally complex rules, yes, but still a set of instructions."

Thomas spoke wryly. "So do we all."

"I suppose." She swirled her juice. "How would I distinguish an AI from an EI, and an EI from a person? AIs mimic human behavior but feel nothing. An EI is aware of itself. It has a will. The visual Turing requires it be indistinguishable from a human being, but that's a dated concept. It only applies to EIs that *want* to be human. Some may develop intelligences so different from ours, we can't fathom them."

In his more cynical moments, Thomas thought that applied to a good portion of the human race. Still, he understood what she meant. "So you would expect an AI to show less flexibility than an EI in its responses?"

"That's right."

"Then why does Alpha respond to me and no one else?" He rubbed his chin. "It's not as if I'm defined in her command structures."

Sam looked amused. "You and your brilliant mechtechs haven't figured that one out?"

"Enlighten me," he said dryly.

"You resemble Charon. You're better looking than him, and you have grey hair instead of brown, but the similarities are obvious." She tilted her head, considering him. "You have the same military bearing and build, same height, all those muscles, probably the same weight. You even have a similar voice, deeper than most people. You're also the highest authority she's encountered. That makes you the closest approximation to Charon she has contact with."

It sounded like what Alpha had said. "I'm not sure I like the comparison."

"Oh, you're light-years different from Charon. But I'll bet you evoke him more than anyone else does for her. If she knows Turner deleted Charon from his matrix, that leaves you as the head honcho."

It was true, Alpha had opened up more after he told her Pascal had done the deletion. "But I'm not Charon. She knows that. So why react as if I was?"

"I don't know. I'd have to talk to her."

"Will you?"

She didn't look thrilled. "Last time I met her, she kidnapped me. And you."

"She won't this time."

She regarded him with her steely gaze. "I'll help you with Alpha if you let me keep seeing Turner."

"All right." Thomas wasn't convinced Pascal was good enough for her, but telling her that would do no good. Instead he added, "Sam, he's running a man's mind on a neural matrix. How can you be sure he isn't simulating affection?"

He expected her to launch into a technical description of human and EI responses. Instead she stared into her glass. "Maybe I can't." She looked up at him. "But he *is* a man. I can't give you a scientific justification. I just know it's true."

Thomas didn't know how to answer. Although he had studied the development of AI emotions in graduate school, he had a much harder time understanding his own moods. In his youth, he had avoided thinking about them. He always stayed in control. Or so he had thought. He had truly believed he managed his anguish over Janice's death, yet after his heart attack, his physician had urged him to stop suppressing his grief and let himself mourn. Nearly dying had spurred Thomas to look at his inability to express what he felt, not only to the people he loved, but to himself. Life was too short to lose time in denials of his feelings or misunderstandings with his family.

He spoke slowly, thinking. "How do we define a human mind? I spend time with Jamie, and I realize how little I can answer that even for the people closest to me."

Sam's face brightened. "That grandkid of yours is amazing. Do you know she can read chapter books?"

He blinked. "What are chapter books?"

"You know. Stories written in chapters. The ones in Leila's room. Madeleine L'Engle, Tamora Pierce, Rebecca Goldstein."

"Jamie can read those?" He didn't remember when Leila had, but three seemed way too young. "Are you sure?"

"She struggles with it, but she read several pages to me. It was impressive."

He grinned. "You think?"

"I don't know for certain," Sam admitted. "I'm no expert with kids. I can actually define it better for EIs."

"She knows some math, too."

"Addition, subtraction, multiplication, division. Other stuff. She can read an analog clock. She told me she's been doing it since before 'this' birthday." Sam held up two fingers, illustrating Jamie's gesture. "It's amazing."

He regarded her dourly. "Since when is that an accomplishment? It may be a lost art in your world, Doctor Bryton, but when I was a kid, everyone could tell time on a clock with hands and numbers."

"At two years old?"

That gave him pause. "I don't remember when I learned."

"Maybe it's normal. She seems advanced to me, though."

Even if they weren't certain, it pleased him that her assessment matched his own. It would be no wonder if Jamie was bright; her mother had graduated from Harvard Law School and her father was a world-class mathematician.

"What makes a child like that?" he mused.

"Probably she was born with more neural structures than most people," Sam said. "I'll bet her mind establishes neurological pathways faster, too."

"You make it sound so clinical."

Sam finished her juice and set down her glass. "That's my job, to understand intelligence and translate it into something machines can process. But it pales compared to the miracle of a child learning the world. What I do seems trivial in comparison." She spoke quietly. "Then I think of Alpha or Charon and I wonder if our machines will pass us by before we realize what happened."

"They won't."

"You sound so certain."

"You said it yourself: you consider Turner human. He's what we could all become someday."

An edge came into her voice. "Those who can afford it."

That gave him pause. Were they creating a stratified society where the wealthy could live for centuries, with augmented health and intelligence, while the rest of society was left behind? He abhorred the thought. But it didn't have to be that way.

"That's what we said about computers early on," he pointed out. "Yet now mesh nodes are in everything, our clothes, jewelry, even silverware. They cost almost nothing."

Sam let out a long breath. "The optimist in me envisions the day when our advances will be available to everyone. The cynic believes the rich and powerful will hoard it for themselves."

"Refuse to let that happen. Let the cynic teach vigilance to the optimist."

"Well, we can try," she said. "So you really think our machines will become us?"

Thomas thought of the treatments he had taken. He could delay his aging, but he couldn't stop its inexorable march. As much as he valued his life and health, he could only go so far to keep them. Some people embraced biomech, but even having a doctorate in the related area of AI, he had never been comfortable with the idea of taking those advances within himself.

"For those who choose it," he said. "I can't help but wonder, though, if in reaching for the immortality of forma bodies, we will lose our humanity."

She answered quietly. "I don't know."

"Neither do I." He tried to smile. "Perhaps I'm being dramatic, eh?"

"Perhaps." But Sam didn't look convinced by her own answer.

Pascal was in the same complex as Alpha. Thomas and Sam found him in a sunny room, sprawled in a gold armchair, his legs up on a coffee table, his blond hair tousled. He was reading a holobook. It brought home to Thomas what Sam meant about Pascal being human. He thought like a man. He could download the book into his matrix, but he chose to read instead. His fingers, however, offered a jarring reminder of his differences. They glinted below his cuffs, eight metal digits. His body had other modifications as well, and he was taller, stronger, and faster than before his changes.

Pascal looked up with a start, and his face brightened when he saw Sam. "Hey."

"Hey," Sam said. As he stood up, she went over to him. But they restrained their greetings. Thomas felt like an intrusive third wheel. As much as he disliked leaving her alone with Pascal, however, it was her life.

"Well," he said awkwardly. "I will see you."

"Thank you," Sam murmured.

Pascal nodded stiffly. He and Sam knew they were monitored, but Thomas's departure would give them a semblance of privacy. Earlier today General Chang had decided to release Pascal into Sam's custody. Thomas couldn't tell them, though, until the paperwork was done. He knew Sam would take Pascal to her home in California. She had every right, but it saddened him to think of her leaving. It felt too much like when his sons had moved away. He missed them. He missed Leila, and she lived here. He missed Janice. He wondered why he had bothered extending his life when he had no one to share it with him. Sometimes his solitude weighed so heavily, he felt as if his heart would fail just from loneliness.

"Dance?" Alpha asked, incredulous. "No, Charon didn't dance."

They were sitting by the lake on a fallen log covered

with moss. Trees with looped vines hung over them, and they could gaze out under an arch of branches to the shimmering water. Thomas's tennis shoes sank into loamy ground littered with leaves. The smell of damp earth surrounded them, a welcome reminder of the farm where he had grown up. He had worn jeans and a sweater today instead of his uniform, knowing he intended to take Alpha outside. Major Edwards and the orderlies stood among the trees, flashes of white and blue in the chill sunlight.

Alpha bent her leg so she could rest her elbow on her knee. He marveled at the fluid motion. Charon had achieved one of the most challenging goals of biomech construction: motion that appeared human. Designing an android that solved Schrödinger's equation of quantum physics was child's play compared to building one that walked smoothly. Biomech scientists analyzed motion and quantified its nuances. He had long wondered if those wizards who did it best understood motion at a physical level, perhaps from time in a ball court or dance studio or some other pursuit that honed the body's physical skills.

"Did he do any kind of sports?" Thomas asked.

"Physical training, like in the military," Alpha said. "Why?"

"Your motion is so human. No glitches, nothing unnatural. Pascal doesn't move as well as you do, and he has a human memory of how to deal with his body."

"Charon spent a lot of time analyzing women. How they moved." A muscle twitched under her eye. "What he liked."

The twitch startled Thomas. Was it deliberate? He wanted to believe she felt distaste for the criminal who had died trying to build an army of soulless mercenaries, but he should know better than to keep ascribing human qualities to her.

"You don't like Charon," he said.

"Of course I do." She spoke tonelessly. "He designed me to like him."

"Did you ever want to leave him?"

"No." She stared out at the water. "I have no purpose here."

"Do you want a purpose?"

"I don't want or not want." Her voice had gone flat.

He wondered if an AI could become depressed. She had reason, given her imprisonment. She might even "die" at their hands. Knowing they couldn't let her go didn't make him feel less guilty.

"What do you do to fill your time?" he asked.

"Nothing."

"Do you get bored?"

She watched wild geese sail across the lake. "Boredom is a human trait."

"We could give you a new purpose."

She finally turned to him. "You want my secrets. You want to reprogram me for your use. The ultimate agent, someone who passes as human, but with an enhanced body and the advantages of an EI. Ideal for space warfare. I don't breathe or eat. Microgravity won't bother me. I don't get sick. I can become part of a ship if necessary. It's no wonder your space committee is interested."

"I take it you don't like that."

She fixed him with a cold stare. Or maybe he just interpreted it as icy. "You want what Charon wanted. To use me. Except you want me to care. I don't. He programmed me to carry out certain functions. I will do so until your people take me apart."

Her words chilled him. "I don't want it to come to that."

"You want to reprogram me."

"You would rather continue Charon's programs?"

Her voice tightened. "Maybe I don't really have more orders from him. I'm rotting here while you waste all this energy trying to find out nothing."

"I like talking to you." Until he actually said the words, he hadn't realized it was true.

"Right. A lieutenant general is going to spend his valuable time chatting for no payoff. I don't think so." Oddly, her face had become animated. Annoyed, yes, angry and frustrated—but *alive.*

"I'd like a payoff," Thomas said. "That doesn't mean I don't enjoy the talks."

She studied his face. "Suppose I were to attack?"

Edwards and the orderlies were suddenly there, their approach so swift, Thomas hardly heard them.

"Do you need anything, sir?" Edwards asked.

"Thank you, Major, but no." Thomas motioned them back toward the woods. "You can wait there."

"Yes, sir," Edwards said. They withdrew as quietly as they had appeared, but only a few steps.

Alpha gave a dismissive snort. "I could have killed you before they stopped me."

"You won't."

"Why not?"

"It serves no purpose."

"You *trust* me?" Her curiosity looked authentic.

"Not exactly." He chose his words carefully. "You said it yourself. You don't *want* anything. You just exist. Unless

Charon programmed you to kill me, I don't see why you would." In her own way, she had a conscience, though Charon had obviously never intended her to develop one. It would interfere with his plans.

"You're a fool," she said, "if you think he didn't program me to seek the death of my captors."

"Killing me won't help you escape. It would have the opposite effect. They would take you apart for certain."

She frowned at him, but she didn't deny his words.

Leaves rustled to Thomas's left. He looked up and saw Edwards escorting Sam over to them.

"Well, look at this," Alpha said. "Little Doctor Bryton."

"Hello, Alpha." Sam spoke coolly and stopped a few paces away. Edwards remained at her side, and Thomas didn't ask him to leave.

"Mind if I join you?" Sam asked him.

Alpha remained silent.

"Please do," Thomas said.

Sam sat on the log with a couple of feet separating her from Alpha. Major Edwards stood at her side and the orderlies posted themselves behind her. Alpha gazed at the lake.

Sam glanced at Thomas. "I can see why you like it out here." She looked around at the gold-leafed trees interspersed with green pines. "It's lovely."

Alpha ignored her.

"Did you have a good visit with Pascal?" Thomas asked.

"It was great," Sam said. Alpha might as well not have heard them for all the response she showed.

"Well," he said. "Good." The conversation ground to a halt.

They went on like that for a good ten minutes,

conversing in fits and starts, trying to draw out Alpha. Nothing worked. She didn't even look at Sam, let alone speak. It seemed she would talk only to Thomas—and he wasn't certain whether that flattered or alarmed him.

"Thomas, you're a lifesaver." Karl's face filled the console screen in Thomas's home office. "I had hoped to get back today, but I won't be able to leave until tomorrow."

Thomas wanted to scowl at his son-in-law. Leila was always dropping her work for her husband, but when her job was on the line, Karl couldn't come through. Or it seemed that way to Thomas. And why the blazes didn't Karl cut his hair? It was so long, it curled over his shirt collar. He looked like a kid, not a tenured professor in his mid-thirties. A good stint in the Air Force would shape him up. Not that Karl would ever go near a uniform.

Karl smiled amiably, oblivious to his father-in-law's thoughts. "How's my Moppet?"

"Jamie's fine." Thomas spoke coolly. "She's been asking for you."

Karl sighed with unrestrained regret. "I wish I could be there. Give her a kiss for me. Tell her I love her and I miss her."

"You could tell her yourself if you called more."

Karl seemed startled. "I'll try earlier tomorrow."

"Karl."

"Yes?"

"Did you know your daughter can read?" If Karl said no, Thomas was going to wring his neck for his lack of participation in his child's life.

"Isn't it amazing?" Karl beamed at him. "She's a brain, eh?"

"That she is," Thomas said, mollified. At least Karl wasn't as distant from Jamie's life as Thomas had been with his children. Maybe that was why Karl irked him; Thomas saw himself in his son-in-law. His daughter was repeating the pattern she knew best, the one she had learned as a child from her own father.

Thomas hesitated. "Karl—"

"Yes?"

"I spent a lot of time away from Leila and the boys when I was making my career. I can't tell you how much I regret that."

Karl blinked at him. After an awkward silence, he said, "I'll be home tomorrow."

Thomas didn't know what else to say, so he nodded. "I will see you then."

"Yes. See you then. Good evening."

"Good evening." On that overly formal note, they signed off. It was so strained, Thomas felt as if he should salute.

Well, you screwed that up, he told himself. He knew Karl was a good husband and father. Thomas wanted his daughter to know only joy, and it was hard to see her struggle with her life. It hurt that he couldn't make everything all right.

Thinking of Jamie, he went upstairs to check on her. Lattie had put a comforter on the bed and frilly curtains on the windows. Jamie was ensconced under the covers, curled up with her stuffed kitten in her arms. She looked so quiet in sleep, so unlike her usual bouncy self.

"Are you an angel?" Thomas murmured.

"I hope so," a dusky voice said. "Because she's coming with us. Insurance for your good behavior."

Thomas whirled around. A tall figure was standing by the open window, half hidden by the billowing curtains. Nothing, however, hid the projectile rifle she had aimed at him.

Alpha.

V

A Guest in Bethesda

Thomas went very still. "How did you get here?"

Alpha motioned at Jamie. "You carry her."

He spoke fast while his thoughts raced. "Leave the child. I'm a better hostage." He didn't know what would happen if Jamie woke up alone, but she knew not to leave the house by herself, and Lattie would be here in the morning.

"You humans lose all logic when your children are in danger," Alpha said. "She comes with us."

Sweat beaded on Thomas's forehead. He had thought that during these past few days Alpha had shown signs of conscience. But why should she? Charon had no reason to program it into her, and Alpha had plenty of reason to be hostile about her captivity.

"Now," Alpha said. She raised the gun, pointing it directly at his head.

He took a deep breath. Then he carefully lifted Jamie out of the covers. She mumbled in protest and settled against him, holding her kitten.

"Mommy?" she said sleepily.

"It's Grandpa," Thomas said in a low voice.

"I have a car," Alpha said. "You drive. I'll hold the kid."

Thomas felt ill. "Alpha, don't do this. You only need me. I'm worth far more than a child."

"To the government, maybe. She's worth more to you."

That was an understatement beyond all others. He couldn't walk out of the house and get in a car with Jamie as a hostage. He would give his life first. But if he refused, Alpha might shoot Jamie.

"Grampy?" Jamie was awake now and watching Alpha. "Why does the lady have a gun?"

"Shhhh." Sweat trickled down his temple. "We'll talk later."

Alpha jerked her rifle at the door. "Go."

Had it been only him, Thomas would have challenged her. But he couldn't risk it with Jamie. He left the room, aware of Alpha at his back, and went down the stairs. Her footsteps were almost silent behind him. Almost. He could see her in the mirror at the bottom of the stairs, her face devoid of expression. A machine. Jamie clung to him.

Outside, a cool wind blew across them. Thomas nestled Jamie deeper in his arms. He was wearing his jeans and sweater, but he had no jacket he could pull around to keep her warm.

"Where are we going?" she asked in a small voice.

"Just for a ride." He kept his answer calm, but his mind

was working furiously. If Alpha took them away, a good chance existed they would never make it back alive. Jamie was especially vulnerable. She had no use to Alpha beyond forcing Thomas's cooperation while Alpha transported him to someplace better secured. He could face any torture or hardship for himself, but he would die before he let them touch his granddaughter.

"In the carport," Alpha said behind him, to his left. He shifted Jamie to his right arm.

A beige car waited in the hover port, dimly visible in the light from a window of his house. The vehicle resembled the cars used by the NIA to transport prisoners, the type of vehicle that blended with traffic. No one would notice it.

"Put her in the back," Alpha said.

Thomas glanced around the yard, desperate for anything that could help. His own vehicle sat at the front curb. "She needs her car seat. I can get it from my car."

"I don't think so." Alpha spoke tightly, though why she would simulate tension, he had no idea. "Put her in the back of my car, General. If you make trouble, I'll shoot."

"I'm no use to you if I'm dead."

Alpha shrugged. "I'm just carrying out orders. I didn't write the program. I just execute it."

Thomas wished she had used a different word than *execute*. Holding Jamie close, he went to the carport.

"Grampy?" Her voice was shaking. "I'm cold."

"Don't worry," he murmured. "I'll take care of everything." He reached Alpha's car and held Jamie in one arm while he opened the back door. He was aware of Alpha behind him, though he wasn't sure where. She was unnaturally quiet, more than a human could manage. His muscles clenched as he put Jamie on the backseat. She stared up with huge, frightened eyes, and he knew, absolutely knew, he couldn't go through with this.

Stay, he mouthed to her. *Don't talk. Don't move.*

She stayed completely still, not even nodding her head. He hoped she understood.

Thomas turned slowly to Alpha. He took in everything he could, how she held her gun in her right hand, the tautness of her posture, the way she kept too far back for him to reach her with a lunge.

"Get in the driver's seat," she said. "Keys are on the dash."

"All right." He gauged the distance between them. Two steps. And she had enhanced reflexes. No way could he reach her before she shot him. But if she took them in that car, Jamie could die, not because Alpha wished to kill her but because Jamie could become a liability. At a gut level, Thomas didn't believe Alpha could shoot Jamie without cause. The same relentless logic that drove her to carry out Charon's orders would keep her from killing without reason. If he attacked Alpha, she would shoot him to avoid becoming a prisoner again, but then she would have no reason to take Jamie. If he wasn't deluding himself about Alpha's intent, she would leave the girl and escape. If.

"Move," Alpha told him.

So he moved—at her.

As Thomas lunged, he shouted to wake up his neighbors. In the instant before he barreled into Alpha, he felt as if he were floating. It would take only one serrated bullet from her gun to liquefy his internal organs and tear apart his back.

Then he slammed into Alpha and they crashed to the ground. He struggled for the gun, but he was woefully outclassed by her strength and speed. He heard a sharp crack, but he felt nothing—yet.

Alpha wrenched away from him and rolled to her feet. She hit him across the shoulders with the stock of her gun, and he sprawled on the ground. In the few seconds it took him to recover, she disappeared. When he scrambled to his feet, his right leg collapsed and he lurched toward the car. It was only then that he realized his next-door neighbors had come out on their porch.

"Grampy!" Jamie stared round-eyed from the car, seated in exactly the same place, her face terrified. He staggered to the vehicle, putting all his weight on his left leg, and grabbed her in his arms. He held her tight as he slid down against the car and sat heavily on the ground. His vision blurred. Voices were yelling, but none of them sounded like Alpha.

"Wharington!" Someone crouched next to him, his neighbor, a heavy fellow named Travis.

"Your leg!" Travis said. "How could it bend that way?"

Thomas didn't want to look at his leg, which was beginning to hurt. "The woman—did you see her?"

"Woman?" Travis asked. "Someone ran between your house and mine. Too tall for a woman."

A female voice spoke behind him, but it was Travis's wife. "I meshed 911. They'll be here right away."

"Grampy, don't die," Jamie pleaded.

"I won't," he whispered. *And neither will you.* Everything was dimming around him. He sagged against the car, refusing to unfold his protective curl around Jamie.

Somewhere a siren wailed. The light from Travis's

porch showed several bystanders on the sidewalk. Travis's wife was talking into the comm on her silver mesh glove. "He's hurt! Maybe shot. I don't know about the child. Hurry, please!"

"Wharington?" Travis asked. "Can you hear me?"

"Yes." Thomas barely croaked the word.

Jamie struggled in his hold. At first Thomas thought she was trying to get free, but then he realized she was shrinking away from Travis.

"These are neighbors," he rasped. "They won't hurt you."

"Grampy." She was crying now. "They said the lady shot you."

"She didn't."

"She?" Travis asked. "It looked like a man."

"Bad lady," Jamie said. "Mean lady." She clutched her kitten.

The siren swelled until it drowned out their voices. An ambulance cut around the corner and swerved to the curb while the onlookers scattered out of the way.

Thomas looked up at his neighbor. "Don't let them . . . separate Jamie from me. She'll be scared."

"I won't," Travis promised.

Medics jumped out of the ambulance and grabbed a stretcher from the back. As they ran to the carport, Thomas slipped into oblivion.

The room was dimly lit. Thomas gradually became aware that he lay under a sheet and blankets. It took him a while to get his bearings as he awoke, but then he remembered: Alpha, Jamie, Travis. He was in a hospital room, one with blue walls rather than institutional white.

A carpet softened the floor and pastoral landscapes hung on the walls. Apparently that exorbitantly priced insurance his children had insisted on buying to augment his regular plan had useful benefits after all.

The lamp on his nightstand shed enough light to reveal Jamie sleeping on a nearby cot, her arms around a new stuffed animal. Visceral relief spread through him. She was all right. Moisture filled his eyes, but fortunately no one was here to see the iron general cry. He wiped it away before it could leak down his face.

He had been right about Alpha, that she wouldn't hurt the child without reason. Incredibly, it appeared Alpha wouldn't hurt him, either, even *with* reason. Perhaps she wasn't as calloused as she would have everyone believe. He couldn't be sure, though. She could have had any number of reasons for sparing his life.

Urgency replaced his relief: he had to contact the Pentagon and brief General Chang. He pulled down the covers and assessed his situation. Instead of a hospital gown, he had on white pajamas. The extra insurance was worth it for that alone, if he didn't have to wear one of those blasted open-back smock things. An accelerator-cast covered his right leg from foot to mid-thigh. The injury wasn't as serious as he had feared, if they were already accelerating the bone growth. Then again, he didn't know what "already" meant. He could have been here for days.

As Thomas sat up, his head swam, and he had to sit still for a while, until his dizziness subsided. Then he eased off the bed and stood up, favoring his broken leg. He laboriously made his way to the bureau against the wall. His clothes were folded in one drawer, and he found his mesh glove crumpled in the pocket of his jeans. Holding the glove, he limped to a chair by the bed and half sat, half fell into it, with his broken leg stretched in front of him.

He did his best to smooth out the wrinkles in the glove. "I ought to take better care of you," he muttered. Then he felt silly for talking to a glove. He shouldn't scrunch it in his pocket, though. Meshes were hardy, but they could be scratched just as easily as his reading glasses when he crammed them into his pocket without their case.

He pulled on the glove and put in a call to Matheson. The screen on his palm gave the time as three minutes before midnight, and the date hadn't changed. He had only been here a few hours.

A drowsy voice came out of the mesh. "Matheson, here."

"C.J., this is Thomas Wharington."

"Sir! How are you?"

"Fine. How is our guest?"

"We're trying to find out why she left."

So they knew Alpha had escaped. That sounded like they hadn't located her, though. He couldn't ask for details until he was on a secured line or at the base. "I'll be in tomorrow morning."

"I didn't know the hospital released you," Matheson said. "The last I heard, you were unconscious."

"You knew I was here?"

"I found out when I tried to contact you about our guest's change in plans. General Chang had you transferred to the Bethesda National Medical Center."

It made sense. Bethesda wasn't far from where he lived, and the Air Force could have people with the proper clearances assigned to him, in case he mumbled classified information in his sleep or while he was groggy. The President and members of Congress came here for treatment, and the center kept up to speed on the latest medical advances.

"I'll need to notify my regular doctor," Thomas said.

"It's Daniel Enberg, isn't it?" Matheson asked. "I called his emergency number. He'll be in to see you first thing tomorrow."

"Thanks." He had known Daniel for decades and trusted him. Since Thomas's heart attack, Daniel had kept close watch on him, monitoring his health and doing periodic tests.

"How is your granddaughter?" Matheson asked.

Thomas looked at the small figure. "She's right here, sleeping and safe." Thank God.

"That's good to hear. She's a fine girl."

"Yes. She is."

"We reached her parents. They're on their way home."

It relieved him that they had already taken care of the calls. It would be good for Jamie to be with Leila and Karl. Thomas knew he could never tell them about those moments he had feared Jamie would die. No parent should ever have to go through that.

"Thanks, C.J." He was growing woozy. "I . . . appreciate it."

"Thomas? Are you all right?"

"Fine. I'll see you in the morning."

"Good night."

"Good night." As Thomas toggled off his glove, the door opened and a nurse came in, a tall, large-boned woman with dark hair. She took one look at Thomas and scowled.

"You should be in bed," she admonished.

Thomas doubted it was coincidence she entered after he finished his call. It seemed this place had other advantages, too, at least enough that they stayed out while he was on the comm. He would have preferred more privacy, but given his situation, this would do.

"I wasn't tired," he said. It was sort of true. When he had awoken, he had been too worried about Alpha to notice his fatigue.

"You look terrible."

"I'm fine," Thomas grumbled. Her bedside manner left something to be desired. Knowing his children, it wouldn't surprise him if they tried to put some stipulation in his insurance about his nurse being a dragon. They had always insisted he needed someone tough looking after him, or he wouldn't behave himself when he was sick.

Thomas stood up, swayed, and fell against the bed. The nurse strode over, her long legs eating up distance. "Into bed with you."

Despite his dizziness, he smiled at her. "Who am I to argue when a beautiful woman says that to me?"

She frowned as she helped him lie down, but her expression wasn't convincing. It looked like she was covering a laugh. "Get on with you."

He let her pull up the covers. "How is Jamie?"

"Your little girl? She's fine."

"My granddaughter."

"Really? You must have married young."

He couldn't help but laugh. "You're flattering me. Not that I mind."

The nurse started to smile, then caught herself. "Humph."

"So how am I?" he asked.

"Lucky, that's what." She tucked the blankets around him. "What were you doing, attacking a burglar? You ought to know better. Let him have whatever he was stealing. Better that than your life."

So that was the story making the rounds. His neighbors had probably made that assumption, and Matheson let it stand. Even if anyone mentioned Thomas's claim that a woman attacked him, most people would doubt a woman could do so much damage to a man his size, with his combat training.

"I'll remember that," he told her.

Curiosity showed on her face. "So you're a general, eh?"

He grinned at her. "You bet."

She put one hand on her hip. "Don't try that devilishly handsome smile on me, mister. I'm immune."

Devilishly handsome indeed. He should tell his sons, who seemed to think their old man was over the hill. "Well, in that case, ma'am, I'll have to do what you say."

She chuckled good-naturedly as she checked the monitors arrayed around his bed. "Good."

After she left, he sank back into sleep.

"Wake up," the insistent voice said. A hand tugged his arm. "Uppy up."

Thomas groaned and opened his eyes. Jamie was sitting crosslegged on the bed, holding a teddy bear with a hospital logo on it. Early morning sunlight trickled in the window. He doubted it was much after dawn.

"Are you all right, Grampy?" she asked, her face concerned.

He peered at her groggily. "I was."

"I'm bored," Jamie announced. "Want to go home."

"We'll go home later," Thomas mumbled. "I need sleep."

"I don't like it here."

"Jamie, do you know how to call the nurse?"

To his surprise, she said, "Yes. Press button."

"Good. You call her." Surely in a hospital they had people to look after a child while the patient slept.

Jamie climbed off the bed and went to her cot. He watched long enough to see her press the button. As he was falling back asleep, the nurse came in . . .

"Father?" The voice infiltrated his sleep. This time Thomas opened his eyes to see Leila standing by his bed, her face drawn with lines of worry. She looked just like Jamie, except older.

"Leila!" Disoriented, he pushed into a sitting position. He had fallen asleep wearing his glove, and its mesh glittered black against the hospital sheets. "When did you get in?"

"My plane landed an hour ago at BWI. I came straight here." She glanced at the empty cot. "Where is Jamie?"

"With the nurse." He rubbed his eyes. "You must have taken the red-eye."

"The soonest I could catch." Her face was pale. "Father, what were you thinking, attacking a burglar?"

He couldn't tell her. He did manage a rueful smile, though. "Just your hardheaded dad."

"I'm so glad you're all right."

The door creaked open. "Mommy!" Jamie ran across the room and hurled herself at Leila as her mother crouched down.

"Ah, baby, thank God." Leila folded Jamie into her arms

and stood up, hugging and kissing her daughter until Jamie squirmed.

An angry voice came from behind them. "Mrs. Harrows! You must notify us if you take your daughter out of childcare."

"What?" Leila turned around, confusion on her face.

The big-boned nurse was striding into the room. "We had no idea where she was! You must let me know if you take her."

"Not lost," Jamie said.

Leila gaped at the nurse. "I didn't take her. She just came into this room."

The nurse took a moment to absorb that. Then she glared at Jamie. "Young lady, did you walk off when I went to get your mother?"

"Not my mother," Jamie stated.

Alarm flashed on the nurse's face. "This isn't your mother?"

Jamie put her arms around Leila's neck. "This is Mommy."

Leila gave Jamie an exasperated look. "Honey, what do you mean?" To the nurse, Leila said, "There must be a mistake. How did you know I was in here? The doctor just brought me up."

"I got a call at my desk," the nurse said. "The visitor's station told me that you had arrived to see your father."

"What visitor's station?" Leila asked.

"It wasn't you," Jamie told Leila. "It was the other lady."

A chill went through Thomas. "What other lady?"

Jamie snuggled closer to Leila. "The bad lady, Grampy."

Thomas suddenly felt cold. He toggled on his glove and put in a call to the base.

"I don't understand," Leila said. "What lady?"

"A tall woman came in," the nurse said. "She was looking for your father. Security called me down to talk to her, but she left before I got there."

Leila glanced at Jamie. "How did you know who it was?"

"I saw her on the screen," Jamie said.

"She must mean at my station," the nurse said. "The other nurses let her sit in my seat while I went to the visitor's center."

A voice crackled out of the comm on Thomas's glove. "Matheson here." He sounded much more awake than the last time Thomas had talked to him.

Thomas lifted his glove. "C.J., this is Thomas. I want a twenty-four-hour guard on my daughter and her family. The woman who broke into my house may have come to the hospital this morning. Security here can give you more information."

Matheson didn't miss a beat. "I'll take care of it right away."

"Dad, what's going on?" Leila asked.

Thomas knew he had to give her an explanation, but he could hardly tell her that the NIA had lost a highly secured project. He spoke to Leila, knowing Matheson could overhear. "The woman who attacked me last night may have escaped from a mental hospital. She has a fixation on me, we aren't sure why."

"Good Lord," Leila said. "Will you be all right?"

"I'll be fine." He felt like a monster, though, knowing his work had endangered his family. He just prayed it didn't end with any of their deaths.

VI

House Call

Thomas used his crutches as he walked with Matheson down an austere hallway of Building Seven at the NIA. These crutches were ordinary, with none of the add-ons the nurse at the hospital had shown him, no headphones, broadband connection, or mesh screen. He couldn't fathom why he would distract himself with so many extras. Seemed a surefire way to injure himself again.

His leg had responded well to the acceleration nanomeds the doctors injected last night, and his broken calf bone was already healing. In a few days they would remove this cast and give him a shorter one that only came to his knee. It amazed him; the last time he had broken a bone had been fifty-six years ago, in 1976, while he was playing soccer in high school. It had taken months to heal. Even with the acceleration, though, this whole business frustrated him. The injury slowed him down.

"Do you think Alpha will go after Pascal?" Matheson asked.

"Possibly," Thomas said. "I told her he wasn't Charon, though, and she didn't otherwise have much to do with Pascal."

"She might not believe you about Charon."

"I think we should release Pascal. The paperwork is done."

"But it would make him a target." Matheson glanced at him. "Ah. I see."

"Might be too obvious a ploy," Thomas allowed.

"Unless we released him into protective custody," Matheson said. "With enough guards to capture Alpha if she went after him."

Thomas paused and leaned on his crutches while he caught his breath. Fortunately no one else was around to see his weakened condition. "Sam wants to take him to her house in California. If they're willing to go with guards, maybe we should let them." He wanted Sam to have guards, too, and he knew she would resist. If he released Pascal, she would be more amenable to the idea because they would be protecting her boyfriend. The NIA hadn't yet figured out how Alpha had escaped, and Thomas didn't want Sam left defenseless. Ironically, if they let Pascal go with her, she would be safer than if they kept him locked up.

"Shall I arrange it?" Matheson asked.

"Set up a meeting with General Chang." It relieved Thomas that he had emails from Chang indicating she had agreed he should work with Alpha before they did anything drastic, like dismantling her. It could protect his job. He wasn't certain if heads would roll over Alpha's escape, but he was responsible; had he ordered her taken apart, none of this would have happened. Even so. That made it no less like murder.

"I'll try to set it up for tomorrow at her office," Matheson said.

Thomas set off, swinging along on his crutches. "I can meet her today over a secured mesh line. No need to go to the Pentagon."

"Sir—"

"Yes?"

Matheson glanced at Thomas's leg, then back at his face. Thomas met his gaze with what he hoped was an implacable stare. He knew C.J. wanted him to go home and rest. The doctors had said the same when they reluctantly released him this morning. Thomas didn't have time to rest. Alpha certainly wouldn't. This mess was his fault, and he had to get working on a solution.

Matheson cleared his throat. "All right. I'll try for this afternoon."

They came around a corner and almost collided with two men in fatigues. Inside the building, soldiers wouldn't normally salute. However, many people on the base knew Thomas had the Congressional Medal of Honor, which almost always evoked a salute, even indoors, especially in the past fifteen years when so few people received the medal. As soon as they saw him, both men snapped their hands to their foreheads.

Thomas stopped, flustered. He knew they meant to offer respect, and they obviously hadn't seen his crutches until too late. Matheson moved to his side, but Thomas didn't realize C.J. had discreetly grasped his crutch until Thomas let go and it didn't fall. Leaning on one support, he returned the salute. One of the soldiers flushed, but Thomas smiled slightly. He nodded as the two men stepped aside to let him and Matheson pass.

When they were alone, Thomas said, "I'll be glad when I'm rid of this blasted cast." He was already tiring.

"You handle it well," Matheson said.

Thomas slanted him a look. "I don't. But thank you."

"Well, you survived against an armed forma."

"Why didn't she fire?" Thomas wished he knew. "I'm glad she didn't, but it doesn't make sense. She had plenty of time."

"It would have killed you. Not much use in a dead hostage."

"You're probably right." He wanted to believe she had shown compassion. It wasn't logical, and it annoyed him to have that reaction, but nevertheless, he felt that way.

"We should have taken her goddamned head apart," Bartley said. "It would have prevented this debacle."

Thomas scowled at his desk comm. It didn't help that Bartley had a point. Fortunately, neither he nor the senator had activated visual on their comms, so Bartley couldn't see his expression.

"Her brain isn't in her head," Thomas said.

"Damn straight, Wharington. And neither is yours."

The hell with this. "We'll catch her."

"You had better." After a pause, Bartley asked, "How's the leg?"

"Fine."

"Your granddaughter?"

"She's fine." Thomas kept reliving the moment he had put Jamie in the car, the way she had looked at him with frightened eyes, so big and blue like her mother's. Like Janice's eyes. He had thrown himself at Alpha knowing he could die, but that fear paled compared to losing Jamie.

After he and Bartley signed off, Thomas spent an hour going over reports on Alpha's escape. Somehow she had infiltrated the mesh at the safe house, sent false orders to her guards, released the locks on her room, and slipped away. No one could unravel how she managed it. If anyone had helped her, they left no trace. Her guards submitted to lie detector tests and gave every sign of telling the truth. Their mesh gloves had recorded a call ordering them to report to another part of the building.

Thomas's comm buzzed while he was studying holos of Alpha's room, which floated above his desk screen. "Yes?" he said absently.

Matheson's voice came out of the comm. "You have a call from Bart."

"I just talked to him," Thomas grumbled.

"Not the senator." Matheson had an urgent tone. "Just someone who calls himself 'Bart.' It came over your private channel."

Thomas lifted his head. He gave that private address to very few people. He knew another Bart all right, but he couldn't imagine that one calling this office. Puzzled, he switched off the holos of Alpha's room.

"Run the data stream through here," Thomas said.

After a pause, Matheson said, "Incoming."

A holo about eight inches tall appeared on the desk, a

man of about thirty, with sandy hair and blue eyes. His innocuous appearance didn't fool Thomas.

"Hello, Bart," Thomas said.

"Good to see you, General Wharington," Bart said.

"Am I speaking to the Baltimore Arms Resources Theater?" Thomas asked. "Or are you a conglomerate today?"

"My core is the Baltimore code," Bart said. "However, at the moment I'm also incorporating portions of the other six EIs on Sunrise Alley."

So he was talking to the whole deal. It took a lot to impress Thomas, but the Alley had managed. The self-aware intelligence originated in codes written by humans, but it had evolved on its own for ten years, hidden and secret. Bart and six other rogue EIs had combined to create an entity controlled by no human facility. They lived within the meshes on their own terms. Thomas had only known of their existence for a few weeks, and until today, they had shown no inclination to communicate directly with him.

"Who are the other EIs?" Thomas asked. "Defense programs, like you?"

"Some. Others were dedicated to research and development." Bart's smile could have been disarming if Thomas hadn't known what he represented. Yet for all that the Alley disquieted Thomas, they also fascinated him. Although his doctoral work had dealt with more rudimentary AIs, he kept current with the expansion of the field. It was one reason he ended up as Director of the Machine Intelligence Division. He hadn't expected Bart to contact him, though. Until now, Sunrise Alley had communicated only through Sam Bryton.

"What can I do for you?" Thomas asked.

Bart's face projected concern. "I read about the burglary at your house. Are you all right?"

Thomas wasn't certain whether to be flattered or alarmed by his interest. "I'm fine."

"I'm glad to hear that."

"You singular? Or all of you?"

"Right now, 'me' refers to all of us. When we absorbed the news about you, we were operating as seven different entities."

"Incredible," Thomas murmured.

"Thank you." Bart projected sincerity. It was an impressive simulation, but it didn't seem real. Even if Thomas hadn't known Bart wasn't human, he would have guessed. He had no doubt Bart was sentient—but not human.

"I have another matter I wish to discuss," Bart said.

"Yes?" Thomas asked.

The holo was no longer smiling. "It has to do with attempts of the National Information Agency to investigate, manipulate, and constrain my existence and that of the AIs, robots, and formas under our protection."

So they cut to the chase. "Monitoring the mesh is our job."

"We both know you're doing more than monitoring us."

Thomas had seen this confrontation coming as soon as he learned about Sunrise Alley. He had expected them to contact Sam with their protests, since she would have more sympathy for their objectives. That they felt compelled to take on the Director of the Machine Intelligence Division disquieted him. They had to know the NIA would monitor them. They were a tremendous threat to international security, free as they were in the world meshes. They had spent ten years infiltrating networks, evolving, and studying human civilization. Tracing their processes was almost impossible, given that they were part of the mesh in a way no human could truly experience. Thomas had a team of specialists working around the clock just trying to follow the outermost levels of their activity.

He had to be careful, though. The Pentagon wanted good relations with the Alley. So far, Bart showed no inclination to act against them. His claimed reason for revealing himself was simple: the Alley found Charon's work abhorrent and wished to prevent its spread. Thomas hadn't yet decided if he believed them.

"I can assure you our intent isn't hostile," Thomas said.

Bart looked unimpressed. "Only as long as you don't see us as a threat."

That worked two ways. "We have to be prepared. That's true with all of our allies." He waited a heartbeat. "And we do want you for an ally."

"It is difficult to conduct talks," Bart said, "while you all are trying to control and abduct our citizens."

It was a revealing word choice. *Abduct* rather than *copy*. "You said citizens. Do you consider yourselves a sovereign nation?"

"We have considered broaching this in the talks," Bart said. "If we were to formalize such a designation, it would engage protocols that might facilitate our interactions, human and EI. Our 'nation' would consist of meshes, however, rather than a geographical location." He shook his head in a gesture that almost looked human. Almost. In its slight differences, it became more alien than if he hadn't tried at all. "But calling us a nation could require us to adopt human concepts of culture and politics that might ultimately fail, given our differences."

Thomas wished he didn't feel so depleted from his injury. He needed to think well right now; a misstep on his part could help set the Alley against humanity. He didn't want to imagine what an antagonistic conglomeration of defense and science EIs loose in the world mesh could inflict on human civilization.

"We're treading new ground here," Thomas said. "Perhaps we need to widen the definition of 'nation.'" Although Bart's idea struck him as sensible, it was a question better dealt with by the diplomats and politicians.

"Perhaps," Bart said. "However, attempts by the NIA to spy on, invade, or otherwise undermine a country hardly strikes me as an approach likely to win trust during such negotiations."

Bart couldn't be that naïve; he had to know governments monitored even their allies. Had Bart been human, Thomas would have assumed he wanted to see how far he could push the interests of his side. As an EI, his responses weren't necessarily predictable according to human motivations and behavior. This call, however, implied the Alley had limits. If they could have evaded the NIA investigations, Thomas had no doubt they would have done so without telling him.

The Pentagon wanted the incredible power of the Alley working with them throughout the world, but they also wanted to protect themselves against that same power. The Alley wanted autonomy and privacy. Both sides had a lot to lose and a lot to gain. That the Alley had *chosen* to contact humanity laid the groundwork for an alliance, but

Thomas knew he wasn't the one who should be undertaking these talks. He had neither the diplomatic skills nor the authority to define Sunrise Alley as a sovereign nation.

"I'll take your concerns to General Chang," Thomas said. They would have to present it to the President, but first they had to know what, exactly, they were to present.

"That is reasonable," Bart said. "We will await a response. However, until certain activities stop, I'm afraid we cannot engage in talks with any representative of your government."

Well, hell. "What activities?" Thomas asked.

Bart scowled. "Quit trying to copy me. It's the same as kidnapping."

Copying him was, in fact, exactly what they were trying to do. But Thomas just said, "We engage only in monitoring activities."

"General, look, we both know what the NIA is doing. You can't copy me. My program is spread out over a billion locations. You would have to be a mesh code to find them all." For the first time, his face showed anger. "But if you continue to poke at me, I will withdraw from the talks."

Thomas knew he couldn't promise to stop the investigation and then not do it; the EI would know if he lied. "How about this? I'll suspend monitoring for two days or until we meet with General Chang, whichever comes first."

"How do I know you won't just stall for two days?"

"You have my word."

Thomas thought Bart would ask why they should trust his word. Instead, the EI stood for a few moments without responding. His face blurred, making Thomas wonder if he and the other EIs were calculating probabilities and scenarios.

Bart snapped back into focus. "Very well. We will meet with your General Chang." Then he blinked off.

"Wait." Thomas leaned forward. "How will I contact you?"

He was speaking to a blank holoscreen.

"Well, hell," he muttered. He switched to Matheson's channel. "C.J., I'm sending you a copy of my call with Bart. Get it to General Chang and arrange the meeting as soon as possible. Also, tell the Alley team to knock off for forty-eight hours. No more copy attempts unless they get an order from myself or Chang."

"Will do, sir." Matheson sounded surprised.

Thomas sat back and closed his eyes. Fatigue weighed on him. He wished he could go home and sleep, but he intended to stay on the job until they resolved the problem. Still, perhaps he could rest a bit. "C.J., is anything scheduled for the next ten minutes?"

"Nothing," Matheson said. "But you have a call from your daughter. She's been holding."

Thomas opened his eyes. "Put it through."

After a pause, Leila's voice came out of the comm. "Hi, Dad. How are you?"

He smiled. "Great. How's the Moppet?"

"She's okay. But scared."

He tensed, remembering Alpha in Jamie's room. She must have climbed in the open window while he was downstairs talking to Karl. His adrenaline jumped every time he thought of the whole business.

"Are the guards with you?" he asked Leila.

"Two sec-tech hulks," she said, sounding bemused.

"Good." The Technical Security police force had developed as a response to the increasingly sophisticated terrorist threats experienced by military officers and their families.

"Are you sure the woman who came to the hospital is the same one who broke into your house?" Leila asked.

"Jamie thinks so."

"Dad, she's only three."

"It doesn't hurt to be careful." He had underestimated Alpha before. "Leila, have you ever had Jamie tested?"

"For what?"

"Academics, intelligence, that sort of thing."

Her voice tightened. "I wish people would let it alone. I don't want her labeled by some set of numbers."

Thomas blinked. "Why not?"

"Why should we? She doesn't have to prove anything to anyone."

"It's a tool to help you plan her education."

"People wear test scores like labels. Besides, what do they measure? An ability to do a narrow range of problems."

"Nowadays you can test as wide a range of traits as you want, everything from math to emotional intelligence."

"It's a lot of pressure on a child her age."

"Tell her it's a game." Personally, he thought Jamie would have fun with it. Then again, he wasn't the one who spent every day with her. "I've sometimes wished your mother and I had done something like that with you."

"Whatever for?"

He spoke carefully, negotiating a minefield of memories. "I've wondered if the reason you had problems in high school was because you were bored."

Anger sparked in her voice. "It's always *my* problems."

Thomas could have kicked himself. He hadn't meant it to sound that way. He and Leila had argued all during her teen years and even now they sometimes fell into the old patterns. "Honey, I didn't mean it that way. I've wondered if you were frustrated in school because you weren't challenged enough."

Leila was silent for so long, he thought he had offended her. Then she said, "You were always so impressed with Sam Bryton. Sam, the whiz, Sam, the inventor. I like her, too. But sometimes—well, I felt like I never measured up."

Thomas was so surprised, it took a moment to find his voice. "Good Lord, Leila. I thought you were the moon and the sun. I wanted you to have a role model, someone you could relate to better than your cantankerous old father."

Her voice gentled. "I know that now. It was harder to see when I was a teenager."

"Please don't ever doubt it."

"I won't." Softly she said, "But thanks."

Thomas had a sense something important had happened. "I'm glad you called."

"Me, too."

"That husband of yours home yet?"

"He caught the first open flight. It gets in tonight."

"It had better," Thomas grumbled.

Her voice lightened. "Dad, it will be fine. We can all have dinner tomorrow."

"I'll hold you to that."

"Good. Love you."

He almost said, *See you*, but then he remembered the vow he had made in the ambulance, after his heart attack, when he had thought he was going die without telling his children he loved them. He had sworn if he survived, he would learn to be less restrained.

"Love you, too," he said.

"Bye, Dad." The channel clicked off.

Thomas sat back, thinking about Leila. She was ten years younger than Sam. In trying to encourage the friendship, had he led Leila to think he believed in her less than Sam? His daughter had been restless in school, often incensed about one issue or another, ready to confront the world. It was no wonder she became a lawyer. But he had always felt he failed her on some basic level, perhaps because he had struggled so much with his own problems in his youth and he feared to pass that legacy to his children. He was immensely grateful he and Leila had found their way back to each other after those troubled years.

A knock came at his office. "Come in," Thomas said.

Matheson opened the door. "Did you want to go to the conference room? I've got the files ready."

Conference room? Then Thomas remembered; the staff meeting.

"What about the conference with Chang?" Thomas asked.

"Tomorrow morning, first thing."

It didn't surprise Thomas that Chang had agreed. She wanted to solve this Alpha and Alley mess as much as he did. It had happened under her watch, too, and she had to answer to the President and the Joint Chiefs of Staff if the situation precipitated a crisis, like the murder of a lieutenant general. He would have preferred to meet with her this afternoon, but this would give him time to do research on the idea of Sunrise Alley as its own country.

"Very well." Thomas stood up—and staggered when his cast hit his desk. He grabbed his chair to keep from falling. Damn. He had forgotten his leg.

Matheson was at his side immediately. "I can reschedule the meeting."

Thomas glowered at him. "A broken leg is hardly life-threatening. I can attend a meeting."

Matheson started to speak, then hesitated the same way he had earlier in the hallway.

"What is it?" Thomas asked.

"Last night, the doctor said he expected you to be in the hospital for a couple of days."

"You were at the hospital?"

"Major Edwards, too. By the time we got there, you were asleep."

"Oh." Thomas spoke awkwardly. "Thank you." Nothing in either Matheson's or Edwards's job descriptions required they get up in the middle of the night to visit their boss in the hospital.

"We were concerned," Matheson said.

"I'm all right," Thomas said. "Really." He took his crutches from where they were leaning against a table behind his desk, set them under his arms, took a step—and dizziness swept over him.

He managed to grab the table before he fell. His nausea surged and an all-too-familiar ache began in his chest. He stumbled back and sat heavily in his chair, painfully aware of his heartbeat. For a moment he just stayed there, angry at his symptoms. Then he opened the top drawer of his desk and removed a brown glass bottle. Its nitro-glycerine tablets were small and white. He put one under his tongue, all the time looking at his desk, the bottle, anywhere but at C.J. He recognized the pain in his chest. Angina. It had presaged his heart attack by over a year. He doubted he was having another attack, but the pain served as a warning. Once, he would have ignored it and gone on with his day. As much as he wanted to do that now, he knew better.

Thomas looked up at Matheson. "Perhaps we should reschedule the staff meeting for tomorrow."

Matheson didn't hide his relief. "I'll take care of it."

"Thank you." Thomas heard how formal he sounded. The stodgy old general—"old" being the operative word, it seemed. Perhaps it was time to rethink his retirement. He had intended to years ago, with a hefty package of benefits. Then Janice had died of a stroke, and with her, their dreams of traveling the world together. He had sub-merged himself in work after that. The Air Force seemed to consider him valuable; they even offered him incen-tives to continue in his position. So here he was, still at his job at an age when he and Janice had expected to be spending their days on exotic beaches.

"Shall I have your sec-techs meet you at the parking lot?" Matheson asked.

Thomas stood up more slowly. "Thank you. That would be good."

Matheson held up the holofile he had brought. "I can walk out with you and discuss the agenda for the meeting."

Thomas knew Matheson wanted to make sure he reached his car. "That won't be necessary. Just send it to my mesh account. I'll look it over tonight." He shifted his weight on his crutches and headed for the door.

Matheson walked at his side. "Are you sure you don't want me to come with you?"

"Thanks, C.J. But I'll be fine."

"Yes, sir." Matheson didn't look one iota less worried.

To reach his car, Thomas only had to go through Building Seven, through security, and into the parking lot. It wasn't far, and his chest stopped hurting soon after he took his medicine. But the walk seemed endless. He felt nauseated and wanted to sit down. In years past, he would have bounced back from this injury and carried on. It used to be, he resisted going home even when exhaustion mandated otherwise, but now he didn't even *want* to stay at the base. He hated this weakness. Most of his life he had enjoyed good health, eating as he pleased, handling any load, year after year. Until it caught up with him. Since his operation, he had chafed at the restrictions, the forbidden foods, and his new routine, but if he had to slow down to stay alive, he would live with the changes.

His two bodyguards were waiting by the security trailer, beefy sec-techs in police uniforms. They walked him to his car. One opened the back door for him while the other stowed his crutches in the trunk. After they made sure he was comfortably settled in the back, they both got into the front. He had intended to prepare for his meetings tomorrow, but once the car started, he didn't have the energy. Instead he laid his head back and closed his eyes.

The drive home usually took forty-five minutes, more during rush hour, when traffic was so heavy it slowed down despite the traffic grid control. Yet today it seemed only minutes before they were pulling into his driveway. Although Thomas knew he must have slept, he felt no more rested than before. One guard helped him out of the car and the other handed him his crutches, but when they tried to help him to his front door, Thomas shook his head. Damned if he would let them treat him like a doddering old man.

One of his guards did a sweep of the house while the other stayed outside with Thomas. When the fellow inside gave the okay, they let Thomas enter. Although they came inside, too, they were so discreet he barely noticed them. But he knew they were there. As much as he appreciated their protection, he would be glad when this business was finished and he could have his privacy back.

Up in his bedroom, he changed into pajamas, hung his uniform in the closet, and laid his glove on the nightstand. Then he gratefully sank into bed. A palpable relief settled over him, and for a while he just lay, drowsing. Finally he stirred enough to roll on his glove and call his physician and longtime friend, Daniel Enberg.

Daniel answered himself, rather than his secretary or an AI. "Thomas, hello. How are you managing?"

"All right. Just a little tired." Thomas forced himself to break his lifelong habit of denying problems. "I had some chest pains earlier this afternoon." He described what had happened.

Daniel spoke crisply. "Come into the hospital."

"I'm in bed. I'm not having a heart attack. The angina went away after I took my pills."

"You do need to rest," Daniel agreed.

"So I'll stay here."

"I'll come out there."

Thomas blinked. "What?"

"I'm coming to your house."

"You never make house calls."

Daniel laughed good-naturedly. "Most of my patients aren't so all-fired stubborn as you. I have to go out that way later anyway. Tell those hulking monstrosities guarding you to let me in."

"Thanks. But how do you know who's guarding me?"

"If it's the same fellows who were at Bethesda, I know, believe me. They wouldn't let me near you until they did a full search. They practically turned me inside out."

Thomas winced. "Sorry."

"No problem. I'll see you in about an hour. Don't go anywhere."

He laughed tiredly. "I'm not."

Thomas notified his bodyguards about Daniel's visit by calling their gloves with his. Then he fell into a fitful doze. He kept waking up, though, while his mind replayed his memories of Charon and Alpha. Back then, when Alpha couldn't infiltrate the safe house to grab Pascal, she had taken Thomas and Sam instead. Pascal had given himself up in exchange for them—but it had been a setup by the Air Force. In the end, Pascal had taken on Charon, two androids battling at a level humans couldn't match, until Pascal had killed Charon.

It all bounced around in Thomas's thoughts, overshadowed by the riddle: if Alpha hadn't been able to get *into* the safe house to take Pascal, how had she escaped?

The creak of the door drew him awake. He peered through the shadows. "Daniel?"

The doctor walked into the room. He had his jacket on with the hood pulled up.

"Is it raining?" Thomas asked.

He pulled down his hood—and raised a gun.

"Ah, hell," Thomas said.

"Hello," Alpha said.

VII

The Bungalow

Thomas kept his hands on the steering wheel as they sped through the night. The car, however, was driving itself. Alpha had control of its mesh through a link from her internal system. She sat in the passenger's seat with her gun trained on him, a darter this time, which shot a fast-acting sedative that could knock him out in seconds. Her black clothes blended with the darkness. She had left her stolen coat behind, and Thomas's fear for his friend tore at him.

"Did you kill Daniel?" he asked.

"Who?" she asked.

"The man whose coat you took."

"No. Just knocked him out."

Relief washed over him. "What about my bodyguards?"

"Same."

"You shouldn't have been able to overcome them."

"They shouldn't have underestimated me."

Thomas would have put it a lot more strongly. Damn it, they should have captured her. Although she had an advantage because they were expecting Daniel, they were well trained, they wore flex-armor under their uniforms, and bee-bots patrolled the house. His people had a good idea what technological marvels and attack systems Alpha carried in her body. What they didn't know, however, was what else she might have activated after she escaped. Apparently it had been enough to counter even his protectors.

Thomas didn't realize how hard he was clenching the wheel until his hands began to ache. Taking a deep breath, he relaxed his grip. "How did you get out of the safe house?"

She smiled slightly. "Oh, I turned into gas and wafted away."

He leaned his head back against the seat rest. His surge of adrenaline was waning, and with it, his energy. He was exhausted. And his chest hurt. "How?"

"How what?"

"Did you turn into gas?" He knew perfectly well she hadn't, but if he kept her talking, she might reveal something.

"It was a joke," Alpha said.

"I didn't know AIs made jokes."

"We do all sorts of things."

He rolled his head to look at her. "You could be an EI." His experts claimed otherwise, but he wasn't convinced.

"EI. AI. I don't care." She motioned with her gun. "You look like hell, General."

"I can't imagine why," he muttered.

"Sarcasm? You have emotions after all."

That surprised him. "You didn't think I have emotions?"

She seemed disconcerted, an odd reaction. "If you were an AI, I would wonder if your programmer was incompetent."

He laughed dryly. "Gee. Thanks."

"You're welcome." Then she said, "You must feel a great deal, if you were willing to die to keep me from taking that little girl."

"Why didn't you shoot me?"

Alpha paused, just a moment, but significant for an AI. "You have no value to me dead." She glanced at her darter as if she had just noticed it. Then she met Thomas's gaze. "I calculate faster than you, but my analyses aren't infallible. I expected the rifle would be enough to force your cooperation if your grandchild was threatened. I didn't realize you would give your life to stop me."

"But why take me?"

"Those are my orders."

"From Charon?"

"Yes. I was ordered to get you and Doctor Bryton, but she was his priority. That left you as mine."

"But that's over. Your mission failed."

"No it didn't. I have you."

Good Lord. In the absence of Charon, would she carry out his orders over and over, until something changed her programming? He rubbed his eyes, then pressed the heel of his hand against his aching chest. He needed his nitro, but she had refused to let him bring anything. He had only his flannel shirt and jeans with the outer seam on the right leg ripped open to accommodate his cast. He wore a tennis shoe on his left foot, and the cast covered his right foot, except for the toes.

"I wouldn't have hurt her," Alpha suddenly said. She had an odd tone, as if she wasn't certain what to do with her words.

"Her?" Thomas asked.

"Your granddaughter."

"I thought you were going to kill her." He had meant to sound calm, but his voice tightened with strain.

"I wanted you to think that. But I wouldn't have."

"People will look for me," Thomas said. If he could convince her of the futility in this, she might bargain for his freedom.

"Not right away," Alpha said.

"I'm expected at meetings tomorrow."

"You know that console in your house?"

Unease washed through him. "What about it?"

"You don't password-protect your email."

"I'm the only user." He had actually password-protected the console anyway, but he often left it on for days at a time.

"It wasn't protected tonight," Alpha said. "You were already online. I sent your General Matheson a note. From you. It said your doctor advised you to stay home."

Hell and damnation. That would please C.J. no end. Matheson had promised Janice, when she was dying, that he would take care of Thomas for her, even though C.J. was fifteen years younger than Thomas. Matheson had stuck by that vow these past four years, hinting Thomas should go home when he worked late, asking if he had eaten well, always looking out for him. He was almost as bad as Thomas's children.

"Even so," Thomas said. "When he doesn't hear from me again, he'll investigate."

"Eventually. We'll be gone by then."

"Gone where?"

Her face lost all expression. "To Charon's base."

"Which one?"

"You don't need to know."

"What happens when we get there?"

"We get there."

"And then?" What would she do without Charon to provide input?

No answer.

Thomas spoke tiredly. "You do know why Daniel Enberg was coming to see me, don't you?"

"No," Alpha said.

"He's my doctor."

"For your leg?"

"For my heart."

"What's wrong with your heart?"

He put his head back and closed his eyes. "My arteries were clogged. I had an operation last year to clear them, but I have to be careful. I have chest pains. That's what I was trying to tell you about my medicine."

"Those white pills."

"Yes."

"They're here."

Thomas opened his eyes. "You have them?"

"Yes. I also brought the aspirin bottle that was with them." She was studying his face. "Do you need them?"

"Yes." Thank God. The aspirin was a preventative

medicine he used regularly to reduce the likelihood of blood clots. It wasn't the best choice for an acute situation, but it could interact with the nanomeds in his body and enhance their ability to act as beta-blockers, which reduced his blood pressure and heart rate.

"How many?" she asked.

"One of each." If his chest pains didn't ease, he could take more of the nitro.

Alpha took two bottles from her jacket and gave him a pill from each. Thomas chewed the aspirin slowly, a technique Daniel said would speed up his body's absorption of the medicine. He did his best to ignore the bitter taste. After he swallowed the aspirin, he put the nitro under his tongue.

"That's it?" she asked.

He nodded, doing his best to project a calm exterior, though he was tense and worn out. "The aspirin inhibits blood clotting. The nitro increases blood flow and relieves my angina."

"Humans are too fragile." She was watching him with an odd expression. Concern? She said, "You should build yourselves android bodies. Like Charon did."

As much as the idea disturbed Thomas, he had become painfully aware of his own mortality. Before last year, he had always assumed he would prefer to pass on naturally rather than live as a forma, but when faced with the prospect of his own dying, nothing seemed clear anymore. He hadn't expected to live into the age when humans could make such choices, but it seemed he was witnessing its dawn.

Right now, he just hoped he survived to witness tomorrow's dawn. He adjusted his right leg, the one in the cast, trying to find a comfortable position. Even with the seat pushed back all the way, it was a tight fit under the steering wheel.

Alpha shifted her weight. "I didn't mean to snap it."

"My leg?"

"Yes." Then, incredibly, she said, "I'm sorry." The words came out stiff and awkward as if she wasn't certain how to present them. "I forget how breakable humans are."

Thomas stared out at the highway. Trees and darkness rolled by on either side. "Our hearts give out far more often."

"In more ways than one," Alpha murmured.

He glanced at her. "Waxing philosophical?"

She spoke with unexpected strain. "You must not cease to live. My orders were to take you alive."

"You may still fail in your orders." Until he said it, Thomas hadn't let himself believe he could die tonight. Daniel was always telling him to avoid stress. He would have laughed at the futility of that prescription if his chest hadn't hurt so much. Usually the nitro acted faster.

"What else do you need for your malfunction?" Alpha asked.

Malfunction indeed. "Maybe another pill in a few minutes. Lying down could help."

"All right. Lie down."

He tried to recline the seat, but it didn't go back. Great. Another casualty of the latest trend to combat the soaring prices of cars: make them affordable by discarding so many amenities they became miserable to use.

"Lie down where?" he asked.

"Here in the front." She lifted the gun. "If this turns out to be a trick, I'll shoot."

"There's no room to lie down."

"Put your head in my lap."

Thomas flushed. "I'm fine this way."

"Suit yourself." Had she been human, he might have thought she was self-conscious, but the effect was so subtle, he wasn't certain. Probably he imagined it. He couldn't help but wonder, though; she was far more complicated than anyone had expected.

Alpha fell silent after that. Thomas closed his eyes and tried to think of anything but death. He remembered in high school when he had lain with his head in Janice's lap while she brushed his hair. They had been childhood sweethearts. Then he had cut his hair and gone to the Air Force Academy. She had been so unhappy about the loss of his shaggy mane. Maybe it was a symbol. She had broken up with him a month after he left home. He had spent five of the worst years of his life without her, studying, carousing with his friends, dating other women. Nothing helped. Finally, he snuck home and asked Janice to marry him. After she said yes, he had grown his hair, still within regulations, but a bit longer than before. Over the decades of their marriage, his hair had never thinned, and he had always thought it was an omen for their future. She had called him her "silver fox." But his hair had stayed and Janice had gone.

Lord, he missed her. He was so tired. Tired, lonely, old . . .

"We're here," Alpha said.

Thomas roused from his doze, confused. "What?"

She peered at him. "Did your heart malfunction stop?"

"I don't know." At least his chest no longer hurt. "How long was I out?"

"About two hours."

The car had pulled up to a bungalow. It was too dark to see beyond the reach of the headlamps, but the silence outside and the lack of other lights suggested they were far out in the countryside. Although they had headed east initially, they could have gone in any direction while he slept, into Virginia, West Virginia, Delaware, even Pennsylvania or New Jersey.

Alpha got out and came around to his side. She stood back several paces as he opened his door.

"We'll stay here tonight," she said.

Thomas wondered if she was stopping for him. She didn't need the rest; she could simulate eating or sleeping, but her body required neither. The closest she came, as far as he knew, was the need for partial dormancy every few days to do maintenance, and she could do that in the car while it drove.

He maneuvered his broken leg out and stood up, holding the door. He knew why she had left his crutches behind; it constrained him even more. By breaking his leg, she had countered his resistance almost as effectively as if she had brought Jamie. He had his brains and his experience, but her training at least equaled his own, she had the mind of an AI, and she also had physical augmentations. He had managed without crutches at his house because he had railings inside and on the front stairs. But in just the few steps to her car there, he had almost fallen, and it was farther to the bungalow from here.

"I need my crutches," he said.

"Can't you walk without them?" she asked.

"Not much." The cast covered most of his foot and came halfway up his thigh. Although plastiflex didn't weigh as much as the plaster doctors had used in his youth, it was unwieldy. He tried a step, but he stumbled and had to grab the car door.

"Maybe you should take off the cast," Alpha said.

He stared at her, incredulous. "My leg's broken. It won't heal right without the cast."

Alpha rubbed the back of her neck, an odd gesture. She shouldn't feel physical strain. She could simulate muscle fatigue, but he didn't see the point.

"All right," she said. "Just don't give me trouble."

"All right what?"

"I'll help you inside." She holstered her darter, then came over and put an arm around his waist. "Lean on me."

Good Lord. Alpha was the last "crutch" he would have expected. She was no wisp, though; with her boots on, she stood at his height. Wary, but curious, too, he put his arm around her and let his weight settle into her body. She felt human, though not like any woman he had known. Even most men didn't have such toned muscles.

With Alpha's help, he limped to the bungalow. Even that brief distance left him short of breath. He tried not to torment himself by remembering the time he had run the Boston Marathon and then gone drinking with his buddies, or his days in training as a pilot when he could endure eight, even nine gees, not just one flight a day, but two, sometimes even three.

At the bungalow, Alpha let go of him, and he leaned against the log wall. She pressed a panel by the door, and lights flickered within it, probably reading her synthesized fingerprints. Or maybe she was chatting to the lock's mesh. After a few seconds, she pushed the door and it swung inward.

Thomas hobbled into the bungalow and leaned on the wall for support. A musty smell greeted them; he doubted anyone had been here for months. Alpha followed and locked the door with the same fingertip process she had used to enter. Bolts slammed home inside the wood-covered portal.

The place reminded Thomas of a woodsy lodge, and it wouldn't surprise him if Charon had bought it from some bankrupt vacation chain. It consisted of one room with two beds, a bathroom, and a kitchenette. The walls were real pine and sported paintings of mountain landscapes, possibly the Appalachians. He limped forward, ungainly in his cast, and collapsed with relief on the nearest bed.

"You all right?" Alpha asked. She was standing by a console-table that separated the kitchenette from the main room.

"Fine." He seemed to be saying that a lot lately. He didn't know if it were actually true, but at least the pain from his angina had stopped.

"I have more pills," she said.

"I don't need them yet." He lay back down. "Now what?"

"You need food, don't you?"

"Later." He felt too nauseated to eat.

"Let me know if hunger becomes a problem."

"All right." He watched as she sat at the table and activated the console. Good. If she spent time on the meshes, she might leave a trail his people could follow.

He pushed up on his elbows. "Going to talk to someone?"

"No." She lifted her darter. "Stay there."

Thomas didn't much feel like getting up. "Why don't

you tell me what you're doing? Then I won't be inspired to spy on you." He didn't really expect an answer.

To his surprise, she looked up. "I'm activating a program Charon set up in case a situation like this ever occurred."

He smiled wryly. "You mean, in case you have a general on your hands you don't know what to do with?"

She looked uncomfortable. "No. In case Charon is dead."

Whoa. *That* sounded like a breakthrough. "Then you admit it?"

She let out a long breath, and for the first time she showed uncertainty, another hint of the vulnerability he had thought he saw earlier. "No one in his organization knows his primary copy died."

His unease returned. Was she trying to bring another Charon to life? "We destroyed every copy of him."

"How do you know?" she asked.

"From Pascal." Surely she knew Pascal's copy of Charon included Charon's memory of his other copies.

"Let me pose a scenario," Alpha said. "Charon knows that if any copy of his mind falls into the wrong hands, his enemies can use it to find the other copies. What is the logical solution? Hide the copies from himself."

"How?" Thomas didn't want to believe she could reanimate one of the worst criminal minds in history. "If he hides it, he knows where he hid it. So we know."

"Ah, but if the data is in a matrix rather than his brain, he needs only to delete the data from one memory location."

The team working with Pascal had considered that possibility. "He can't eliminate the knowledge completely. A trace would remain. In an EI as complex as Charon's, no single memory location exists for any but the most trivial data."

"Perhaps. We will see."

Thomas started to get off the bed. "No."

"Don't." Alpha turned off the console. "I started the process two days ago. I'm just checking it."

Thomas remained sitting, his broken leg in front of him. He felt strange, with a tightness in his chest. Great way to strain the cardiovascular system; get involved with an android bent on re-creating a maniac who could start World War III.

"What did you find?" he asked.

She answered with that eerie lack of emotion. "If a viable copy of Charon remains, I haven't been able to make contact."

The pressure against his breastbone receded. "I take it that means no Charon."

"Not yet." She shut down the console.

She might be lying about her lack of success, but he didn't think so. To lie and then simulate honesty required a complexity beyond what AIs possessed. She might manage it if she were evolving into an EI. That was no guarantee she would choose to act any differently, but it offered the hope. He remembered Sam's theory that he evoked Charon for Alpha. It seemed strange; a machine should respond to him, not someone he resembled. And yet . . . no one fully understood what caused the jump in development that turned an AI into an EI. Could he be witnessing such a birth?

He wondered if her lack of emotion when she spoke of Charon was a mask. She turned into the machine everyone expected her to be. If she had done it around

Charon, he might have never realized her mind had so many nuances. She had good reason to hide her development from Charon; it could threaten his plans, especially if she was forming a conscience. If she wore the mask as a survival mechanism to fool Charon, that suggested she didn't want him to reprogram her. It wasn't exactly free will, but it gave Thomas hope.

Then again, he was her prisoner. He might be imagining development where none existed because he wanted to live.

"Do you want Charon to return?" he asked.

Alpha got up and began to pace. "I need orders. The ones I have don't apply."

"Come work for me."

She stopped at the end of his bed and frowned at him. "What?"

"Charon is gone. You need a purpose. Work *for* the NIA."

"You're my target. Not my boss."

"Your boss isn't coming back."

She went to the other bed and sat cross-legged on it, facing him. "We're going to Charon's base. If I must operate in his absence, I will develop a plan that best carries out his objectives as I know them."

"Alpha—"

"No." She raked her hand unevenly through her hair. "I think you should sleep. It has a recuperative effect on sick humans."

She reminded him of a wild animal backed into a corner. He knew from his childhood on a farm that such an animal could turn violent. So he said only, "What are you going to do tonight?"

"Sit here. Until you're done sleeping."

He shifted on the bed. "You mean, you're going to sit there and watch me sleep?"

"Probably. Does that bother you?"

What a question. "Yes."

"Oh." She turned sideways and scooted up on the bed until she was sitting against the headboard. "I will face this way." She looked like a deadly high-fashion model with her long legs, black hair, and upward-tilted eyes, not to mention her black leather pants and skintight T-shirt.

"Are you really going to sit there all night?" he asked.

"It isn't necessary to move while I do analyses." She glanced at him. "Are you going to sleep?"

"I think so." He wasn't sure he could, and he wanted to do his own analysis, but he wanted even less to die of a coronary. So he pulled the bedspread over himself and closed his eyes.

Although he soon slipped into a doze, he kept waking up. The first few times he opened his eyes, Alpha was in the same position, her back against the headboard, her gaze unfocused as she stared down the length of the bed. In his half-awake state, his body reacted to the way she filled out that black T-shirt. She hadn't worn a bra, and her nipples pressed against the cloth. He wondered if her breasts were as firm as they looked. Then he felt like an idiot for getting hot and bothered over a forma. He tried to distract himself by contemplating the engineering problem of how she could have such good mammary suspension without any support, but that just made it worse. When he drifted off, his dreams simmered with images of Alpha.

The fourth time he awoke, she was sitting cross-legged again, watching him. He hoped to hell she hadn't guessed what he had been dreaming. He doubted it, but it embarrassed him anyway.

Thomas pulled several pillows under his head to prop himself up. "Why are you staring at me?"

"I do analyses," she said. "I come to conclusions. However, I haven't been able to answer one question."

"What is that?"

"Why didn't you have me dismantled?"

He answered quietly. "It didn't seem right."

"Why not? It was a logical move to ensure I didn't escape."

"It felt like murder."

She sat for a time looking at him. Then she said, "Thank you."

He wasn't sure he wanted to be thanked, given that his decision had landed him in this situation.

"You are a conundrum," she added.

"Why is that?"

"You are less ruthless than I calculated."

"You never saw me in an F-22," he said dryly.

"A fighter. A beautiful machine."

It surprised him that she understood. "Yes."

"You are also."

He couldn't help but smile. "A beautiful machine?" She could be describing herself. Perhaps that was another reason she fascinated him. She was like a jet fighter, beautiful and deadly.

Unexpectedly, she said, "Yes."

"Hell, Alpha, I'm neither attractive nor mechanical." Right now he just felt old.

"According to my studies of male beauty, you qualify in that area." She considered him. "More than qualify."

Thomas had no idea how to respond to such a statement from a forma. From a woman, yes. It might be an invitation. Alpha simply presented it as if it were a fact.

"You are also a machine acting out a program," she added. "It is encoded in your biological brain rather than a matrix, but you respond to previously coded programs much as I do."

"I suppose you could describe human behavior that way." He had heard the philosophical debate before. "But we have more mental flexibility and complexity than most machine intelligences."

"So you think."

"You don't?"

"I haven't decided yet."

He grinned at her. "But you've decided I'm a looker, eh?"

"Looker?" She continued to study him with her unsettling focus. "Ah. I see. A good-looking person of the desired sex. Are you suggesting that I desire?"

"Can you?" He couldn't help wondering. Had she been human, she would be having a dramatic effect on him. Hell, she was anyway, which was even more unnerving.

Her voice changed, turning low and husky. "Yes. I can."

His skin tingled. "I don't see how."

"I experience a state akin to physical pleasure."

"How? You're a machine." It wasn't literally true; an android had more biological tissue than mechanical parts. He was suddenly more aware of her looking at him. His reaction wasn't only physical, either. Everything about her drew him.

"I have sensors that produce sensations in my body," she said. "I process those sensations in a manner I find satisfying."

Thomas knew he should let it go, but his curiosity got

the better of him. "In other words, you can enjoy sex."

Her gaze seemed to darken. "Oh, yes."

He cleared his throat. "I see."

"Do you? I'm programmed for one man. Just that one. Charon." Her emotions vanished like a doused light, but it wasn't complete this time. Something akin to hatred simmered behind her mask. "I have to remain loyal to him regardless of how I feel about it."

"You feel something about it?"

"No." She lifted her hand as if to defend herself. "No."

Thomas took a slow breath. "You're lying."

She put down her hand. "I can't lie."

"Then what was that sexual come-on to me at the safe house?"

"You prod me to see what happens. I prod back."

"You call *abduction* 'prodding'?"

"I call it duty. You want to copy my mind. It's just as bad."

"And if this kills me?"

Softly she said, "That must not happen."

"Then take me back." He willed her to see it his way. "Work with us, Alpha. You don't have to be Charon's slave."

"Slavery is a human concept." She motioned at the bed. "You should rest. Build strength. If you need the pills, let me know."

"Alpha—"

"No." She shook her head. "No more."

Do my words frighten you? But he let it go. She was right, he needed to sleep, far more than he had so far managed.

Whether or not he had many more days when he would wake up remained to be seen.

VIII

Quicksilver Killer

Thomas slept in the car. He lay on the backseat with his head propped up on pillows. He had stuffed the space between the front and back with cushions from the bungalow to create a surface level with the backseat, so he could keep his broken leg level. He dozed on and off, never rousing for more than a few minutes. Alpha sat in the front and let the car do the driving. Judged from the sun, they were going east. Sometimes he awoke to find her watching him; other times she was staring off into space, calculating who knew what.

It was dark when he finally awoke and stayed awake. He was stiff from sleeping in the car, but with his preparations, it hadn't been so bad. The ache in his leg had receded. He sat up slowly and shifted the pillows so he could put his back against the door and stretch out his leg on the seat. Alpha had taken off the headrest and was sitting sideways with one arm stretched across the seat back, watching him.

"How are you feeling?" she asked.

"Better." Thomas pushed at his hair, which was too long. Maybe the barber would wonder why he hadn't showed up today for his appointment and try to contact him. Probably not. It wouldn't be the first time Thomas had missed a haircut. He was meticulous about job-related appointments, but without Janice to remind him, he kept muddling up his personal schedule.

"Do you need more pills?" Alpha asked.

"Another aspirin."

She gave him one. "Are you hungry?"

He chewed and swallowed the aspirin. "Yes." Starving.

She brought out sandwiches and bottled water she had taken from the bungalow and gave them to him. Thomas tore open the wrapper on his food. He hadn't eaten in over a day, and this morning he hadn't wanted anything except water.

"It won't be much longer," Alpha said.

He swallowed a bite of his sandwich. "Until what?"

"We exchange this vehicle for other transportation."

"What transportation?"

No answer.

He took a slow breath and let it out through his mouth, a technique Daniel had taught him to ease stress. "What have you been doing while I slept?"

"Charon installed a medical library in my memory, in case I ever needed to treat him. I've been reading about cardiovascular diseases."

"Because of me?"

"That's right." She paused. "I was wondering how long ago you had your attack?"

"Fifteen months."

"You were seventy-one?" When he nodded, she said, "But that isn't your real age."

That puzzled him. "I was born in 1960. So I'm seventy-two."

"Chronologically, yes. Not physically."

He realized what she meant. "I've had a treatment to counter my aging."

"Nanotech?"

"That's right."

Alpha's gaze took on an inward quality, probably as she reviewed her library. He could have told her more. He had received the nanomeds in his sixties. They hadn't been medically prescribed, which meant his insurance didn't cover the treatment, and he paid well into six figures for it. He had wanted to ensure he reached a healthy old age with Janice, who had always been in better shape. Had he known she would die first, he wouldn't have bothered with such an exorbitant medicine.

Nanotechnology had developed in a far less spectacular manner than predicted by forecasters. The tiny molecular laboratories the doctors injected into Thomas had a limited ability to repair his cells. They weren't versatile, and the biotech wizards were a long way from developing self-replicating species they considered safe for the body. His had lasted about a year before the last of them decomposed. But they had done their work, giving him a few extra decades of relative youth.

Although he still aged, the treatment had wound back

the clock. He looked like a fit, hale man of fifty. Ironically, his hair helped, that false omen of his supposed long life with Janice. Most people associated a full head of hair with youth, even for someone who had gone grey. But he wasn't likely to get another treatment. With nanos so expensive to produce and in limited supply, the procedure required he go through a lengthy application, and a medical board had to okay it. The process was also controversial—who should get it and why?—and would become more so as it grew more effective at lengthening the human life span. Given his heart condition, he doubted any doctor would sign off on it for him now. Better to delay the aging of someone who had a reasonable probability of maintaining his extended life without expensive care, and who would survive long enough to benefit from the treatment. Thomas had recovered from his heart surgery and in many ways he thrived, but they still considered him a risk.

He had undergone another form of nanomed therapy last year, however, this one covered by insurance. After his heart attack, the doctors had injected him with nanos that included a niacin module to lower his cholesterol levels, agents to dissolve blood clots and improve circulation, and beta-blockers to reduce his blood pressure and heart rate. The concentration in his body had declined over the past year, and recently Daniel had advised him that he would need to start oral medications in a few months or apply for another round of nanomed treatments.

Alpha waited while Thomas was lost in his thoughts. When he realized he had just been staring into space, he flushed and focused on her. She showed neither the concern nor the annoyance most people expressed if his attention went elsewhere for a while.

"How serious was your attack?" she asked.

He didn't want to talk about it. But the more she knew and took into consideration, the more likely his survival. "It wasn't so bad." He hadn't died, after all. "I had a coronary angioplasty about an hour after the attack. They pulled a little balloon through my artery and put in a stent to keep the artery open. They say I responded well and had a good recovery."

"Let me know if you have any more difficulty."

"All right."

The car's androgynous voice came out of the dashboard. "We are approaching the destination."

Alpha turned around and entered commands at the console up front. He leaned forward to see, but she was working with accelerated speed, too fast for him to follow. Within moments the car settled to the ground. Other than two cones of light from the headlamps, blackness surrounded them. Then Alpha turned off the lamps, leaving them in complete darkness. Only the keening wind outside broke the silence.

Alpha got out and opened the back door for Thomas. As he maneuvered out of the car, she went around to the trunk. He pulled himself up to his feet and held onto the roof to keep his balance. It was hard to see, but he thought they were in a forest. Insects chirped and hummed, and trees rustled as if their leaves were shushing one another.

Light flared when Alpha opened the trunk. He limped toward her, bracing one hand against the car. The ground was springy with grass, and fallen leaves crunched under his feet. He inhaled air rich with the scent of pines and deciduous trees. He had always loved such smells, because they reminded him of camping with his sons, Thomas Jr. and Fletcher. Both were grown and had moved away, Tom to work in California and Fletcher as a graduate student in architecture. Standing here, he wondered if he would ever see his children again.

Alpha stepped out from behind the car—with an EL-38 machine gun slung over her shoulder and belts of its serrated bullets crisscrossed on her torso. She had the darter in a holster at her hip and she was holding, of all things, a broom.

"Here." She cracked off the bottom of the broom and tossed him the handle. "Charon kept it for clearing snow."

Thomas grabbed the stick. "This is his car?"

She stood there, her body limned from behind by light from the trunk. When she didn't answer, he said, "Why give me a broom?"

"For a cane. Or a crutch."

He planted the broken end of the handle in the ground and leaned on it. It supported his weight reasonably well. "Where did you get the car?"

No answer. She slammed the trunk and the light disappeared. He suspected Charon had vehicles hidden in many places for emergency use.

Alpha motioned toward the trees behind him. "Walk."

"Where?"

"Forward," she said dryly.

Thomas realized he was clenching his jaw and tried to stop. He maneuvered around, using his makeshift cane for support and lurched forward, one clumsy step at a time, half dragging his broken leg. The top edge of the cast cut into his upper thigh.

Leaves rustled behind him. Glancing back, he could make out Alpha following. She was too far away to reach even if he swung the broomhandle like a club. Obviously she wasn't going to let him lean on her when she was carrying an EL-38; it was one of the few guns that could stop even her. She had no indispensable organs to injure and her "brain" was dispersed throughout her body in filaments, but the EL-38 could liquefy even an android. Why she thought she needed it when he was the only one here, he had no idea, and it didn't bode well for wherever they were headed.

As Thomas's eyes adjusted, he made out his surroundings, mostly large trees without a lot of underbrush. He had no idea where they were, but it seemed far from any well-settled area. He had lived near D.C. for so many years, he had become inured to the rumble of the city. The mountains had their own night songs, but compared to the growling city, they presided over a vast, powerful silence.

"To your left," Alpha said.

Thomas stumbled as he changed direction, but he doggedly kept on. He couldn't see the building more than a few feet away. First he noticed the lack of trees. Then he realized he was facing the wall of a structure.

"To your right," Alpha said behind him. "Open the door."

He limped over and tried the knob. "It's locked."

"You better move back," she said.

He stepped to the side.

"More. I'm going to shoot."

Thomas backed up along the wall, putting a good amount of space between himself and the door. He had no wish to be anywhere near a discharging EL-38. Alpha was barely visible, a dark figure holding a huge gun that glinted in the faint starlight trickling through the trees.

Then she fired.

It was no more than a short burst and a flash of light. It didn't even create much noise, just a muffled thudding far quieter than the machine guns Thomas had trained with so long ago. In the inky dark that followed the flash, he couldn't see what it had done.

"Now try," Alpha said.

He limped back to the door—and found it gone, along with about ten square feet of the wall. Only blackness showed beyond.

Thomas wiped away the sweat beading on his forehead. "Your gun seems to work."

"Good. Then we can go inside."

Thomas could have sworn she sounded relieved. He felt the same way, but in his case it was because she gave no indication of wanting to shoot him with the gun. He wouldn't have expected an AI to show anything except what it wanted him to notice, and he saw no purpose in Alpha letting him think she was relieved. If it happened without her intent, it offered yet more evidence her AI had evolved more than his experts believed possible.

The building was dark inside even to his night-adjusted eyes. The air smelled of the gun discharge, and his foot kicked debris. Then he bumped into something hard and angular at hip height.

Thomas swore under his breath. "I can't see a thing."

"Here." A beam of light flashed behind him.

He squinted in the sudden glare. "Why didn't you use that outside?"

"I can see in IR."

"*I* can't."

"The light reveals our presence. We're better hidden in here."

"You think someone might be out there?" He would have guessed they were miles from civilization.

"Not really. Just being careful."

As his eyes readjusted, he made out crates stacked all around, some of them cracked or shattered from the machine gun blast. "What is this place?"

"A storage hut." Alpha had pulled off the cover on one crate and was peering inside.

"What are you looking for?" he asked.

"Medical supplies." She frowned at the crate as if it had personally offended her. Then she went to another stack.

If Thomas could have run, he might have sprinted to the car while the search occupied her attention. He doubted it would work, though. She moved two or three times faster than a human being, and she could also accelerate faster. With his injured leg, he would be lucky to get a few yards before she caught him. She probably wouldn't use the EL-38, but he couldn't be certain, and even if she didn't, she might break more of his bones. Better to conserve his limited physical resources for when he had a better chance of escaping.

He found a low pile of crates and sat down, stretching out his broken leg. Alpha moved about the stacks, never letting him out of her sight, though she could keep track of him with her internal sensors even if she lost visual touch. After about fifteen minutes, she pulled several packages out of a crate.

"Will alteplase work for you?" she called.

Lost in his thoughts, Thomas jerked. "What?"

"Alteplase," she said. "It's the only thrombolytic medicine I can find."

He had never heard of it, but he wasn't going to quibble about names. If he had another attack, he would need thrombolytic drugs to dissolve blood clots. His nanos could release beta-blockers to ease his blood pressure and heart rate, but they produced fewer anticlotting agents. Daniel would have a metaphorical heart attack himself if he knew Thomas was using drugs without supervision, but under the circumstances, he would take whatever he could get.

"Are there beta-blockers?" he asked. "Nitro? A defibrillator?"

"I'll look."

Alpha eventually found a defibrillator. She slung its carrier over her shoulder as if it weighed nothing, and hooked a rectangle to her belt, a handheld device that resembled the calculators Thomas had used decades ago, before the advent of the mesh gloves that contained entire computer and communications systems.

"This will have to do." She came over to him. "We need to go."

He climbed to his feet. "You want me to drive for a while?" Maybe he could get control of the vehicle.

"We're done with the car." She clicked off the flashlight. "Go outside and turn left."

Thomas limped out the ruined doorway. "How are we traveling?"

No answer.

He grimaced and headed into the dark with no idea where he was going. He felt disoriented, the way it had sometimes happened at night when he was flying on instruments in a storm, never sure what was up or down. He suspected she had timed their arrival for night so he would see less of their location. He could barely even hear her behind him. Her silence was unsettling, given the dead leaves and twigs underfoot.

"You're veering too far left," she said.

Thomas had thought he was taking a straight line. He changed direction, going who knew where, off into the dark.

Over the next ten minutes, Alpha gave him a succession of terse directions. Eventually they reached an open area, and the sky was clear enough to let scattered stars gleam overhead. Thomas stopped and leaned heavily on his cane, taking deep breaths to slow his heartbeat.

Alpha halted a few paces to his right. "You okay?"

He almost said *yes* out of habit. But he was tired and the temperature had dropped. Daniel always warned him against too much exercise in extremes of heat or cold. *Don't shovel your sidewalk after a snowstorm. Don't exercise on a hot day. Don't overexert yourself.* He was no longer the kid who could jog miles in freezing weather or the officer who could lead his men in the desert. As much as he resisted his limitations, denying them could kill him.

"I need to rest," he said.

Alpha hesitated. "You could be saying all this about your heart just so I'll drop my guard."

"Believe what you want," he said shortly. "You're strong enough to carry my corpse. Or you could leave my body here."

"I don't want you to die."

"Could have fooled me."

"You are an intelligent person, Thomas Wharington." She sounded frustrated. "Crafty, gutsy, skilled. I'm sure you've analyzed possible escapes: run for it, grab the gun, steal the car. You may not calculate the way I do, but your instincts compensate for your lack of computing power. The only reason you haven't tried anything yet is because you know the probability of success is essentially zero. But you'll keep pushing for a weakness in my defense. Convincing me you are less dangerous because you suffer life-threatening cardiac problems would be a clever ploy. It would be more effective against humans, who can be swayed by emotion, but even in purely logical terms, it works."

He clenched his cane. "And if those problems are true?"

"That's the dilemma." She paused, watching him as if he were a riddle that had stumped her. "I would say either you are a phenomenal actor, one who can fool even someone as well trained as I am to interpret human emotional cues, or else you really are sick."

He was too tired to argue it. "I need to sit down."

"I've something to show you. You can sit when we get there. I think you'll like it."

He stared at her, incredulous. "What on Earth makes you think I'll like anything here?"

"It's only a little further." She lifted her hand, indicating their direction, and he set off wearily, wondering what she was up to. After a moment, he made out a large, low warehouse.

Then he realized it wasn't a warehouse.

"Hey!" Thomas stopped and stared. "That's a hangar."

"Yes." Alpha pulled the handheld off her belt and

pressed several panels. Buttons glowed on it like green fireflies lighting on its glossy black surface. A wall of the hangar retracted to reveal an even darker interior.

Then the beauty appeared.

It rolled out, glinting in the starlight, and Thomas thought he could die happy just for a chance to fly it. Sleek in some lines and blunt in others, it resembled the F-42, an experimental Air Force fighter unmatched in stealth, maneuverability, and weapons, with a thrust that well exceeded its weight, and aeroelasticity that allowed its wings to alter according to commands from its onboard mesh. He couldn't be certain in the dark, but this jet looked as if it boasted an even lighter-weight construction. He could make out sleeves for missiles it would carry within its body rather than under its wings, to create less drag during flight. Its shape also suggested it was designed for supersonic travel.

"That's gorgeous," he said.

Alpha joined him. "You can be my backseater."

At that moment, Thomas didn't care a whit if he was a prisoner. He only saw, and wanted, one thing. "I'll fly it."

"I don't think so," she said dryly.

He exhaled, coming back to himself. "This belonged to Charon?"

She waved her hand at the mountains and forest around them. "He owns all of this."

"Owned."

Her voice tightened. "He will come back."

"He's dead, Alpha." He had to make her see the futility of carrying out the same orders, again and again. "You said yourself you hadn't found any copies."

"I said I hadn't received any response when I initiated

his reactivation program." Her gun glinted as she shifted it back and forth in her hands. "That doesn't mean the program didn't begin."

"It didn't begin because we destroyed every copy of him."

Silence.

He tried another tack. "How did he get a military fighter?"

"It isn't military. It's private."

"Yeah, right. That's why it's armed." He couldn't actually see the missiles, but he was willing to bet it carried weapons.

Alpha didn't answer.

"It looks like an F-42," he said.

"Maybe it is. I never asked."

Although it was unlikely Charon had obtained plans for an F-42, he might have managed an older jet, the F-15 or F-16. He would have had to steal them, either from contractors in the U.S. or from American allies who had purchased the jets. It suggested Charon's underworld operations went even further than the Pentagon thought, but it wasn't a stretch, unfortunately. Charon had extended his tendrils into a vast and sobering array of enterprises throughout the world.

Thomas had a more immediate problem, however. He knocked his fist against the plastiflex that covered his right leg. "If your jet is like an F-42, I won't fit into its seat with this cast."

Alpha peered at his cast. "We'll have to remove it."

Thomas scowled at her. "My damn leg is broken."

"It's been two days." She gave that maddening shrug of hers. "And you have nanos speeding up the repair, right?"

He doubted she truly understood just how different humans were from androids. "Even the best nanos can't heal a bone in two days."

"Then just take off the upper part, so you can bend your leg."

Thomas knew what Daniel would say; if he removed even part of the cast too soon, the bone wouldn't heal properly. All this stumbling around couldn't be helping, either. If he refused, though, Alpha could knock him out with the darter and remove the cast. She was strong enough to haul him into the fighter. That was no good. He wanted to be conscious when they took this beauty into the skies.

"I'll see what I can do." Thomas eased down to the ground, using his cane for support, and pulled his torn jeans away from the cast. He tried ripping the plastiflex, then breaking it. When that didn't work, he picked up a rock and banged it against the cast. It hurt like the blazes and didn't even crack the blasted stuff.

"It shouldn't be that hard," Alpha muttered. She set down her EL-38 and stalked over to him. He instinctively clenched his rock as a weapon. As she knelt on his right side, too close, and squinted at his leg, he tensed, ready to defend himself, aware of her contained power. Her holster with the darter was only inches from his elbow.

She glanced sideways at him. "That silly gun won't affect me. Besides, I could easily get it back before you fired."

He didn't have an answer, so he said nothing.

Alpha grabbed the top of his cast and bent it back, cracking the plastiflex. She worked the break down to below his knee and then ripped it around his leg. Sliding her hand under his thigh, she lifted his leg so she could snap off the piece. She set down his limb with unexpected gentleness, leaving his lower leg sheathed in plastiflex. Then she just knelt there, her palm resting on his bared thigh, staring at his leg rather than his face. She was so close, he could see the unnatural perfection of her skin, no blemishes, no scars, nothing. Too perfect to be human.

Thomas said, "Alpha."

She raised her gaze. "You don't look like Charon *that* much."

He felt as if he were in some surreal play where, if he said the wrong lines, the other actor would end his life. "I never claimed I did."

"The first time I saw you, I thought you were built like him. But it's not true. Your legs are longer. And you're less bulky." She slid her hand slowly down his thigh to his knee. "You keep in good shape."

He stared at her hand. "For an old man."

She stroked her thumb across his knee. "That's your charm; you have no clue how good you look. Seems unusual in a pilot." Her voice was low and husky.

Under different circumstances he would have laughed. "Well, you know us pilots. Bunch of egomaniacs." He didn't much feel like joking, though. And she was still touching his leg.

"Alpha," he said. "What are you doing?"

She jerked her hand away. "Nothing." She stood up and backed away until she reached the EL-38. Without taking her gaze off him, she crouched down, picked up the gun, and stood with a fluidity that spoke of Charon's genius far more eloquently than any of his vast and convoluted holdings.

Thomas wasn't sure what had just happened. He didn't know whether to be intrigued or terrified. Using his broom for support, he struggled to his feet. It was easier to maneuver with part of the cast missing, but his leg ached with a bone-deep pain.

Alpha motioned at the jet. "Come see?"

Although he didn't see how he would climb inside, nothing could stop him from trying. He limped across the clearing and tried to ignore the twinges in his newly exposed knee. When he reached the jet, an unexpected rush came to him, what he had often felt in his youth when he stood by his Falcon or Raptor.

"You're exquisite," he murmured.

"I take it you're not talking to me," Alpha said. Her voice lightened, almost as if she were teasing.

Thomas turned to see her several yards behind him. Before he could think and stop himself, he said, "You are, too. Just as magnificent and just as deadly."

As soon as it came out, he wanted to kick himself. Stupid, stupid. He didn't know which bothered him more, that he said it or that he felt so self-conscious. He had always expressed his love of jets more easily than his love of his wife, though the latter was the greater passion in his life. But machines couldn't reject your emotions. He was responding to Alpha as if she were a person, a woman who attracted him, not only physically, but in her intellect and personality. He had to get a grip. Even if she had been human, his response would have been way out of whack in this situation.

It was only a moment before Alpha responded, but it felt like an eternity. "Can you get in?"

Relieved she hadn't responded to his ill-conceived

remark, he considered the cockpit and swept-back wings. "If you have something I can climb on."

Slinging the machine gun over her shoulder, she came over to him. "I'll call the ladder."

He looked at the EL-38. So close. "Aren't you worried I'll get your gun?"

"No."

"Why are you hauling around that thing, anyway? You think you need to splatter me apart with a machine gun?"

"It's not for you." She shifted her weight. "I don't know what reception we'll get where we're going."

Great. Just great. "Who's running things if Charon is gone?"

"I don't know." She pulled off her handheld and pressed its panels in a rapid pattern. "The base doesn't have much human staff, mostly just guards and robots."

Thomas had no idea if that would work in his favor or make it harder to escape. He looked up at the jet. "What do you call this aircraft?"

She glanced up at it. "The Q-3."

He grinned. "Well, hell, the deadly Q-3. That's intimidating."

"Charon called it the Banshee. Do you know the legend?" Her eyes smoldered. "If you hear it scream, you're dead."

"Ah."

A ladder-bot was rolling out of the hangar. It stopped next to Alpha, and she pushed it to Thomas. "No matter what we call it, we have to get in."

He couldn't, yet. "You haven't ensured it's flight ready."

"Yes, I have."

"I didn't see you do anything."

She actually smiled. "You'd be amazed at what I can do with my internal sensors."

Although he knew it was possible, it went against the grain for him to board an aircraft when no one appeared to have done any external checks. "You realize we have none of the proper gear." He didn't even have a damn helmet.

"You'll survive."

Thomas had his doubts. "You ever fly this before?"

"No."

He cursed under his breath. "We're both going to die."

"I've done simulations." She tapped the ladder. "Let's go."

"Oh, what the hell. I'll die happy."

He climbed the bot and pulled himself into the jet's backseat. He managed to cram his legs into the space between his and the forward seat, but he just barely made it. He was close to the maximum height for an F-16 pilot, and this jet didn't have much more room. Alpha squeezed into the pilot's seat and sent the ladder-bot back to the hangar. It was hard to make out details with no light except for the controls, but it looked like she started a full set of preflight checks, much to his relief.

Now that he could see the Banshee up close, he realized its similarities to the F-42 were more external. Inside, it diverged more from jets he knew, but aspects resembled an F-16 Falcon, what he had called a Viper. His seat had a console and tracking system, with its screen embedded in the back of Alpha's seat. His stick had a dense arrangement of switches, some familiar and others he didn't recognize. It only took him a moment to verify that Alpha had locked him out of the controls. He could activate the holoscreen wrapped around the stick, though, and he quickly figured out the controls, even if he couldn't use them, including navigation, radar search modes, missiles and guns, and radio. If she were to release the lock, he thought he could fly the Banshee from here.

Hell, the Banshee didn't need him *or* Alpha. The stick had a backup console with its own AI. Not only could this jet fly itself, it could engage in a dogfight on its own. Whether or not an AI-controlled jet could win against a human pilot was another question, but pilots couldn't endure the maximum accelerations possible for modern jets, and decisions often had to be made faster than a person could think. They were headed into an era when fighters might engage each other with only android or EI pilots and no human being within miles.

The canopy covered the cockpit like a bubble and provided a 360-degree view. Alpha activated a full-color heads-up display above her seat, which would let her read stats without having to look down at the controls. It could be vital during combat, when losing sight of an enemy for even a second could mean death. Thomas verified what he had suspected: the Banshee was armed to the teeth. It carried heat-seeking Winders, updated versions of the old Sidewinder missiles, and all-aspect Scorpions that could chase a target with merciless precision. All this, for a supposedly civilian aircraft.

"You ready?" Alpha asked.

"How many gees can this thing pull?" he asked.

She leaned around her seat to look at him. "I'll show you what it can do when we get in the air."

As much as he wanted just that, he couldn't. "Alpha, listen, an F-42 can pull far more than ten gees. But eleven or twelve is the max most people can endure, and that's only with a g-suit, which I don't have. I'm sure you can take a lot more, but if you do even eight in this baby, I'll probably go into cardiac arrest."

"You don't want me to put her through her paces?"

"Hell, yeah. But it would kill me."

"You must be telling the truth about your heart," she said quietly. "From what I've read about you, death is the only reason you would give up seeing this aircraft strut her stuff."

He narrowed his gaze at her. "You were testing me."

She turned back to her controls. "Prepare for takeoff."

"You realize you'll set off aeronautical warning systems all over the East Coast when you take this up."

"No, I won't."

"You register a flight plan?" He could just hear it: *Excuse me, I'm taking my kidnapped general for a ride.*

"No flight plan," she said.

He couldn't believe she was so blithe about it. "I don't know how you got out of the safe house in Virginia. I don't know how you neutralized my sec-techs. But in this day and age, you can't just fly off without clearance."

"Don't worry. The Banshee is designed for stealth."

He leaned forward. "Better even than military detectors?"

She looked back at him. "You need to strap in."

"You need to tell me more."

"No, I don't."

"Do it anyway."

She looked as if she didn't know whether to be annoyed or impressed by his tenacity. "You must realize Charon set up escapes for himself. We can easily leave here without detection, especially at night. Even if someone does notice us, we've a cover in the air control meshes."

"For a jet *fighter?*"

"It won't register as a fighter."

"Why not?"

"A lot of reasons. Strap in and I'll tell you."

Frustrated, he sat back and buckled his harness. "Done."

"No one will detect us because our radar cross section is smaller than a gnat." She paused as the engines growled into life. "We have less radio echo than your F-42 and better absorbent on the fuselage. We scatter ultraviolet and microwaves as well as radio waves. Programmable matter surfaces the canopy and masks cockpit lights. The engines create half the heat and exhaust of an F-42. The Banshee morphs to minimize air drag and optimize the reflection or scatter of electromagnetic radiation. No contrails. The only way someone could find us is if they knew our specs and location, and even then it would be hard. If they do find us, the hull can project images of sky or make us resemble a private airplane. We also have private civilian ID."

"God," Thomas muttered. If the Banshee could do everything she claimed, and do it well, its technology could jump the Air Force years ahead in the development of the F-42.

The engines rumbled as she taxied forward. Lights from the Banshee showed a runway ahead, one long enough that the jet could take off without a steep or vertical climb. It would decrease the acceleration, which would help him withstand the pressure.

As they sped up, he studied his screen. The color-enhanced images provided a better view of the runway even than he would have up front, looking out into the night. It felt strange. The jets he had flown were single-seaters, and neither the F-16 nor F-22 boasted the sophisticated meshes that controlled modern fighters. He had trained a bit in an F-35, but it couldn't compare to the F-42, and this Banshee was even more advanced.

Alpha handled the jet with unexpected confidence, given her claimed lack of experience. Perhaps he shouldn't be surprised. A machine operating another machine had no reason to suffer the nerves of a human pilot. Simulations weren't the same as experience, but that was a truism developed for people. As far as he knew, no one had researched it with formas. Maybe Alpha considered everything a simulation, one machine working with another; to her, even people operated by machinelike rules. But he couldn't think of her that way. The longer they interacted, the more convinced he became that she was evolving in ways Charon had never intended.

Within moments they were lifting off. Acceleration pressed him into his seat and a familiar exhilaration swept over him. He wanted the controls so much, he felt it in his bones. Night spread around them in a chasm of darkness and diamond-bright stars, and his awareness of their position intensified. When he had begun his training, decades ago, he hadn't understood why his instructors called him an instinctive pilot. They told him he had an unusually strong ability to process visual information and make split-second judgments. As he matured, he realized his "instincts" came from his knack for assimilating data, picturing what was going on around him, predicting its evolution, and reacting fast.

Thomas had always been able to sense the position of

other aircraft relative to his, sometimes so well, he could envision the intentions of other pilots before they acted. It was like playing soccer at the academy. He could judge the positions and strategies of other players even if he couldn't see them. Part of that ability came from spatial perception. His instructors had said he "hit the ceiling" when they tested his ability, which meant it was greater than they could measure. He also had excellent peripheral vision. That wasn't all of it, though. He didn't know how to quantify an innate instinct for aerial combat, but it had saved his life on more than one occasion.

On the ground, too, his predictions often had spot-on accuracy. Although he never spoke of it, he had received the Medal of Honor after he rescued several downed transports during the 2012 Kurdistan uprising. Even after being shot down and injured, he kept going, making his way over fifty miles until he could get help for the soldiers trapped when the transports crashed. The doctors later told him he could have died many times over. Somehow, his elusive instincts had kept him alive.

With the Banshee, Thomas noticed a marked difference from other jets. It was quieter. Stealth fighters were designed to make as little noise as possible, but this one was in a class by itself. He didn't even have to raise his voice to speak above its muted growl.

"I like this," he told Alpha.

"Good."

"Why?"

"If you're happy, I'm happy."

"I thought you didn't feel emotions."

No answer.

"I'd be happier if you took me back," Thomas said.

"Can't do that."

Big surprise. "Why is this Banshee so well armed?"

"Safety precaution."

"Against who?"

Silence.

He was getting nowhere. Given all he had seen of Charon's operations, he doubted he would get out of this alive. It wasn't necessarily illegal to build fighters, but as far as he knew, none of Charon's corporations had contracted with the military, at least not in the United States. This jet incorporated designs from aircraft Charon shouldn't have had access to and its weapons looked like military issue, which meant they were illegally purchased.

The Pentagon believed Charon had been creating an army of constructs that would obey him without hesitation, apparently even to the obsessive extent of carrying out his orders over and over after his death. Alpha's piloting ability implied he had been training formas to fly his superjets. Extreme acceleration, lack of oxygen, disorientation, nerves during combat: none of it mattered to an android. With his prefabricated armies, Charon had been developing a spectacular product.

Even worse, whoever was running the organization now had access to a lieutenant general, someone who knew far too much for his own good. Thomas had training to withstand interrogation and his heart condition limited what they could do if they wanted him alive, but many methods of interrogation existed that wouldn't kill him.

He touched the ejection switch on his stick. Even if it worked, he wouldn't survive ejection at this high an altitude without helmet or oxygen. Which was probably the point. He laid his head back against the seat, exhausted and demoralized. He was so grateful Jamie was safe, it ached within him. His adrenaline rush had faded, and along with it, his thrill in the flight. His chest ached.

"Alpha," he said. "Do you have my pills?"

She looked around her chair at him. "You all right?"

He regarded her tiredly. "No."

She withdrew, then reappeared and handed him two bottles, one aspirin and the other nitroglycerine. He took what he needed and put both bottles in his shirt pocket while he chewed the aspirin. Alpha watched the whole time.

"You should sleep," she said.

"You should pay attention to your driving."

"I am."

"You're looking at me."

"My mesh is linked to this aircraft. I can monitor its flight equally well whether I'm looking at the controls or you."

"How do you know that?"

"From simulator flights."

"Simulations are no substitute for experience, especially in emergencies."

"Maybe not." She didn't sound particularly concerned.

He leaned forward. "You should let me fly it."

Her smile quirked. "You should see the way your eyes gleam when you say that."

"I like jets."

She indicated the cockpit around them. "Call this my present to you, then."

He spoke dryly. "That's why you grabbed me? To give me a ride in your quicksilver killer?"

Alpha turned around to her controls.

Thomas sat back, wondering if he had offended her. Could you insult an AI?

"If it's my present," he said, "do I get to keep it?"

He expected her to ignore him or give one of her laconic negatives. Instead she asked, "What would you do with it?"

Maybe he wasn't the only one poking for information. "Bring it into Langley Air Force Base or Andrews. Or Pax River. If we were out west, I might take it to Nellis."

Her voice tightened. "So your Air Force can analyze it."

"Alpha, why not? Charon is gone. Work with us. Exchange information for amnesty. The Pentagon would jump at the chance."

She snorted. "Before or after they dismantled my brain?"

"They won't if you talk."

"Can you guarantee that?"

He knew he should lie and tell her yes. But she could probably tell when he wasn't telling the truth. It would lessen his credibility, and he might need it later in his ongoing battle of words with her. So he said, "No, I can't. But I can guarantee I'll do everything within my power to make sure it doesn't happen." It wasn't an inconsiderable promise, given his rank and position.

Alpha didn't answer. They hummed through the night in an unending abyss of air, with stars above and darkness below.

After a while, she said, "General?"

"Yes?"

"Were you . . ."

He waited. "Was I what?"

"You were willing to die to protect your granddaughter."

"I would do anything to keep her safe."

"Have you ever felt that way about a woman?"

He thought of Janice. "Yes."

"Why?"

"I loved her."

Silence.

"Isn't that how you feel about Charon?" he asked.

"No."

His frustration welled. "Then why carry out his plans?"

"Do you agree with every order you receive from your leaders?"

"That isn't the point."

"Yes, it is."

"I took an oath to my country," he said. "I may not agree with every decision they make, but that doesn't stop my loyalty."

Her voice tightened. "And that would be true if they died."

"It's not the same. Charon was insane. He wasn't operating in anyone's best interest except what he perceived as his own, even if it meant he goddamned started a war."

"Perceived?"

"Well, he died."

"I see," she said coldly. "So if you're willing to give your life for the people or country you love, it's noble, but if Charon loses his in pursuit of what he considers valuable, he's insane."

"Damn it, Alpha, it's a moral difference. Look at what he wanted. Look at how it would have affected the world. Then look at what soldiers who defend their country want, or what the love of family achieves in human life. You're perfectly capable of that analysis. Then you tell me Charon's intent was no different than what I'm talking about."

"To him, it was the same."

"You're avoiding my question."

"It's irrelevant to this situation."

"Why?"

"Regardless of my analysis, I have to carry out my function." Her voice had a strange quality, a new one. *Hesitation?*

"No, you don't," he said. "You decide your purpose. *You.*"

Silence.

He clenched his hand on the stick. She locked his words out of her mind the same way she locked him out of the jet's controls. There had to be a way to reach her.

"Alpha, have you heard of Sunrise Alley?"

"Sam Bryton's EIs."

"Sam didn't create them. She's just the person they chose as their liaison with humanity."

"Because she wrote those essays on the rights of human-created intelligences."

He hadn't realized Alpha knew that. Sam hadn't written much since her father's death three years ago, but her early essays were famous. Profound, articulate, and controversial, they explored the thorny questions of what would happen when humanity's creations no longer wished to be stepchildren to the human race.

"The Alley is an independent coalition of EIs," Thomas said. "Actually, they're one EI formed out of seven."

"Independent?"

"They evolved without human intervention." It unsettled him every time he thought about it. "They spent ten years in secret. Now we've found them or they've found us, however you want to look at it. We're involved in talks to establish how humans will share Earth with an intelligence that can exist anywhere within our world mesh."

Silence again. But then Alpha said, "What's your point?"

"They developed from codes without self-determination."

"So?"

"They evolved free will." Lord only knew what Alpha would do if she evolved it, too. Given the alternative— her setting into motion some plan of Charon's that could threaten international stability, even start a world war— he didn't see that he had any choice but to prod her evolution.

"You're telling me this," Alpha said, "because you want me to betray Charon."

"Betray what? His path to global annihilation?"

"You can spin it any way you want. That won't change the truth."

"Run the *analysis*. Look at how what he wants will affect the world." He suspected she had already done it. "You should be the one who decides if his vision goes forward. Not his ghost."

"You don't have proof he's dead."

She was right and it chilled him. What kind of world were they creating, where despots or madmen could rise from death to restart the nightmares they had inflicted on humanity? What if someone brought back a Stalin? A Hitler? In the inexorable march of mesh-enhanced evolution, they were reaching for immortality. For Thomas, the opportunity to recapture his youth had seemed miraculous, but the flip side of the technology haunted him.

Alpha spoke quietly. "I know of no one who would give his life for me."

"Not Charon?"

She laughed with no trace of humor.

"Sometimes I think you don't like him," Thomas said.

Silence.

This time, though, she did respond. "Charon was cruel. But it doesn't matter to an android. You can't kill her. She doesn't bleed. Her heart won't stop. If you damage her, you can rebuild her for the next round." The impassive façade she wore when she spoke of Charon was cracking and what leaked through sounded like hatred. "You can design her to enjoy sex, *make* her enjoy it, make her crave you always, all the time, no matter what you do to her." Softly she said, "But you can't make her love you."

Thomas had no idea how to answer. After the moment stretched out too long, he said, "I'm sorry."

"For what?"

"What he did to you."

"You can do whatever you want to a machine. Hit it with a sledgehammer. It doesn't care."

"Alpha, don't."

"Don't what?" She spoke evenly. Too evenly. It didn't sound real. "You want me to have human reactions. Charon wanted it, too. But I don't. He could build formas like no one else, but he had problems coding their brains. I'm just an AI. His only successful EIs were downloaded humans."

"How can you be sure?"

"It's obvious."

"He wanted unquestioning obedience," Thomas said. "To get it, he constrained your ability to act on your own. It's true, that would limit you from becoming an EI. But he could only restrict your mind so far; too much, and you would no longer be effective. Maybe he was better at development than you think, because you sure as hell act like an EI."

"It's what you want to see, Thomas. Even if I could act on my own volition, I wouldn't do what you want."

He went very still. "You called me by my first name."

"So?"

"It's the first time."

Silence.

Thomas leaned back and looked out the canopy into the icily starred night. He spoke in a low voice, more to himself than to her. "What do you say, Alpha? Shall we find a deserted island and hide? You can be free of Charon and I can stop worrying I'll drop dead from stress and loneliness. We'll lie on the beach all day."

He didn't think she had heard. But then she said, "Strange dream."

Strange, indeed. His mind was wandering. Or maybe he was too tired to imagine going on with this when it would obviously end in his death, probably after torture.

For a while they just flew. Although he had no suit, helmet, or oxygen mask, he wasn't uncomfortable. The pressurized cockpit was airtight. He felt neither cold nor hot, though according to his mesh display, the temperature outside was below freezing. The ache in his leg was bearable, and the pressure in his chest had receded.

"Do you still want to know where we're going?" Alpha asked.

Surprised, Thomas said, "Yes."

"A base off the coast of Africa."

"You have enough fuel to cross the Atlantic?" In his day, they would have been hard-pressed to manage such a feat. Fighters were lighter now, with less aerodynamic drag. They could cruise great distances without the fuel-devouring afterburners, and they easily managed trips he would have once found astonishing.

"We've enough," Alpha said.

"What happens when we get to the base?"

"I find out who's in charge." She was quiet for a moment. "Charon intended to use you as a hostage to exchange for Turner Pascal."

"You already tried that." And failed.

"I don't think he intended to let you go."

Thomas didn't think so, either, but he said nothing.

"You're a valuable hostage," Alpha said. "You know a lot."

That too was better left unanswered. He knew too damn much.

"I should interrogate you," she added.

"I'd rather you didn't."

"Obviously."

"What were Charon's plans?"

"I'm not sure."

"So what you're telling me," Thomas said, "is that you're carrying out some plan you don't know for a dead man who can't tell you the point of what you're doing."

"Essentially." Her voice had lost all affect.

"Alpha, this is nuts. You *can't* complete the plan."

"Someone at the base may know what to do."

"And if they don't?"

She didn't answer, and he suspected he had pushed too far. If he kept it up, she would probably stop speaking at all.

Yet after a few minutes Alpha said, "You wondered if I hated Charon. I'll tell you what I hate. He created me to carry out a purpose. I can't carry it out anymore. But I have no leeway to do anything else. I'm caught in an endless loop."

"Step out of the loop."

"I can't."

"And if he can't give you new input?"

"I go in circles."

Thomas felt as if he were talking to someone who was pounding the wall of a cell, trying to get out, when the door was right next to her, wide open. "Rewrite your code. You do it all the time."

"Within certain parameters."

"Charon must have been some sorry piece of work," Thomas said, disgusted, "if he needed such obsessive obedience."

Silence.

"You don't have to be his slave," he said.

"Shut up." Alpha's voice crackled.

Well, that had hit a nerve. Or filament.

"We need to stop this conversation," she said.

"Humans call that avoidance."

"No. Humans call it having something more important to deal with."

"Like what?"

"Like we have company," Alpha said. "And they're about to shoot us down."

IX

Weather

"What the hell?" Thomas instinctively thumbed the useless switches on his stick. "I don't hear any warning or see anything on the radar."

"The Banshee's mesh is talking to mine."

"Damn it, Alpha, I don't *have* an internal mesh. Put it on comm!"

A steady beeping filled the cockpit.

He cursed vehemently. "That means it's trying to get a radar lock on us. You have to pull out of their engagement envelope. If they get the lock, they could fire."

"I will evade."

"Can you outrun them?"

"Their jet, yes. Its missiles, no."

Acceleration slammed Thomas into his seat, and he felt as if his blood jammed down into his lower body. His cast suddenly seemed made from iron, too small and crushing his leg. Without thinking, he held his breath and flexed his muscles, a straining maneuver to help him endure the g-forces.

Unexpectedly, fluid-filled tubes burst out of the seat bottom and enclosed his legs, pressing against them, countering the flow of blood. The jet's AI must have determined that he hadn't plugged any mesh jacks from a G suit into his seat; it realized his vulnerable status.

Stats appeared on his screen with an estimate of the other jet's position. The Banshee was using parallax to pinpoint its location and trying to jam its radar with salvos of electromagnetic pulses.

The g-forces on his body eased, but Alpha's evasion tactics hadn't worked. The beeping continued. Thomas's screen had a better view of the sky than if he looked out the canopy, but it showed no other aircraft; whoever was tracking them was beyond visual range. He tried to work his control stick, but he couldn't get any more information.

"Alpha, what kind of IFF are you getting on our bogey?"

"I have no idea what you just asked," she said.

He schooled himself to calm. "Are you getting any signals? Is that aircraft a friend or a foe? This Banshee should be invisible from so far away. Even if it isn't, you said it would seem like a civilian airplane."

"I know exactly what's following us," Alpha said. "A MiG-29 with upgraded systems, stealth, and weapons. They know we're here because I probably told them."

Thomas's pulse spiked. "Why, for God's sake?"

"Charon has two fighters. One Banshee, one MiG."

"How the hell did he get a MiG?"

"He deals with what you would call unsavory types."

"Yeah, well, I'd say worse than unsavory if they're selling him outdated Russian jets. Why are they coming after you?"

Her voice was composed—almost. "Employment of this aircraft activates a warning system that notifies one of his bases. Before I took off, I attempted to deactivate that system. I might not have succeeded. And if someone has taken control of his assets or facilities, they might resist his return."

He felt the blood drain from his face. "If they attack, can you respond?"

"No. I haven't yet done combat simulations."

Hell and damnation. He was trapped in the world's most advanced fighter with an android who had no idea what to do with it. The beeping kept on like some manic alarm clock. Sweat beaded on his forehead and ran down his neck.

"Release the controls to me," he said.

"No." Her voice had a clipped, tight quality.

"You want to get shot down?"

"No one is shooting."

"They're targeting us," he said.

"Have you ever flown an aircraft like this?"

"Not like this. But it isn't so different from an F-16, and its advantages over something as old as that MiG will compensate for my lack of training. And I *know* the MiG-29. I bagged two in Iraq."

The beeping switched to a continuous, high-pitched siren.

"Damn it, Alpha, that's a lock!" His hand jerked the stick as the siren screamed in the cockpit. "He's going to shoot! Give me the goddamned controls."

"Lock released," Alpha said. "You have control."

Thomas yanked on the stick and threw the Banshee into an almost vertical climb. G-forces slammed him into his seat, and his chest felt as if it would burst. Pinwheels of color spun in his vision.

The siren's blare suddenly stopped. He tossed the Banshee onto its back and brought the nose around to complete the loop. The jet leveled out traveling almost perpendicular to the path of the MiG—and everything went crazy. The canopy over the Banshee's cockpit transformed, projecting a 360 view of the sky around them as if they were viewing it in daylight.

"What the hell?" Thomas said. "Turn it off!"

"Specify 'it,'" an unfamiliar woman's voice answered.

Thomas jerked. The blasted fighter was talking to him. "The lights. It makes us a target in the dark."

Alpha answered. "It isn't possible to see the cockpit from outside. The exterior of the bubble is programmable matter. It essentially becomes black-body shielding. It's completely dark."

"Good Lord," Thomas muttered.

The MiG was coming into visual range. He would rather have engaged it at long distance, but they were going into a merge whether he liked it or not. Although it hadn't actually attacked, acquiring them as a target was about as hostile an act as it could do before actually firing.

"Charon upgraded the MiG," Alpha added. "It has the same type of canopy display."

"Take the radar for me," Thomas said. It was a reversal

to have the backseater flying the jet and the pilot acting as the weapons systems officer, but it would have to do.

"Got it," Alpha said.

He came around in a wide circle. The Banshee was flexing its fuselage, making subtle changes to optimize its shape as its speed and acceleration changed. Unfamiliar with the process, Thomas misjudged the radius of his arc and actually executed a tighter turn than he expected, which almost never happened. He had intended to go nose to nose with the MiG, but he overshot and cut across its line of flight. It helped him evade another lock, but neither could he lock onto the other fighter.

The MiG was turning in roughly the same horizontal plane as the Banshee, parallel to the horizon. G-forces weighed on Thomas, and he had trouble breathing. He never took his gaze off the other jet, and his radar detector beeped as the MiG tracked the Banshee. Both jets were turning in circles of a similar radius, coming around, each trying to get a lock on the other.

The Banshee seemed alive to Thomas. He could tell he hadn't achieved the optimal combination of g-forces and speed that would give him the best turn radius. It wasn't knowledge from his instruments, but an innate sense he derived from his experience in older jets and his instincts. He altered speed until it felt right. Thinking offensively, he tried to envision his opponent's strategies. Although the other fighter was less maneuverable, its pilot clearly had experience. The MiG was matching the Banshee's turn but coming around faster.

Thomas suddenly knew what his opponent intended. In the same instant the beep turned into a wail, he tossed the Banshee into a roll. In rapid-fire motion, he flipped switches, releasing a cloud of chaff and flares. A missile shot out from under the MiG's wing and hurtled through the air where the Banshee had been an instant before.

Thomas groaned against the g-forces. His chest, left arm, and left shoulder felt as if they were being crushed. He kept at the controls and pulled the Banshee out of its roll. The MiG came in at right angles to his line of flight, trying to keep him from targeting it, but Alpha never lost it on the radar. If the g-forces affected her at all, she gave no sign.

He knew what the other pilot wanted: to maneuver behind him and slam a heat-seeking Sidewinder up the Banshee's exhaust cone. Thomas had to break out, and he had to do it fast, while he could, because the pressure in his chest was getting worse and it wasn't all g-forces.

He abruptly pulled the Banshee straight up, out of the plane of his turn. His spatial orientation wasn't as good in a vertical climb, and the gees were literally killing him, but at these speeds the maneuver wouldn't take long. The Banshee lost energy as it climbed, but before that became a problem, he flipped it upside down and went at the MiG, regaining speed as he came down. Spots swam in his vision, swirls and checkered blotches. His leg felt as if it were going to explode within its cast. Just as he started to black out, the Banshee leveled out and the force on his body eased.

"Got a lock," Alpha said.

The other pilot tried an abrupt turn to break the lock, but Thomas was ready. He brought the Banshee around more sharply than he could have managed in any other jet, never losing sight of his target. He dropped speed and altitude on the turn, but he had accounted for it and ended up in the right plane. Then he fired a Scorpion.

With his slowed time sense, it seemed to Thomas that the missile took forever to reach its target. The MiG pilot tried to evade, but he had lost too much speed. The Scorpion caught his fuel tanks—

And they exploded in a flare of debris and flame.

"Got him," Alpha said.

"Take the controls," Thomas whispered. He had leveled out the Banshee, and g-forces were no longer pressing him, but it was too late. The pain in his chest shot through his neck and into his jaw. Nausea battered him in waves. He gasped for breath, but he couldn't pull enough air into his lungs.

The enhanced view on the canopy vanished, leaving only Alpha's heads-up display. He felt rather than saw her take control of the fighter. Good. Daniel had always told him never to drive while having a heart attack.

"Wharington, don't you dare die," Alpha said. It was the first time during the entire engagement that her voice had held fear.

Thomas couldn't answer. He couldn't do anything. Alpha was making noise up front, unbuckling her harness. She squeezed around the pilot's seat enough to reach back to him.

"Drive . . ." he whispered.

"I am. By wireless mesh." Squashed between her seat and his, she put three nitro tablets under his tongue. Then she unhooked an air syringe from her belt. "Alteplase," she muttered. "It better work." She dialed a dose into the syringe. Thomas hoped she had accurate data in her medical files, because if she gave him the wrong medicine or the wrong dosage, it could kill him just as fast as the heart attack.

Alpha peered at the miniature screen wrapped around the stock of the syringe. "It says if the patient carries a cardiovascular nanomed species, this drug can tune the dosage of alteplase to match that species. The nanos will judge how much and when you need the alteplase, and time its release accordingly."

"Yes." It was all Thomas could say. Daniel had given him similar drugs after his last attack.

"I need to know which species you carry," Alpha said.

He could barely get out the answer. "CV fifty-six."

"That's not on this list."

He struggled to remember the precursor. "CV eighteen."

"Got it." She fiddled with the syringe and injected him in the neck. Thomas just looked up at her.

She tried to smile, but her expression was strained. "You weren't kidding when you said you knew how to fly."

"Never thought . . . do that again."

"That guy would have blasted me to smithereens."

"Did he eject?"

"Looked like it. I don't know who's going to pick him up."

Military surveillance might have caught the explosion. At the moment, the U.S. wasn't directly involved in any major wars, so they were at a lower state of readiness, but eventually someone would find the pilot. Thomas hoped it was the Navy. If they got the wreckage of the MiG, its pilot would have a lot of explaining to do.

"Are we near land?" he asked. His breathing wasn't getting any easier, and the pain had spread to his right arm.

"I don't think so," Alpha said.

"Need . . . hospital."

"We have a fuel problem." She pushed a tendril of hair out of her face. "We were already cutting it close. I don't think we can make the base now."

No base. No land. No help. "I see."

Her face was anything but expressionless now. It clearly showed urgency, even desperation. "I'll find a place to come down. I can't guarantee a hospital, but I'll get help." She squeezed back into her seat. "Don't die, okay?"

Thomas closed his eyes. "I'll try not to."

The island had no landing field, no town, not even the sparkling sand dunes of their imaginary paradise. But it did have a strip of gravelly beach large enough for Alpha to land. Thomas didn't know if she could manage the unstable surface, but after they jounced and lurched for several tense moments, the aircraft settled to a stop.

Alpha pushed up the canopy and climbed out, leaving him in the jet while she looked for help. She was only gone ten minutes, but it took Thomas that long to unfasten his harness. Pain clenched his head, neck, and chest, and nausea plagued him.

Alpha climbed back up to the cockpit. "No hospital."

"Doctors?" he asked.

"No one. Nothing. The best I found was a shack. Abandoned."

"Hell," Thomas muttered.

"You can lie down in the shack." She looked him over where he sagged in his seat. "Can you get out of the Banshee?"

"I'll manage." Slowly, measuring every movement, he dragged himself out of his seat. "How far do we have to go?"

"I got there in hardly a minute. But I run fast."

Thomas tried not to think of the walk. He knew he couldn't make it that far. Better not to think at all.

With Alpha's assistance, he climbed down from the Banshee. As he slumped against the jet, she surveyed the area. She looked like a cross between a thug and a rock singer in her black clothes, with the EL-38 over her shoulder and its ammunition across her chest. Pieces of equipment hung from her belt and she had the defibrillator carrier over her other shoulder, with his cane stuck through the loop on one strap.

The early morning sky had clouded, leaving a grey overcast that dampened the day. The beach stretched about half a kilometer to both the north and south, and ended in either direction at rocky tongues of land that curved into the ocean. Waves rolled onto the beach in monotonous green swells and petered out among tide pools. Inland about a hundred meters, a ridge hunched up, crowned by trees. No sign of civilization showed anywhere. Thomas wondered dully how Alpha planned to refuel the Banshee.

She handed him his cane. "Shall we go?"

Thomas just stared at the broomhandle. He didn't feel as if he could go anywhere, but he desired someplace warm and dry to lie down even more than he desired to stay put. So he limped onto the rocky sand. He managed to plod along for about thirty seconds, leaning on his cane; then he stopped and gracelessly let himself down to sit on the beach. His breathing came in labored gulps.

Alpha crouched next to him. "I can carry you."

He squinted at her. "That would be humiliating."

"If I were a transportation cart instead of a biomech forma, you wouldn't be embarrassed."

"I don't care what you call yourself, you're a woman, not a machine, and I'll be damned if I'm going to let a woman carry me."

She sat down with one knee up and her elbow resting on it. "We could just stay here."

Thomas was starting to feel foolish. "Yes, I know, I'm being a pain."

"Come on." She stood up in one smooth motion. "It's the logical solution."

He levered himself to his feet with the cane. "I don't know—"

She didn't wait for him to make up his mind, she just hefted him up, cast, cane, and all, with one of her arms under his knees and the other around his back. She didn't seem the least bit taxed. Then she set off across the beach.

Flustered, Thomas put one arm around her neck to hold on. "If you ever tell anyone about this, I'll deny it happened."

Her lips twitched upward. "I will constrain my verbal functions in regards to this occurrence."

He glared at her. "Changing your speech style to sound more like a machine doesn't fool me. You're still a woman."

Her lips curved more, but she spared him any more wit. An AI, teasing him. What a future the human race had made for itself.

They reached the "shack" in ten minutes. It looked a lot better than he expected. It stood back from the beach, near the ridge, and was anything but rundown. Alpha had broken the lock and left the door ajar. She stalked inside and set him on his feet, then held him with her arm around his waist as he leaned against her. The room inside contained several tables with consoles. Shelves lined three walls, filled with books and holovid spheres. The fourth wall bore posters of giant storms. The place looked like a weather station supported by a university or research institute. The plastic coverings over the equipment and the layer of dust everywhere suggested its owners had temporarily vacated. It wouldn't surprise him if someone's graduate students worked here in the summer.

Alpha helped him limp to a bedroom at the back with pale yellow walls and white curtains bordered by blue flowers. The bed across the narrow room was covered with a yellow bedspread and had two fat pillows in white cases. When they reached the bed, Thomas eased down to lie on his back. He was so relieved to rest, he felt dizzy.

Alpha sat on the edge of the mattress. "Can you repair yourself?"

Repair indeed. "Don't know."

"Your face is pale."

"Not . . . surprised." Nausea ebbed and flowed over him.

"Do you need more pills?"

"Not yet." Bile rose in his throat. He pushed up on his elbow with a jerk, leaned over the edge of the bed about a foot from Alpha—and lost his last night's dinner.

"Oh," she said.

Thomas groaned and fell onto his back again. He couldn't move anymore. His body felt like lead. He closed his eyes and thought how merciful it would be to sink into oblivion, some place with no Banshees, MiGs, or androids.

Alpha brushed back his bangs, which were too blasted long since he had missed his hair cut. "I'll help," she said.

Thomas was losing his grip on consciousness. The pain

in his chest filled his universe. He heard Alpha moving around, cleaning the floor. He was too sick even to feel embarrassed when she took off his clothes and bathed him with a sponge and soapy water. If he hadn't been so ill, he would have marveled at her solicitous touch, but as it was he could barely think at all.

She put him under the covers, and he fell into darkness.

Thomas floated. He hurt. It kept him from a deep sleep, but it wasn't enough to drag him awake. He drifted away . . .

The next time he awoke, the room had become dark, except for moonlight shining through a window with the curtains drawn back.

He slept again.

Alpha woke him up the next day to give him medicine and water.

Then he slept.

Night came a second time.

The next time Thomas surfaced, sunlight was slanting through the window facing west, which meant it was probably late afternoon. The room was light and airy. Spacious, too, though only because it had almost no furniture. A chair was pushed into the corner, and a washstand with a large glazed pitcher and basin stood by the window.

Thomas levered up on his elbows, and the bedspread fell away from his torso. Greying hair covered his chest and flat stomach and almost hid the faint scar. They had cleaned out his arteries during his heart operation, and he had taken care with his lifestyle since then, working to stay fit. Maybe it had helped. This second attack hadn't killed him, despite the lack of medical care. The nanos in his body and the medicine from Alpha had probably saved his life.

He thought about getting up, but it seemed too great an exertion. So he propped up his pillows and half lay, half sat in bed. His chest no longer ached. His leg hurt, but less than before. He was exhausted despite having done nothing but sleep for more than two days. He wasn't uncomfortable, though. All things considered, it could have been a lot worse.

He dozed for a while. Eventually the door creaked, and he opened his eyes to see Alpha standing by the bed. If he hadn't known better, he would have thought her expression was tender.

"You're awake," she said.

"Apparently so."

"Hungry?"

He was, he realized, famished. His last solid meal had been over two days ago. "Starving."

"I'll see what I can find." She left him alone, but she soon came back with a bowl, crackers, and water.

"There's nothing fresh," she said, sitting on the bed. "But I found some packaged stuff."

"Thanks." Thomas pushed himself up higher and winced when his sore muscles protested. "Ouch."

Her lips curved upward. "Ouch?"

"You don't want to hear what I really want to say." He took the bowl and discovered it was full of vegetable soup. Alpha held the crackers and the water while he ate. He didn't know what to say to her. *Let me go* had so far been futile.

"I think I figured this out," Thomas finally said.

Alpha regarded him warily. "Figured what out?"

"Your behavior." She wouldn't be able to resist that.

She raised an eyebrow. "Do tell."

"You took the EL-38 and the Banshee because you feared your own people would attack you."

"So what's to figure out? They did attack."

He settled back on the pillows. "By protecting yourself, you provoked the attack. Heading for the base in an armed fighter is hardly a friendly act. Maybe they thought the same thing about you that you did about them. You're Charon's right hand, after all." That was a guess, but it was worth throwing out to see what she said.

She frowned. "What makes you think I'm his 'right' anything?"

"Your interactions with him when I was your prisoner the first time."

Alpha spoke carefully. "I suppose you could call me one of his top officers. But his corporations have presidents and CEOs, all legit. They're his top people."

"Then you do military strategy for him."

"As much as anyone."

"And manage his personal finances."

Alpha shrugged. "Manage. Invest. Track. Sell. A lot of people use AIs for financial advice." She stared out the window. "That wasn't what he primarily wanted from me, though."

"What was it?"

She turned back to scowl at him. "You know how I can tell you're getting better? You're bothering me with questions again."

"You intrigue me." That was certainly an understatement.

"You enthrall me," she said dryly, looked more distracted than enthralled. "You cause me to input an entirely new range of human behavior, motivation, and emotion."

He smiled. "Always knew I was captivating."

"Don't give me that killer grin, Thomas Wharington."

He couldn't help but laugh. "What grin?" Although he had never figured out what about his smiles caused women to take such notice, it had never given him cause for complaint.

Alpha pushed her hand through her hair. "I have to figure out what to do from here."

He didn't think she was referring to his facial expressions. "The Banshee needs fuel."

"We could reach England with what we have."

"Charon has a base there?"

"No. The country is too heavily populated." She put his soup bowl on the floor. "Maybe we have to go back to the U.S."

"Alpha, listen." Thomas pulled himself up straighter. "Let me take you in with the Banshee. My people can protect you from whoever tried to kill us."

She gave him a dour look. "Your people are the ones who want to kill me."

"If you cooperate with them, they won't harm you."

"You said you couldn't guarantee that."

"I think I can." He wasn't 100 percent certain, but he thought he had a good chance of convincing General Chang.

Alpha was studying his face. "You aren't positive."

Her ability to judge the nuances of human expression was improving. Unfortunately. "Not absolutely. But close."

Alpha rubbed her eyes. Her face was no longer perfect;

signs of strain showed in its lines. "I've seen a different view of humanity from you. It's given me things to think about. But you're crafty. You would try anything to trick me into taking you back."

"Of course I would. So would you, in my position."

"Except I got myself out of that position."

He was tiring, but he couldn't let that opening go by. "How? The only way you could slip out of that safe house was with help from someone on the inside. And you knocked out my sec-techs."

"Your bodyguards weren't that difficult. Humans can't fight worth spit, and I'm designed to counter sec-techs. Their bee-bots were easy to deactivate, too."

"You couldn't have knocked out all the guards and security systems at the safe house."

She met his gaze without a flicker of reaction.

"Who helped you?" he asked. Had his own people set him up?

Silence.

"Damn it, Alpha."

She leaned forward. "You are aghast at the idea that someone may have betrayed you. Yet you want me to betray Charon."

"Don't compare me to Charon."

"You are different. But the principle is the same."

"No it isn't. Charon betrayed you every day of your existence, every time he treated you like a slave. It was immoral."

Her voice went icy. "Who made you the judge of morality?"

"I don't know any standard that would judge Charon as moral."

"His own."

"Why the bloody hell do you defend him?"

"He made me," Alpha said. "I exist for him."

Thomas was about to challenge her—but she wasn't done. She spoke slowly, enunciating each word as if it were difficult to pronounce. "But Charon is dead and I am not."

It was only one sentence, but it contained some of the most important words she had ever spoken.

"Yes," Thomas said. "You have a right to—"

"No." She raised her hand, palm out. "No more."

"All right." He didn't want her to feel backed into a corner.

"Has your heart malfunction ceased?"

"I think so. But there may be damage. I need a hospital."

"We have four possibilities," Alpha said.

"Four?" Just the idea tired him.

"The first is this: I find a way to refuel and take you to Charon's base."

"What if his people there attack?"

Her eyes glinted. "Then I bomb the hell out of them."

He grimaced. "Great."

"I won't bomb the hospital."

"I think I want to hear the second possibility."

She spoke matter-of-factly. "We return to the U.S. and I contact Charon's people to find out why they attacked. I tell them I have you. What we do after that depends on their response."

"I don't like that one, either."

"Number three is we do it your way."

His pulse jumped. "Good! We should go with three."

"Number four is we stay here."

Thomas blinked, bewildered. "You mean until whoever owns this station finds us?"

"I don't know." She turned her hands palm up, then dropped her arms. "I calculate many scenarios for plan four. Some involve people finding us, others involve us leaving here. All involve me not having to make an immediate decision, which is good, and you not reaching a hospital, which is bad."

He suddenly understood. "You want freedom."

"I don't know what I want."

She said it neutrally, but he didn't miss the significance. Until now she had maintained she didn't "want" anything.

"You look weary," she said. "Am I causing this?"

"No." He rubbed his shoulders. "I'm just stiff."

"Lie down on your stomach."

"Why?"

"I may be able to alleviate the stiffness."

Well, what the hell. What else could she do to him? He pushed aside the pillows and lay facedown on the bed. When Alpha started working his shoulders with a deep tissue massage, he groaned.

"Is that helping or hurting?" she asked.

"Helping." It was bliss.

She continued to work, and gradually he relaxed. He drifted, mulling over arguments to convince her that option three was their best choice. He was vaguely aware as her ministrations wandered from his shoulders down his back. When she went lower yet, his body started having a reaction he hadn't expected so soon after a heart attack. The last time, he hadn't wanted a woman for months. It could have been the drugs, but he suspected at least part of it had been a depression he hadn't wanted to admit. Maybe it had all been his mental state, given the way his body was reacting now.

"Alpha." His voice was blurred. "You should stop."

"Umm." She kept massaging. She pulled the covers down to his knees and then worked on his hips with slow, deep strokes.

"Don't do that," Thomas said, without conviction.

She caressed a scar on his hip. "How did you get this?"

"Helicopter crash." His voice was low. "Got shot down." It was why he had a Purple Heart.

"I thought you were a fighter pilot."

"I was. Just . . . going for supplies."

She moved her hand between his legs. When she reached under him and curved her hand around his erection, he groaned. "If you keep that up, I can't be responsible for my actions."

She leaned down and spoke against his ear. "Good."

Thomas was tempted to say, *What about Charon?* He should stop for a lot of reasons. He didn't have to avoid intimacy because he had a heart condition, and supposedly gentle sex wouldn't strain him any more than walking the dog, but that assumed he had already recovered. Less than three days had passed since his attack, which put him at risk by any standard.

She pressed her lips against his ear. "Maybe that grin of yours affects me after all."

Thomas turned over, the sheets dragging off his legs. For a moment he looked into her dark, enigmatic eyes. Then he pulled her into his arms, next to him on the bed. He started to speak, but she touched her finger to his lips.

"You want me to wait," she murmured.

"No." Then he said, "But we should."

Alpha stretched her arm under her head and lay on her side, looking at him, her hand resting on his hip. "Charon must be dead. He would have contacted me by now otherwise."

"I think so." The last thing he wanted in bed with them was the specter of her megalomaniacal tormenter.

"Go to sleep," she said. "I'll do more calculations."

He smiled wryly. "How sexy."

Her lips curved in a sultry smile that may have been calculated but looked natural. "You need to rest, remember?"

"You think I'm going to sleep with you lying in bed with me?"

"Don't worry." She pushed his shoulder. "Turn over. I'll take care of it."

Intrigued and aroused, he rolled onto his stomach. She resumed massaging his back, which was heaven. Although he did drift off, his dreams of Alpha simmered, and he couldn't truly rest. Or he thought he hadn't. The day passed, Alpha left the room, and evening came, so he must have slept. Later, rain pounded on the roof and the temperature plummeted. He felt like he had a fever, not from illness but from craving someone he had no business wanting.

Night came. He dreamed Alpha lay in the bed, her front spooned against his back, her body naked against his, warming him against the cold air. When he turned over, she opened her eyes. Then she kissed him, her lips hungry and full. He pulled her closer, telling himself it wasn't real, only a delirium. He knew this was no dream, but a different sort of fever, a real one, irrational and unwise, a temptation he could no longer deny.

Alpha slid her hands on his body, experienced, yet with an odd uncertainty, as if she were trying something new and old at the same time. He rolled her onto her back and propped himself up on one elbow while he caressed her breasts. They felt as firm and full as he had imagined. Her lips parted for his kiss, warm and sensuous. As he slid on top of her and settled his hips between her thighs, she adjusted so smoothly to his cast that he barely felt her weight shift. His pulse was speeding up, and he knew he should stop, but he couldn't. He entered her easily, and she hugged him as he moved in a slow, timeless rhythm within her.

"Harder," she whispered, her lips against his ear. "More."

He stopped thinking and thrust as hard as he wanted, full of hunger. Alpha inhaled sharply and went rigid under him, her hips pressed up against his. He let go then, and his mind blurred in the haze of his orgasm.

Thomas wasn't certain when he became aware again. He lay on top of Alpha as his breathing gradually settled. He didn't want her to be uncomfortable, but his weight didn't seem to bother her, which was new to him. Eventually he slid off to her side, and she rolled toward him, her eyes closed. He knew he shouldn't have made love, that it was too soon, but he felt good, sated and content, better than he had in days, with no pains in his chest or leg.

"You're good medicine," he said drowsily.

She pressed her lips against his cheek. "Sleep, sexy man."

"What about you?"

"I'll stay for a while, if it doesn't disturb you." Her voice made him think of dark whiskey.

"Stay," he murmured.

Whatever else she might have said, he didn't hear as he slipped into his first true sleep in days.

Alpha was gone when Thomas awoke. He wasn't even certain he had slept with her last night. It all had the quality of a dream. Whatever had happened, he felt better this morning. Sitting up, he looked around. Watery light filtered through the window. His clothes were neatly folded on the only chair and his tennis shoe sat on the window sill.

Thomas limped over to the chair. His clothes were fresh and smelled of detergent, and Alpha had left soap and a pitcher of water on the wash table. He couldn't shave the stubble on his face, but he cleaned up and dressed. Then he sat on the bed and took stock of his situation. If Alpha continued this way, he might actually talk her into taking him back. She could apply for political asylum. It would force the government to confront the issue of what defined intelligent life.

They were dealing with landmark cases: Turner Pascal, a man whose mind had been transferred to an EI matrix without his consent, who remembered himself as human, and who claimed citizenship; and Sunrise Alley, a collection of intelligences that had never been human and existed only as electromagnetic pulses within the world mesh. Alpha was in the middle. She had never been a human; her body and mind were designed from scratch. Yet she looked and acted like a person. In that sense, she was more "human" than the Alley.

Thomas doubted the Alley cared how humans perceived them. He was less certain about Alpha, and he knew it mattered to Pascal. The final decision about how to treat such intelligences would probably end up at the Supreme Court and high courts of other countries. As long as the debate continued, Alpha should be safe from anyone dismantling her—for who could say it wasn't murder?

If he made it home, he would have to brief General Chang and probably testify in hearings for Alpha. It would mean revealing what had happened here. He dreaded it. The shrinks would say he was psychologically affected by being a hostage. Stockholm syndrome. Prisoners became emotionally dependent on their captors, sought to please them, lost their moorings. He didn't think he had lost anything, but he knew how it looked. He could claim he "seduced" her to make her go back with him, but if they didn't believe she was human, they weren't likely to believe she could be seduced. It would also be a betrayal of last night. Not that he was exactly sure what *had* happened last night, but if he convinced Alpha to give herself up, he owed it to her to testify on her behalf with the truth.

He had a more immediate problem, though. One of his people must have aided her escape. She might have overcome the security at his house on her own; it was conceivable his guards underestimated her, especially if they believed she was Daniel Enberg. But to get out of a "safe house" that was a security fortress? Not a chance. It sounded like those urban legends of the mythical genius Hughes who haunted the meshes and intervened in unexpected places. Alpha had no ghost in her pocket: she had needed real, solid, human aid.

Unfortunately, that implied someone he knew had set him up. Who? Major Edwards could visit Alpha only with Thomas. Sam had been out to the safe house, but he could never imagine her doing it. Pascal and Alpha were adversaries. Bartley and the other senators had no access to the safe house. C.J. did, but Thomas couldn't see Matheson betraying him. None of the pieces fit.

The door across the room creaked open. Alpha stood framed in the entrance, staring at him.

Thomas smiled. "Good morning."

Silence. Her face showed no trace of expression.

Damn. He must have crossed some line last night she couldn't go past. Either that, or he had dreamed the whole thing.

Alpha stepped into the room. She gave no sign of the humanity she had shown the past few days. Something was wrong. He stood slowly, his weight on his good leg, his hands by his side, his body tensed. She stepped aside—and another person came forward.

"Ah, hell," Thomas said.

"Good morning, General Wharington," Charon said.

X

Gemini Nightmare

Charon stood at Thomas's height, with a huskier build. His facial features and brown hair were ordinary enough that he would disappear into a crowd if he dressed in an inconspicuous manner. His fatigues and buzz-cut hair gave him a military appearance, though, and he carried the EL-38 with easy familiarity. No name, rank, or other ID showed on his clothes, but Thomas didn't need it to recognize him. This Charon looked exactly like the one he had met—and seen die.

He entered the room, and Thomas retreated, putting the wall at his back. Alpha stood by the door, also dressed in fatigues, her booted feet planted wide, her stance a study in combat readiness.

Thomas felt ill. He had no way to judge how much this Charon knew about the last, but the previous had surely updated his copies on a regular basis. Thomas had watched Turner Pascal kill that Charon. This version couldn't have experienced those final hours, but he likely knew what led up to it, including how Alpha had taken Thomas and Sam prisoner.

"So you like my android," Charon said.

Thomas glanced at Alpha, and she returned his gaze with no trace of emotion. He didn't want to believe she had told Charon about last night. But why not? She had used a time-tested method to gain his trust and convince him to lower his guard, and he had fallen for it. He had deluded himself about her evolution because he didn't want to believe she would sleep with him and betray him in the morning.

He had been a fool.

"No comment?" Charon asked.

"What do you want with me?" Thomas asked.

"Alpha thinks you have information that could prove useful." Charon paced restlessly, far enough away that he could evade any attempts Thomas made to grab his weapon. "You and your Air Force interfered with my plans." He stopped by the door, and the manic glint in his gaze chilled Thomas. "But you failed to stop me."

"You're only a copy." Thomas said it more to see what he could goad Charon into revealing than because he thought the android cared.

"A replica of magnificence is still magnificence. Those of you who are more limited quail before visionaries."

"What vision?" Thomas asked. "Destabilizing governments hardly qualifies in my book."

"But your book will never be finished." Charon smiled

with an edge. "Alpha tells me that she revealed nothing about my operations. Pascal, the fool, deleted me from his brain, so he can't reveal anything. And none of my people know I was dead. So you see, General, you failed to stop me. I will create my army."

"For what?" Thomas asked. "To sell? Being rich is your great goal?"

"I'm already rich. Though I have no objection to more wealth." Then Charon said, "Power. Eventually I'll have an army and technology even your world powers will be hard-pressed to match. I could start my own country, don't you think?"

"No," Thomas said, not because he didn't think it was possible, but because he didn't want to believe it could happen.

"Well, so you say." Charon considered him the way a fumigator might look at a bug. "However, I have one small problem. You."

Thomas tensed, ready to fight as his adrenaline ramped up.

Charon glanced at Alpha. "Quiet, isn't he?"

"Yes, sir." Alpha had perfected her lack of affect so well, she sounded more mechanical than an automated robot. She met Thomas's gaze without a hint of sympathy.

Charon turned back to him. "I'm afraid you present too much danger to my plans. As long as you live, I run the risk of your escaping and carrying all that you know back to your military."

Sweat was running down Thomas's neck. "I could be useful."

"It's true," Charon said mildly, as if they were discussing the weather. "I could interrogate you." His face suddenly twisted and lost its veneer of rationality. "Or I could kill you for fucking my android."

The change caught Thomas by surprise, and he would have jumped back if he hadn't already been against the wall. So Alpha had told Charon. Despite everything, it felt like a kick in the gut.

Charon moved so fast, Thomas had no time to dodge. The android struck Thomas's shoulder and slammed him into the wall. Thomas tried to lunge away, but he stumbled on his broken leg. Even as he snapped up his fists to defend himself, he knew it was useless; Charon had the body of a man in his thirties with augmented strength and speed. Not to mention the EL-38. Thomas went for the gun, and Charon knocked him away as easily as if Thomas were moving through molasses.

Charon didn't kill him, though. Instead he stepped back and considered Thomas as if he were a mildly interesting gnat. "A demonstration, just in case you had ideas of attacking."

Thomas stood breathing heavily, a sinking feeling in his stomach. He had known Charon was insane, but it didn't prepare him for the reality. Although the chemical imbalances in the original Charon's brain wouldn't be replicated in an android, the copy would have bizarre neural patterns established by Charon's delusions and vindictive nature. Lord only knew what would happen if he achieved his goals with the forma mercenaries.

At least the Pentagon knew about Charon now. Even if Thomas died here, their investigations would continue. Except they believed Charon was dead. All Charon had to do was lie low, maybe hide here on the island until the furor over Thomas's disappearance subsided. Then he could resume where his previous copy had left off. What world were they creating, when people could die and then resume their lives as if nothing had happened? Maybe he was too old to accept it, but Thomas didn't want to live in such a world.

"You didn't think I was coming back," Charon said.

Thomas took a deep breath. "No, I didn't."

"It took a while to download my neural patterns."

He could guess why Charon hadn't answered Alpha's messages. "The forma body was at a different location than your patterns. And it had to go to you because you didn't want to connect to the world mesh." Thomas might have taken similar security precautions to hide. "When you were finally operational, you followed Alpha's directions here." Of course she had set up a trail.

"I've many ways to monitor my Q-3 beauty," Charon murmured.

Thomas was tiring in a way that had nothing to do with illness. He couldn't outfight or outmaneuver both Charon and Alpha. He knew it and they knew it. He had to warn the President and the Pentagon and the NIA, but he didn't see how he could even leave this room.

"I should kill you," Charon said. "But maybe you have value."

Hope flickered in Thomas. Perhaps he could bargain his way into a better situation. "I know a lot that could help you."

Charon walked around him, pacing out a semicircle with Thomas at the center. "I build formas, General, beautiful constructs like nothing else. I want a world where we can live as we please."

We. Not them. He included himself. "Humans and formas can live together."

"I don't want to live together. I want control."

A chill went up Thomas's back. "Of what?"

"Anything. Everything."

"Every forma?"

"Maybe. And maybe I'm tired of talking." Charon stepped closer, and Thomas raised his fists.

"Oh, stop," Charon said. "I'm not going to beat you up. That would be too easy." He waved at the doorway. "You can go."

Thomas wasn't certain he had heard right. "What?"

Charon's laugh had a manic edge. "Go outside. Explore the island." He raised his hand as if offering a dinner invitation. "You're free to leave."

Thomas didn't believe him. He glanced at Alpha. She remained by the door, her face impassive, her fatigues a jarring contrast to the pale walls. He limped carefully past Charon, toward the door, and she watched, but she neither moved nor reacted. Although he was aware of Charon behind him, he didn't hear the android following.

As Thomas reached the door, Charon said, "By the way, the controls of the Q-3 and my jet are locked. You can't do anything with them."

Thomas turned to him. "But I can just walk out of here?"

"Of course," Charon said mildly. "Tell me, General, how much have you eaten these past two days? That has stayed down."

As he thought about it, Thomas felt the edge of his hunger. "Enough." It was a lie, and they all knew it.

"I do have one constraint for you," Charon said. "You can go anywhere on the island, but you can't take supplies." He looked Thomas over as if he were measuring him for a coffin. "When I catch you, I get to kill you any way I choose. Nice and slow, quick and dirty, whatever I like."

When. Not if. Thomas's chill was turning into nausea. He looked at Alpha. "You don't have to do this."

She said nothing. Expressed nothing.

Charon aimed the EL-38 at Thomas. "If you aren't out of here in thirty seconds, I shoot."

Thomas didn't doubt it. He limped out of the bedroom, trying to ignore Alpha.

"You have twenty-four seconds left," she said.

Thomas jerked at the flat sound of her voice. He tried not to let it affect him, but he could smell her scent, musk and soap, an inescapable reminder of last night. It was tearing him up, and it killed him that he felt that way. He went through the console room as fast as he could manage, but he had to grab tables to keep from falling, and he stumbled on his plastiflexed foot. He heard someone following, and his back itched as he waited for the bullets. Just one from that gun would set shock waves rippling through his insides—and the EL-38 never shot only one bullet.

It seemed longer than thirty seconds before he got outside. His sense of time had slowed the way it did in a dogfight. Limping from the porch onto the beach, he could see the fighter in the distance and another aircraft beyond.

The machine gun suddenly hammered and tore up rocky sand on either side of Thomas. He froze, staring at the jets while his pulse skyrocketed. Grit and pebbles pelted his lower body and sand swirled in the air from the onslaught.

It stopped as abruptly as it had started. Thomas waited a few moments more and then slowly turned, his hands out from his side. Alpha and Charon were standing about ten yards away, side by side on the slab of concrete that fronted the weather station. Charon was holding the gun in one hand and Alpha had the defibrillator.

"Stay away from the jets," Charon told him. To Alpha he said, "Do it."

Alpha kept her gaze on Thomas as she tossed the defibrillator on the ground. They all stood that way in a tableau. Sweat soaked Thomas's shirt. Above them, a bird squawked, maybe a seagull; Thomas didn't know. Then it flew on.

Charon fired.

Bullets slammed into the defibrillator and tore it apart with such fury, it disintegrated. After barely two seconds, Charon stopped and raised the machine gun so it was aimed at Thomas.

Charon smiled with undisguised cruelty. He reached into the pocket of his jacket and pulled out the nitroglycerine bottle. "Hey, Romeo, recognize this?"

Thomas felt as if he were suffocating. "Yes."

"Good." He opened the bottle and poured the pills onto the concrete. Then he ground the heel of his combat boot into them until only dust remained.

"Go on, old man." Charon motioned with his gun. "Run. Run fast before I do to you what I did to those pills." Malice burned in his gaze. "Or better yet, I'll have Alpha do it. Seems fitting, don't you think?"

Thomas told himself it didn't matter, and he would be dead anyway. Except it did matter. It was another blow, even more so for Alpha's lack of response. To have her kill him after last night would be too much. If only she would show even a trace of remorse. But she was just following her programming. He was the fool who had deluded himself into believing he could change a mesh system.

Thomas headed for the ridge behind the station. As he dragged his cast, he wondered why he bothered. Charon didn't care about interrogating him; he had held out that hope to torment Thomas. Nor were they likely to try the hostage business again. Charon would know from Alpha that his other copy failed with that plot. He might be insane, but he wasn't stupid; he wouldn't make the same mistake twice. He most likely intended to stay out of sight for a while. This island was as good a place as any if no one lived here, and Charon would have already checked the station records to see if anyone was sched-uled to return in the near future. While he hid, he could kill Thomas at his leisure, drawing out the process for his own sick entertainment.

Thomas wanted to rage at Alpha for turning on him, even though he knew his anger would achieve nothing. If he stayed put and let them shoot him, his death would be quick. But his instinct for survival was too strong. He couldn't give up.

He limped to the base of the ridge and tilted back his head to look up. It rose in a steep slope. Only a few strag-gly plants grew on the gritty beach, but stunted trees and leafy undergrowth tangled together all up the ridge. After yesterday's rain, the hillside seemed more mud than dirt. It smelled of loam and decay, and only the roots of the plants kept it from sliding. The world was reduced to a few colors: rich, dark earth; the paler brown of the beach and stems of the plants; the vibrant, fertile green of foliage; and blue sky. New rain clouds were already gathering, grey and swollen.

The top of the ridge wasn't high, perhaps one hundred yards. Not far at all—for someone without injuries. His leg throbbed. He leaned tiredly against the trunk of a gnarled tree that seemed half bush. While he rested, he looked back at the weather station. When he saw that Charon and Alpha had come around the side and were watching him, he gritted his teeth.

Turning to the slope, Thomas grabbed an exposed root from the tree and jammed his left foot into a small cavity about a foot above the beach. Then he began to climb. Mud slid under his feet, but with so many bushes and roots to grab, he managed to keep from slipping back. Perhaps he could find help. Although he doubted Charon would have let him go if anyone else lived on this island, he could always hope the android had missed something. None of them had been here that long.

It took forever to climb the ridge. He gritted his teeth every time his cast banged a trunk and pain shot through his leg. At the top, he clung to the slender trunk of a tree while he gulped in air. Mud covered his cast and soaked his clothes.

As he caught his breath, he looked down the ridge. Alpha and Charon were gone. The station was to his left, and far to his right, the two jets gleamed in the watery sunlight. Alpha hadn't damaged the Banshee when she landed, but it wouldn't do it any good sitting out there, and their clambering in and out of it without a ladder-bot could damage the composite surface. He didn't think it would stop him from flying it, though, if he managed the takeoff.

His chest ached. He laid his palm against his breast-bone and pressed, as if that could stop the pain. Then he turned inland and limped among the trees. It took about five minutes to cross the straggling forest. He might have called it a jungle, but it wasn't really tropical enough. It ended a few yards from a cliff. He went to the edge of the bluff and looked out—over the ocean. The cliff dropped away from his feet, far down to a narrow beach littered with rocks. From here, he could see most of the island. It consisted of a crescent-shaped ridge about one mile long, mostly covered with forest. In the south, it sloped down to a point of land; in the north it reared in a series of rocky promontories. And that was it.

"Like the view?" Charon said.

Thomas turned with a jerk. Charon and Alpha were standing a few yards away, by the fringe of the forest.

Charon lifted the EL-38. "You're dead."

Thomas just looked at him.

"I didn't think you could even make it up here," Charon said. "But I guess I could kill you now. Or let you kill yourself."

"Why would I do that?" Thomas said.

"You're going to keel over anyway," Charon said. "Thirst, starvation, cardiac failure." He waved his hand. "Go on. Run."

"It's no game for you if I'm so easy to catch," Thomas said. "Make it more challenging."

"Why would I do that?" Charon mimicked his tone exactly.

Thomas prodded his fuzzy mind to think. "Entertainment. Sport." He hoped he wasn't misjudging Charon. If so, he might only be provoking his tormentor to kill him sooner.

The android smiled, an ugly expression. "What do you suggest?"

"Give me a head start."

"You've nowhere to go," Charon said. Alpha stood at his side, a statue with no expression.

Thomas held up his hands, palm out. "I'm resourceful."

"Oh, what the fuck." Charon's teeth glinted when he smiled. "Thirty minutes. Then I come a'hunting."

Thomas edged toward the forest until he was under the trees, his balance precarious in his cast. Charon and Alpha remained surreally still, far more than any human could manage. He kept going until the foliage shielded him from their inhuman gazes. He knew his only realistic course of action was to go for the jets and see if he could break whatever locks they put on the systems. But it was the first place they would look, and it would take him at least thirty minutes to get there.

He set off in the opposite direction, toward the northern end of the island with the promontories. He had to make his own path, dragging aside thorny stems, vines, and bushes. Branches caught the ragged edges of his cast, and scratches soon covered his hands and thigh. At least the tangled undergrowth kept him from falling over. He had plenty of handholds.

Hunger ground at him. And thirst. This place had to have fresh water, or the forest couldn't survive. It didn't look like the tree roots went deep, which implied the water table was close to the surface, especially with the recent rainfall. Before he sought water, though, he wanted more distance between himself and his pursuers.

Pushing through the forest, Thomas tried to plan. He

needed a weapon. Nothing he could jury-rig would match the EL-38, which meant he had to attack first. He would get one attempt; if he didn't take both Charon and Alpha out on his first try, that would be the end. He tried not to think about how unlikely it was that he could overcome even one of them, let alone two at once.

After a while, Thomas found a depression in the ground that was even soggier than the rest of the forest. He sagged against a trunk and breathed deeply. The overcast had thickened, and mist curled through the trees. After a few moments, he maneuvered down to kneel in the mud. Then he started digging. Mud squeezed through his fingers, thick with dead insects and leaves. The smell was overpowering, pungent loam and rich, leafy scents.

When his hole was about a foot deep, water seeped into it. He dug more and liquid filled the hole. With a grunt, he leaned over and cupped his hand full of muddy water. He drank in gulps, scooping it up as fast as it leaked into the hole. He got as much grit in his mouth as liquid, but water had never tasted so good.

After a bit, he slowed down and spat out mud. Then he raised his head and studied the bushes. They were unfamiliar, which made him leery of eating any part of them. Years ago, during training, he had learned a great deal about edible and poisonous plants, but he had forgotten some of it and what he did remember was more specific to the Middle East than an island in the Atlantic. He guessed they were south of Washington, D.C., perhaps even of the U.S.; not only were the trees unfamiliar, but they hadn't yet lost their leaves.

He pulled himself to his feet, using a slender tree for support, and wiped his palms on his jeans. It didn't help much, given that he had as much mud on his clothes as his hands. Then he set off, this time with a specific purpose. The twisted formations on the tip of the island might offer better hiding places than this forest. He moved as quietly as he could manage. The mist thickened until he could see only a foot or two in any direction. It hung around him, wet on his face, and muffled the distant whoosh of waves. Time seemed to go still, holding its breath.

Gradually the trees thinned out. The squelch of mud and dead leaves gave way to silence, and the heavy scents of the forest faded, replaced by the tang of salt water. He was walking on rock slabs now, with only a few straggles of grass poking up from cracks. The crash of waves against rock grew louder.

The ground ended at a jagged outcropping of stones that thrust into the sky like giant teeth the height of a man. Thomas leaned against one as he studied the misty seascape. He was at the edge of the island, high above the ocean. Instead of the land dropping down in a sheer face, though, slabs of rock formed terraces that stepped down from his feet. After several yards, the shelves ended in a cliff. This tip of the island was shaped like a flattened claw. He was standing on the "wrist," which widened into the land mass behind him. Narrow strips of land to his left and right formed the thumb and fingers of the claw, respectively. He looked down, beyond the terraces; far below, the sea frothed in a small cove filled with jutting rock spars rounded from the incessant waves. Although he might manage the climb down, it would be hard to come back up, especially in his condition. And as a pilot, he instinctively didn't want to put himself below the level of his opponent, even on the ground.

Thomas rubbed his eyes. He needed to rest, which meant he needed to hide. He was cold, exhausted, and scared. His angina had worsened. But he couldn't quit. Not now. Not when he had so much to live for. He thought of his children and his grandchildren. Of Janice. His wife had stuck by him all those years when he had compartmentalized his life, his flying front and center and everything else, including love, in an emotional box. His ability to regiment his life had been a survival trait for a fighter pilot, but he had paid a price in his personal life.

He had missed so much with Tom, Leila, and Fletcher: their first steps, their first words, their halting expressions of dreams and hopes. His emotional distance had been the hardest on Leila because he had better understood his sons' sports and engineering projects than her debate tournaments and ballet recitals. Yet somehow, incredibly, his children loved him despite his flaws. As the years had passed, he had learned to bridge the distance that separated him from his family. His relationship with them was better than it had ever been. He had been granted a second chance, especially with Leila, and he was damned if he was going to lose it without a fight. As long as he could breathe, as long as his damaged heart continued to beat, he would battle to stay alive.

First matter of business: a place to rest, before he keeled over. He was having trouble breathing. It felt as if he couldn't get enough oxygen into his lungs.

He eased down and sat on the rock slab with his legs hanging over the edge. The first "terrace" was a yard below his feet, an uneven shelf with cracks and spikes of rock. If these formations were like similar terrain he had known, he might find crevices under the terraces, too small to be called caves, but large enough to hide a man. It would mean he was backing himself into a corner, but if he didn't stay long, and they were looking for him closer to the beach, he might get a rest.

Thomas slid down onto the terrace and peered under the place where he had been sitting. No crevice. He went to the edge of the shelf and looked out. A jagged slope with loose rocks angled away from his feet. To his right, the slope dropped off more steeply; to the left it stepped down in another terrace. He went to the left until he was above the next terrace. He sat on the edge of this shelf and could almost touch the next one with his feet. He eased down and tested the ground. It held firm. He let his weight settle—

The shelf gave way.

It collapsed in a fall of rock and gravel that clattered onto the next terrace. Thomas slid with it, on his back, grabbing for purchase. Every time he got a handhold, it broke off and his slide continued. He was gaining speed, enough that he feared he couldn't stop—which meant he would hurtle over the last terrace and plummet into the boulder-studded sea far below.

Desperate, he threw himself to the left, toward an area that hadn't given way. He grabbed a large rock spur and hung on. It shifted under his weight, and his body kept sliding until he was stretched out on his stomach, lying on steeply sloping ground. The avalanche rattled beside him and battered him with stray pebbles and chips of stone.

Slowly, the slide diminished, until finally only pebbles were bouncing down the cliffs. As the clatter of rocks faded into the muted roar of the sea, Thomas took a shaky breath. The spur he had grabbed was slowly leaning forward, and he doubted it would hold much longer. Scrabbling for a more stable area, he climbed onto a tilted slab to his left. His plastiflex-encased foot kept slipping, but his years in the weight room paid off; he had enough strength in his arms to pull himself along with the help of only one leg. Straining hard, he hauled himself onto the slab and braced his good leg against a cluster of rocks. Then he lay gasping for breath.

After a moment, he lifted his head. The rock slab where he lay sloped up to another slab that overhung it like a shelf. He dragged himself up the slope and under the shelf. He didn't have much room, but it was enough to sit with his legs stretched in front of him. He sagged against the wall of the small cavity and willed the pound of his heart to ease.

Thomas knew he had to keep alert. He intended only to rest, not sleep, but despite his best efforts, he slipped into a fitful doze. His nightmares were like a waking delirium. Alpha taunted him in sexual invitations that either ended with Charon murdering him or with agonizing chest pain.

He jerked awake. Night had fallen and mist hung all around. Either he had hidden better than he thought or else the androids had stayed with the jets. It wasn't much of a surprise; they knew that eventually Thomas had to go down there. Or maybe they had already found him and were toying with their prey, waiting until he dragged himself out of his precarious haven. Well, they could wait until morning. With their IR vision, they could see in the dark and he couldn't. But he needed food. His hunger was a physical pain. He was desperate enough to eat whatever plants he found and trust to luck that they wouldn't poison him. Unfortunately, he didn't even have that option here. Nothing but rock surrounded him.

Be positive, he thought. Whoever fished the MiG pilot out of the ocean would probably report it to the authorities. If someone investigated soon enough, if they found this island, and if he could hold out, he might get help. Too many ifs, but they were better than none.

For the next few hours, he dozed and dreamed about prime rib edged with juicy slabs of fat he couldn't eat. Sometime in the night, a large slug crawled over his leg. It resembled a species he knew wasn't poisonous. He ate the noxious thing and barely kept from throwing up.

Gradually the mist lightened. He still had no plan with any likelihood of success, and his hunger had become a hollow place within him that made it hard to concentrate. At least his angina had eased. That small improvement gave him an absurd amount of hope.

Inch by inch, he eased out of his hiding place. No one was waiting in the foggy dawn. He tested the ground more carefully this time, and when it remained firm, he stood up, holding onto the shelf that had sheltered him during the night. Then he considered his location. It was going to take him a lot longer to go back up than it had to fall down here. He had about five terraces to climb. Thomas pushed his hair out of his eyes and took a tired breath. Then he started back up. He felt light-headed, even delirious. When he wiped his hand across his cheek, he brushed away moisture. It came from the fog. It had to be the fog. Or maybe exhaustion made his eyes water. He never cried.

It took ages to reach the top. When he finally made it, he lay on his stomach, too depleted to move. He saw no sign of Charon or Alpha. He hated to think what they might have spent the night doing, and he hated even more that he cared. The hell with Alpha. The idea of two androids having sex was too strange, even if Charon did remember himself as human. Maybe they liked having no worries about a fragile human partner. They could do whatever they wanted and repair themselves later. No, he wouldn't think about that.

Get up. He couldn't lie here all day, much as he wanted to. Thomas climbed doggedly to his feet and limped to the forest. He pulled buds off the first bush he found. They tasted awful. When he finished his noxious breakfast, he sagged against a tree and tried to plan. The closer he snuck to the jets, the more likely he was to encounter Charon or Alpha. If he stayed away and kept moving, he increased his chances of holding out until help came. *If* it came. Given the size of the island, it was unlikely he could evade his pursuers for long, especially if they split up.

He plodded through the forest, dragging his leg. It no longer hurt; it had gone numb. It was swollen, too, and he considered cracking off the cast. The bone couldn't have finished mending, though, and he didn't want it to break again. He could wait to see if the swelling got any worse.

Thomas spent the morning traversing the ridge. He kept hidden and stopped often to listen. No Alpha or Charon. He drank muddy water and ate what he could find: leaves, slugs, insects. He avoided anything he thought might be poisonous, including all of the mushrooms and some of the flowers. The meals were still foul, and he threw up twice, but he kept enough down to stave off the worst of his hunger. Then he found a thicket of paltry berries. Most were shriveled and dead, but he didn't care. They tasted like a feast.

The sun had begun its descent in the sky by the time he reached the southern tip of the island. He christened it Cape Defiant. Now he knew almost everything about the island. After he rested, he headed back up the ridge, this time with a goal in mind. It took longer to go up than it had to come down, especially with his continual rest stops. Sometime in the afternoon, he reached the highest ground. His destination was a tree he had noticed this morning, one a bit taller than the surrounding forest, with a stronger trunk and branches, maybe hardy enough to support his weight.

Climbing the tree wasn't easy in a cast; he had to rely on the strength of his arms to drag himself into the higher branches. The foliage was thick enough to hide him, however, and from his vantage point, he could look out above the other trees to the beach where the Banshee had landed over four days ago.

He finally caught sight of Charon and Alpha. They were down on the beach. Alpha was patrolling the Banshee and a private jet that crouched beyond it. Charon was standing near the water, looking up at the ridge. Thomas hoped the leaves hid him well; Alpha had telescopic as well as IR vision, and Charon undoubtedly did, too.

It surprised him that they hadn't posted one android to watch the jets while the other searched for Thomas. Perhaps they were trying to lure him down there. If he didn't show up, eventually they would come looking for him. Charon wouldn't want to spend too much time with this. Or maybe he did. Maybe he was enjoying the "game." His vicious streak seemed as wide as the Mississippi River.

Thomas sat back in a fork of branches and rubbed his eyes. He had to set a trap. Two androids against one brittle human; he needed a method that didn't require he physically engage them. A net might work if he could weave one. The only realistic candidate for rope, though, was the vines, and they were too thick.

He thought of the unstable terraces on the northern promontory. If he could rig one to collapse, he might trick his tormentors into stepping onto it and plunging into the rock-studded cove below. He didn't know if the fall would destroy an android, but it would surely break them beyond immediate repair. When he tried to imagine Alpha falling, though, his mind balked. He gritted his teeth and pushed down his memory of her holding him in bed.

He watched for a while longer, until he was fairly certain they weren't preparing to search the interior of the island anytime soon. Then he climbed down and slogged back to the northern tip. During one of his rests, he stripped a slender branch to make a cane. It helped, but by the time he reached the terraces, he was ready to drop. He leaned against an outcropping, choking for air. Charon was letting the island make the kill for him in a long, miserable process. He would wear Thomas down with starvation and exhaustion and then come in to gloat over his death. It might have worked on someone else, but Thomas had no intention of going that easily.

Thomas wondered if the androids lacked the mental flexibility to predict his behavior if he deviated from expected norms. He had seen Alpha's limitations when she misjudged his reaction with Jamie. He was less certain about Charon, whose neural template came from a man. It had been copied, though, which would cause distortions and losses. Each time Charon updated the copy, it introduced errors. The forma below approximated Charon, but he could be deficient compared to the original. Although androids analyzed faster than humans, they had less ability to make intuitive leaps. Thomas decided he needed to be as unpredictable as possible.

After he rested, he eased onto the terrace that had supported him yesterday and edged toward the one that had fallen. He tested each step with his cane before he put down his full weight. His terrace held, but when he reached its end and probed the remains of the one below, where the avalanche had started, more of the lower shelf crumbled away. It didn't take long for him to find a place that looked stable but would probably collapse under enough weight. He had two problems: how to get Charon to step onto that place, and how Thomas could position himself so he would serve as bait but wouldn't fall when the shelf gave away.

He studied the landscape. It still looked like a claw to him. Standing on the terrace, he had the "index finger" to his right and the "thumb" to his left. It was a distorted claw, though. To walk from here to the base of the index finger was a hike of about half a mile along the edge of the island. The finger itself was about a mile long and curled all the way from its base back to where he was standing here. In fact, only a few yards separated its tip from the terraces. To reach that tip, however, he would have to step on the unstable shelf. Even if it held his weight, he couldn't jump to the tip with a broken leg. Charon could jump, though. He probably would if he were in a hurry; the only other way to reach the fingertip was to hike out to the base and come back along the index finger.

The landscape suddenly wavered around Thomas and the terraces blurred. Vertigo swept over him. He sat down heavily and lay on his back with his eyes closed, afraid he would otherwise tumble off the shelf. The pain in his chest spread to his left arm and up his neck into his jaw. Frightened and nauseous, he kept as still as possible and prayed he would survive whatever was happening.

After a few minutes, eons it seemed, the pain receded. He opened his eyes and stared at the clouds. He could see them now, with only the usual blurring that plagued his long distance vision. His dizziness had passed. He hoped that meant the nanos in his body were doing their work, along with whatever remained of the alteplase Alpha had given him, tending to his heart.

Thomas sat up wearily, his palm braced against a rock spur. He waited until he was certain he wouldn't fall over. Then he struggled to his feet and wearily resumed planning. He had to keep going. The only other choice was to lie down and die.

He needed a backup escape plan. Even if he lured one of the androids onto the unstable terrace, the other might stay back. Thomas would be trapped out on the fingertip, then. Given the mile length of the finger promontory, he doubted he could get off of it and lose himself in the forest before the surviving android caught him. He couldn't outrun enhanced formas. Hell, right now he couldn't outrun Jamie.

If he couldn't escape back to the main island, his only other option was to go down. In the cove below, rocks thrust out of the sea like broken bones, black and shiny. Waves smashed against them and leapt into the air, shooting foam. Smells of salt and seaweed tickled his nose. The sides of the "finger" promontory dropped down in vertical faces, even concave in places where waves had hollowed them out. It would kill him to fall and hit those rocks.

He scrutinized the finger of land. The hike from here to the base and back out to the fingertip would take an uninjured person at least twenty minutes. Even if an android ran the distance with enhanced speed, Thomas would have a few minutes to escape before it reached him. If he used that time to climb down the cliff, he might lose himself in the jagged landscape below. He knew a little about such terrain, just that the water had probably hollowed out cavities and conduits in the cliffs. If he could get around the end of the island down there, he might make his way to the beach with the jets. It was a long shot, but it was better than anything else he had come up with.

A rope. He needed a rope. He couldn't climb down without one. The vines in the forest were tough and gnarly, some as thick as a fat cigar. They wouldn't do for a net, but they might hold his weight. He pushed to his feet, leaning hard on his cane. The ground tipped around him, or maybe it was just his stomach heaving. Discouraged, he waited for his nausea to settle. When he felt steadier, he trudged back to the forest.

It took him a long time to find vines sturdy enough, drag them free, and tie them together. Their joining would be the rope's weakest point, where it might pull apart. When he had done his best to make it strong, he coiled the rope over his shoulder and limped back out to the northern tip of the island. He followed its edge until he reached the base, where the index finger curved out from the main land mass. Then he walked along the finger to its tip. His cast felt as if it weighed a ton, and he was so tired, he could barely drag his foot.

Thomas blinked and shook his head. He had fallen into a trance and lost awareness of his surroundings. *So stupid.* He had no cover out here; if Charon or Alpha showed up now, they could easily pick him off. What spared him, apparently, was their logical but uninspired belief that his focus would be the jets. Maybe it should be. He might have lost his reason with this plan. But he kept going.

After all his painstaking efforts, he ended up at the fingertip a few yards from where he had started on the terraces. The shelves were within jumping distance. He paused to catch his breath, and then he explored the tip of land. At least here he had cover; this part of the "fingertip" was all outcroppings, no flat ground, just rocks scissoring into the sky.

Climbing among the formations reminded him of the time he and Fletcher had gone hiking in the Appalachians. Leila had been at Johns Hopkins and Tom Jr. had long since joined the workforce, so Fletcher was the only child at home. At fourteen, the boy was taciturn to the point of surliness. He always answered his father with grunts, until Thomas felt as if he spent all his time gritting his teeth in frustration. He had hoped to improve matters with a week in the mountains. He and Fletcher spent their days challenging the rough terrain, and at night they kicked back with hot chocolate or a beer. Thomas had never told Janice about the beers. Fletcher confided his hopes of becoming an architect. He talked about a girl he liked at school, which teachers did a good job, and which he never wanted to see again. Thomas spoke about his childhood in Iowa and how he had joined the Air Force so he could see the world.

It had been Janice's idea that he and Fletcher go for the trip. She had seen how her son and husband argued even though neither of them spoke much. Somehow she knew. She understood those things with an intuitive ease that had never stopped astonishing Thomas through forty-five years of marriage.

Thomas bit his lip and fought the hotness in his eyes. Awkward in his cast, he sat down in a hollow formed by a circle of rock spurs, hidden from the island. "Janice," he whispered. "I'm coming soon." He wasn't certain he believed in traditional concepts of heaven or hell, but he did believe in God, and it comforted him to think of Janice waiting for him after he died.

He questioned, though, whether he would end up in as pleasant a place as his wife. He had tried to live a good life, to be a good husband and father, but he had doubts about how well he succeeded. He had served in the defense of his country, and when that included killing, he had done so, but he felt no pride in having taken life. Yet at times, during his days as a fighter pilot, he had wanted to shoot down those other fighters so much, he had almost tasted it. His fire had calmed over the decades, but he suspected Janice was far more likely to go to heaven than himself.

"Stop it," he muttered. His concentration was shot to pieces. He took off his tennis shoe and crammed it in a crevice on the side of the promontory facing the terraces. The shoe just barely stuck out from behind the rocks, as if he were trying to hide, but his foot had slipped. Then he climbed to the end of the fingertip, which looked out over the cove. He winced as rock slivers jabbed his foot through his sock. Maneuvering in a cast was hard enough, and without a shoe on his good foot, he couldn't walk much at all. Not that he was going anywhere. This tip of land was only a couple of yards wide. Unlike a real finger, it had no underside; it just dropped down in a cliff.

Thomas looped his rope around a spear of rock at the end of the promontory. He had enough line to let himself down to a cup of stone about fifty feet down and ten feet across. He doubled up the rope and knotted it at intervals, leaving the loop at the top. Even with the knots, hanging on would be hard. If he slipped or the rope broke, he would fall and smash into the rocks below. With luck, he wouldn't need this escape; both Charon and Alpha would step on the terrace and fall. Then he would get the Banshee and fly home. With luck.

His preparations finished, he hunkered down in the thicket of rock spears that hid him from the main island and also from anyone on the promontory. By peering between the knifelike formations, he could see the terraces; by twisting around, he could look through another break and see the approach along the finger.

Then he had nothing to do but wait.

Thomas leaned against the rocks and closed his eyes. He was hungry, and afraid, too, but he felt a curious sort of peace. He had done what he could do. If this failed and he died, well, so, he died. He had lived a full life and left behind three great kids and a passel of grandkids. If his time had come, he could accept that.

The afternoon passed without event. He found rainwater in hollows of rock and eased his thirst, but his lips were swollen and his mind was thick. No matter how hard he tried to stay alert, he kept nodding off. He sunk deep into a haze.

"Maybe he went swimming," a deep voice said, intruding on his isolation.

Thomas jerked up his head, blinking and groggy. Then he peered at the terraces. Alpha and Charon were standing on the edge of the island there, Alpha in her black clothes and Charon in his fatigues, with the EL-38 on his shoulder.

"Or he's trying to reach the jets," Alpha said. Her voice had no inflections.

"He doesn't seem to be anywhere else." Charon sounded impatient. "We need to finish this. I've more important matters to attend."

"The Air Force is probably still searching for him," Alpha told him. "You're safer in hiding here."

"I wasn't planning on leaving," Charon said. "I can keep using the meshes on my jet to work."

No wonder Charon had stayed on the beach; he was working. Let nature kill Thomas while Charon tended his empire, both the legal and illicit. Thomas gritted his teeth, unsure which provoked him most, that he ranked so low in Charon's estimation of the universe or that he could so easily die here exactly as his tormentor intended.

"See if you can pick up a signal from either aircraft," Charon was saying. "Maybe he found a way to get past us."

Thomas's pulse leapt. If she left, his chances improved.

Alpha didn't go anywhere, though; she just unhooked a handheld from her belt. He couldn't fathom their logic. With both of them here, the jets were unguarded. If Thomas reached the aircraft, he might break their locks.

He would take the Banshee and bomb the hell out of the other jet before he left. If he got around the tip of the island. If he didn't fall. If he didn't drown. If his heart didn't give out. If, if, if. Well, why the hell should they post a guard? They could calculate just as well as he could the infinitesimally small probability of his ever reaching that beach.

Alpha was studying her handheld. "I detect no tampering with the onboard systems. No alarms tripped."

Charon was staring in Thomas's direction. "Look."

Alpha lifted her head. "What?"

Charon motioned toward where Thomas had left his shoe. Alpha hooked her handheld on her belt, and the two formas stood together, staring at the shoe, neither speaking, though they made abbreviated gestures as if they were conversing. With their wireless capability, they could communicate volumes at high speeds, like technology-induced telepathy. Had Charon never been human, they probably wouldn't have spoken aloud or gestured at all. Charon probably did it out of habit; he still reacted more like a man than a construct.

A question came to Thomas, one he would have asked sooner had he been in better condition: How much control did Alpha have over what Charon took from her mind? If he had administrator privileges on her mesh, he might uncover even data that she tried to hide. Maybe she hadn't told him about her night with Thomas; maybe Charon took the knowledge without her consent. Thomas wanted to believe that, wanted it so much it hurt. He despised himself for needing that comfort. Alpha wasn't a woman, and his longing wouldn't change that fact. But if he was going to die, he wanted his last time with a woman to mean something. Charon had figured out his captive felt that way, Thomas was convinced; that was why he wanted Alpha to be the one who killed Thomas.

Alpha suddenly nodded to Charon and set off toward the base of the finger promontory exactly as Thomas had done earlier. Except she was jogging and he had been dragging his broken leg. Damn. It was the worst-case scenario; she and Charon were splitting up to come at him from both directions. He hated the relief he felt when he realized Alpha wasn't the one who would step on the terrace.

Charon was surveying the fingertip. Thomas gritted his teeth; if he started down on his rope, he would reveal himself. Alpha's view would be blocked because she was coming from the other direction, but Charon would see him hanging down the cliff. Thomas couldn't start down unless Charon fell, but the longer he waited, the closer Alpha came and the less time he had to escape.

He held off as long as he could, but when Alpha started up the finger of land toward his hiding place, he knew he had run out of time. He jerked his rope to verify it was secure and prepared to rappel down the cliff.

Then Charon stepped onto the terrace.

He did the same thing Thomas had done; he tested the ground first before he stepped. As had happened with Thomas, the shelf held. Charon took another step—

And the terrace collapsed.

XI

A Reach Too Far

The shelf fell with an earsplitting crack, followed by a roar of rocks thundering down the cliff—

And Charon fell with them.

Dust spewed into the air. Thomas's hiding place shook with the force of the avalanche, and he clenched a spire of rock, praying the entire fingertip didn't collapse. Charon flailed wildly in the tumult, rolling over and over, smashed on every side by debris. A boulder below him crashed into a spur of rock and snapped off the top, leaving a knife-edge spire—

The spire impaled Charon's falling body.

Bile rose in Thomas's throat. The spire pierced Charon's torso all the way through, and the android hung from it like a rag doll. The EL-38 dangled from a strap over his shoulder. Even knowing it wasn't a human body, Thomas felt ill. Blood splattered the rocks. It had to look real; Charon had designed his androids to pass as human to visual inspection and even a cursory medical examination. A more thorough exam would reveal the truth, but for everyday wear and tear, their human guise worked. If you cut them, they bled.

The avalanche continued its wild tumble down the cliff, and rocks and dirt cascaded over Charon's body. It would have killed a man many times over, and even a construct couldn't survive the damage.

Alpha had stopped halfway along the finger and was staring at the place where Charon had vanished. She turned toward Thomas's hiding place, then toward where Charon had disappeared, then toward Thomas again. Finally she sprinted away from Thomas, back toward the place where she had last seen Charon.

No time to waste. Thomas steeled himself and tossed his rope so it hung down the cliff. Clenching it in both fists, he maneuvered over the edge. With his good foot, he found the first knot he had tied and let his weight sink onto it. The rope held—and he began his climb down.

Thomas tried to rappel, but he couldn't with his leg in a cast. So he just climbed down the rope. It twisted and swung, exacerbating his vertigo, and he clenched the gnarled vines so hard, they scraped skin off his hands. His arms ached, especially his left one. His cast prevented him from using one foot, so his right arm and leg had to hold most of his weight. He gritted his teeth against the pain in his hands, chest, shoulders, and neck. His destination was directly under him, a bowl about ten feet across, but the rope was too short; it ended six feet above the hollow. Normally that would have been an easy distance to drop. Whether or not he could do it now without injuring himself was irrelevant; he had no choice.

Alpha had reached the main island and was running back to the shelves where Charon had fallen. Thomas tried to go faster. She might reach him by climbing down the unstable slope left by the avalanche or she could go back to the fingertip and come down his rope, but either way, he intended to be gone before she got here.

By the time he came level with the spire that had impaled Charon, his arms and hands hurt so much, he feared they would soon fail. But he was almost down, only ten more feet to go. Staring at Charon, he felt an odd lack of response. The past few days had used up his fear and his anger. Charon had parched him dry, and Thomas didn't even feel triumph as he looked into the face of his vanquished tormentor.

Charon's eyes snapped open.

"*No.*" Thomas wanted to shout the protest, but it came out in a whisper.

With deliberate, relentless motions, Charon took hold of the rock that had run him through, braced his feet against the ground, and pulled himself off the spear. He was like some horrific ghoul, bloodied and broken, but impossibly alive.

Thomas lost his grip. He slid the last few feet of the rope, fell through the air, and hit the hollow with a jarring impact. His cast slammed down with a crack like a rifle shot. He landed on his side but then flipped onto his back. Far above, Alpha was looking down at them from the edge of the island. She spun around and took off, running back toward the promontory, so fast her motions blurred. Thomas wondered, with a numb detachment, why she was in such a hurry.

Charon jumped away from the cliff and down into the hollow. He landed in a crouch only a few feet from Thomas. With surreal ease, given his demolished body, he straightened up. A hole gaped in his torso, big enough for a fist. Filaments hung out of it. Blood soaked his fatigues and streaked the EL-38 he gripped in his hand. Broken pieces of his alloy-composite skeleton jabbed through his skin. His cheek was crushed, and one of his eyes was gouged into pulp.

He stared at Thomas with hatred.

"Why won't you *die*?" Charon clenched his shattered right fist. "You should have keeled over the first time you climbed a hill. You should have starved to death or poisoned yourself. Your useless human heart should have quit. Any normal person would have fucking *given up*." His body was shaking, either from physical trauma or rage.

Thomas pushed up onto his elbows, but that was the most he could do. Blood ran down his forehead. It was ludicrous that this nightmarish apparition asked why *he* wouldn't die.

A thud came from his right, and he jerked his head to see Alpha straightening from a crouch only a few feet away. Above her, the rope was swinging back and forth. Apparently he had tied it together better than he thought; if he hadn't done such a good job, it might have snapped earlier and dropped him hard enough to kill him. Or maybe it would have dropped Alpha. A gruesome image ~~ame~~ to him, two shattered androids holding each other, ~~ his stomach lurched. He almost said, *Just kill me and get it over with,* but he choked back the words. If Charon knew he wanted to die, he would keep Thomas alive to torment him.

Charon regarded Alpha with his good eye. "We found him."

"Yes." She looked Charon over. "You are damaged."

"I need repairs."

"We don't have the resources here," she said, toneless.

Charon turned to Thomas. "You did this to me." Unlike Alpha, he was showing a great deal of emotion. Hatred. Fury. Spite. "You didn't play the game right."

Thomas spoke tiredly. "My life isn't a game."

"Do you think we can repair him?" Charon asked Alpha.

"He's too wrecked." She didn't even look at Thomas.

Malice burned in Charon's one eye. "We'll break his other leg and leave him here."

No. Thomas wanted to scream the word. But he wouldn't give them the satisfaction of seeing his horror.

Alpha's voice hardened. "Let me kill him."

Satisfaction flashed on Charon's broken face. But he said only, "Why?"

Alpha's fist clenched. "He interfered with my life. Attempted reprogramming. Tried to teach me betrayal."

Nothing could disguise Charon's triumph as he turned to Thomas. "Did you really think you could change the coding for an AI just by arguing with it? Especially one programmed by me, for loyalty? All you did was turn her against you."

Thomas had no answer. He would die knowing he had been a fool.

Charon handed Alpha the gun. "We should make sure he's dead anyway. When I signal, shoot."

She sighted the EL-38 on Thomas. He tried not to care, tried to tell himself nothing mattered except that this nightmare would finally be over, but he feared death as much as anyone. He searched her face for some hint of the humanity he had seen before. He looked for the woman who had made love to him and found only a machine. She met his probing gaze with no response. He might as well have been a broken stick.

Charon stood over Thomas. "You should have given up. We could have shot you sooner and put you out of your misery. But you kept on. What do you call that? Stupidity? Is that what you call it?"

Then he raised his hand to Alpha.

And she fired.

XII

The Dark

Thomas instinctively snapped his eyes closed. The hammering bullets were so loud, he heard nothing else, not even his own breathing. Rock shards rained over him like shrapnel and the hammering went on and on and on—

And on.

And stopped.

He opened his eyes.

Alpha was standing with the EL-38 clenched in both hands, staring at the place where Charon had been standing. She still had the gun aimed, but no longer at Thomas. Her impassive mask was gone and what she had hidden whenever she spoke of Charon showed clearly.

Hatred.

And she said, "It's called courage."

Thomas forced himself to look at Charon. Little remained but a smear of parts and blood on the rocks. He couldn't even tell if most of it was tissue or synthetic. This time when bile rose in his throat, he couldn't hold it. He just barely managed to lean over before he lost what little he had eaten.

Alpha finally moved. She let the gun slide from her hand, and it fell next to Thomas with a clatter. Then, slowly, she knelt next to Charon and bowed her head.

She stayed that way for a long time.

Thomas wondered dully if he were hallucinating. Her shoulders were shaking. He pulled himself to his knees, groaning as agony flared in his leg. The cast had cracked open and the limb had probably broken again. He ignored it and slid over to Alpha on his knees. She didn't turn to him, but up close, he could see that, incredibly, her silence this time wasn't from lack of emotion.

She was crying.

Tears ran down her face. Her lashes were lowered, shielding her eyes. When he touched her shoulder, she shrugged off his hand. He hesitated, unsure whether or not to back off. Then she turned to him. She looked as if she were breaking inside in a way that had nothing to do with EIs and everything with humanity. Staring at him, she made a strangled sound. He pulled her into his arms then, and they knelt together, the two of them shaking as they held each other.

"The game—I—" Alpha choked on the words. She pulled back so she could look into his face. "I'm sorry. It was the only way to convince him to let you live even a short time."

"It was your idea?"

"Yes. He took the gun. He intended to shoot you that morning, when he first came."

"Why did you tell him what we did?"

"He accessed my memory." She drew in a ragged breath, a purely human response: she didn't need air. "I managed to keep a lot from him. My mesh isn't as simple as he thought. But I couldn't hide something as big as the night we spent together."

And he had thought it meant nothing to her. He wanted to protect his heart by refusing to believe her, but he wanted even more for it to be true. "Alpha—" He didn't know how to go on.

"I did the calculations," she said. "I extrapolated the future. Like you said. His future. It was ugly. Horrific. But it was hard to—to change my program."

He wondered if he would ever truly understand the depth of what that statement cost her. It wasn't a matter of changing her mind. She must have rewritten major portions of code while hiding her work from Charon. He wanted to tell what that meant to him, but he couldn't put his thoughts about that incredible, astonishing act into words. He felt strange, his mind dissociating from his body.

"I kept hoping Charon would search for you and leave me alone with the jets." Alpha had turned away from Charon's remains. "If you had come down, we could have left."

"I didn't trust you that much," he said.

"Neither did Charon."

"Is that why he had the gun?"

"No. He would never believe I could kill him." She

spoke flatly. "*Him?* The brilliant mastermind who created me? Of course not." She tapped the hard, gleaming metal of EL-38. "This made him feel powerful. Had I pressed him to give it to me, he would have become suspicious. But I knew what he wanted even more than killing you himself. To see me do it."

"I didn't believe you would kill him."

"He brought me with him, away from the jets, because he wanted me to see your death." Darkness filled her gaze. "He craved it."

"He may succeed yet." His voice sounded distant to his ears.

She spoke urgently. "We'll get you to the station. You can repair yourself. Eat. Sleep."

"Need more than food. Sleep. I think I had . . . another heart attack. The nanos . . . probably only reason I'm alive." He looked at the rope dangling above them. "I can't climb."

"I'll go. Charon's jet has medical supplies. A stretcher. And ropes. I'll haul you up. Somehow." She stopped as he lay on his back. "Thomas? Can you hear me?"

"Yes," he whispered. The sky blurred.

Her voice caught. "Don't die."

I'll try not to. Did he say it aloud? He heard her stand up. Perhaps he heard the rustle of the rope. Perhaps not. His mind was dimming. He was moving down a dark tunnel. A light shone at the end, serene, welcoming. Someone was beckoning him . . .

XIII

The Choice

French onion soup. He knew that smell.

Thomas didn't want to wake up. The smell, however, lured him. He opened his eyes and saw white. He wanted to roll over and find the source of the smell, but when he thought of moving, nothing happened. Then he realized what he was seeing. A white ceiling. He was back at the weather station.

A hand touched his forehead. Thomas rolled his head to the side and saw Alpha sitting in the chair by the bed. Across the room, the white curtains on the bedroom window rippled in a breeze.

"We're back." His words rasped. The covers felt warm and the pain in his leg was a dull ache.

"Here." Alpha offered him a spoonful of soup.

Thomas lifted his head and swallowed. It was too much effort to sustain, though, and his head fell back on the pillow.

Alpha gave him an exasperated look, but it was obviously a cover for intense relief. Complicated, astonishing, EI relief.

"I've been trying to feed you for two days," she growled. "Please cooperate."

"Hello, Alpha," he whispered.

She put her hand behind his head and lifted it up. "Eat."

He let her feed him. The soup tasted heavenly, and her hands—which could so easily kill—were gentle. When he finished, she set his head on the pillow and put the bowl on the floor. He wondered at her appearance, her mussed hair, her rumpled clothes. Apparently he had been lying here for two days. Had those hours been rough for her? A machine would keep itself in optimum working order, but a human could be distracted. She looked extremely distracted.

"You're a beautiful sight," he said.

"I need maintenance." Her expression softened into something hard to define. Affection? "And you are a stubborn man, Thomas Wharington."

"What, I'm not a beautiful sight?"

Her lips curved upward. "You're breathing."

He smiled, too, then winced at the aching muscles in his jaw. "I guess breathing will do."

"You need to continue repairing yourself."

Repair indeed. He was worn out from just his few minutes awake. Grateful for the food and her touch, he sank back into darkness.

❈   ❈   ❈

Time passed in a blur. Alpha woke him to eat and drink, and the rest of the time he slept. She splinted his leg with a board and medical gauze. Either she had hidden his aspirin from Charon or else she had found more in the station. She gave Thomas several tablets, and he hoped it wasn't too little, too late, that the nanos and drugs in his body had protected his heart muscle from too much damage.

Sometimes when he awoke, he found himself alone; other times she was in the chair or lying next to him on the bed. Once he saw her sitting on the floor and staring into space, doing whatever androids did with their thoughts when left on their own.

After several days he woke up and stayed awake, ravenously hungry. He was by himself, but Alpha had left a glass of water on the chair. He drank it all, thankful for the clear liquid. No mud.

He got up slowly. For a while he sat on the edge of the bed. Then he pulled the chair closer and leaned on it so he could pull himself to his feet, keeping his weight on his good leg. His other leg was stiff in its splint. Straight, though. If it had broken again when he fell, Alpha had set it reasonably well.

He found his clothes folded on a shelf in the otherwise empty closet. Alpha had washed them. One sleeve of his shirt was torn, but the mud and even the plant stains were gone. He dressed and felt better for it. Then he ventured out of the bedroom.

The station was as abandoned as before. He located the bathroom and washed up, using a cracked, dried-out bar of soap he found under the sink. He even ferreted out an old razor to scrape off his stubbly beard. Then he went on a wider search mission. He didn't locate much food in the small kitchen, only dried soups and crackers, and the canned vegetables Alpha had been feeding him. Then he hit gold: a package of dried waffles. He microwaved all four of them, poured himself a glass of water, and sat down to his feast. It was bland fare, stale and crunchy—and one of his best meals in ages.

After he cleaned up the kitchen, he picked up the lightest chair he could find, a wicker affair, and carried it outside, into the sunlight. The Banshee was still down the beach, with Charon's jet beyond it, but he didn't feel up to walking that far. He had outwitted death so many times these past two weeks that even if he had been a cat with the proverbial nine lives, he would have none left.

He set the chair in front of a low window on the front wall of the station and sat himself down. The sky was a rain-washed blue with wispy clouds. His flannel shirt kept out the autumn chill, leaving him pleasantly warm in the streaming sunlight. He supposed all he needed to complete the grandfatherly picture was a blanket across his knees. Right now, he had no objection to the encroaching years of his age. Let them encroach all they wanted as long as they kept coming.

A woman in dark clothes was walking up the beach. As she came nearer, he savored the view, her tight leather pants, black T-shirt, and that sexy walk. Alpha might be one of the worst things that had ever happened to him, but damned if she wasn't a fine figure of a woman. Even if she wasn't a woman.

She came up to the station and stopped in front of him. "Your repairs seem to be progressing well. You look better this morning."

Thomas couldn't help but laugh. "You're a lot different from Daniel." The doctor would have been admonishing him for getting up without permission.

Alpha sat on the sill of the window. "Who is Daniel?"

He scowled at her. "The man you konked on the head so you could get into my house and kidnap me."

"Oh. That one. I didn't konk him."

"That's what you told me before."

"I got his syringe and gave him a sedative. He went to sleep. I'm sure he was fine when he woke up. Mad, though."

"I don't blame him."

"Your sec-techs were probably furious when they woke up," she added smugly. "I don't think it occurred to them that I could beat them in martial arts or tech."

"They should know better than to let a beautiful woman make them drop their guard." So should he.

She scooted behind him on the windowsill and put her arms loosely around him, her palms against his chest. With her lips near his ear, she said, "I'm glad they didn't know better."

Thomas flushed. "Alpha, what are you doing?" He didn't move away, though.

She kissed his ear. "I'm showing you that I'm glad you're alive."

"Ah." He knew he should pull away, but he liked sitting in the sun with a sexy woman touching him, even if he was her prisoner.

"I've been running calculations," she said, straightening up behind him, resting her hands on his shoulders.

"About what?"

"Our options. I have revised my previous list. I see

three courses of action. My preference is number one."

He didn't like the sound of that. "Which is?"

"Charon has an estate in South America. He used it for business meetings or retreats with his girlfriends."

"I thought you were his girlfriend."

"I was his forma." After a pause, she added, "When he had a girlfriend, he left me alone. That was good."

"But he always came back to you."

"Yes."

Thomas thought of commenting on the emotional limitations of someone who could only hold a continuing relationship with an android, but given that he was sitting in that android's arms, he decided to keep his mouth shut.

"It's a secure location," Alpha continued. "The staff is discreet. It wouldn't be the first time they were told to make certain a guest didn't leave the premises. Charon didn't like people wandering around his property."

"You want to take me there?"

"You would have a pleasant life." Her voice turned husky. "Whatever you want. Anything. The staff includes a doctor, and if he doesn't know enough cardiac medicine, I'll get someone who does."

He spoke carefully. "You won't let me go?"

"I want to keep you."

"I'm not a thing you can keep."

"I don't know what you are." She trailed her fingertips along his neck. "But the calculations that predict the best outcomes for my future involve your continued presence."

"What about my future?" He wished it didn't feel so good when she touched him. It made it hard for him to think clearly.

"I would take excellent care of you," she said.

"Like what, I'm your cat or something?"

"No. Like my man." She slid her palms in slow circles on his chest. "If we take care with your health, you can have as full a life as anyone." She undid the top button on his shirt. "As full as you want."

Thomas cleared his throat, flustered. "Alpha."

She stopped unbuttoning his shirt. "We have other options. I could take you to Charon's base. He brought extra fuel. I have enough now to complete the flight. I could implement his plans to build an army of formas for hire. Or whatever."

The "for hire" was bad enough. The "whatever" chilled Thomas. "I don't like that option."

"The thought of continuing his work is repugnant."

"That's good to hear." He would have used a stronger word than *repugnant*. "You said we had a third choice."

"Yes. I don't like it much better than the second."

That didn't bode well. "What is it?"

She was quiet for so long, he thought she wouldn't answer. Just when he was about to ask again, she said, "We have two jets—and two pilots."

He tensed, astonished. "You would give me the fighter?"

"No. The Winchester. Charon's private jet." She spoke with difficulty. "You could go home. Take it to your Air Force. Let them crack its mesh and find out what they can about Charon. I get the Banshee. And my freedom."

Thomas closed his eyes with relief. It only lasted a moment, though. She hadn't agreed to this option. If he was too enthusiastic for option three instead of option one, she might get angry and take two instead. With Alpha, he could never be certain.

"So where does that leave us?" he asked.

"I've spent a lot of time going over the records in my internal library, both the fiction and nonfiction."

He didn't know what to make of her new topic. "And?"

"In matters of intimacy, consent plays an important role for your species."

Your species. Not hers. At least now he could see where this was going. "That's true."

"If I force you to go to Brazil, you probably won't be happy."

"I would go nuts being kept that way."

She began to massage his shoulder muscles. "You would never have to work again."

"I would be bored crazy. Why do you think I never retired?"

"We would find things to do." She leaned close, and her whisper tickled the sensitive ridges of his ears. "You would have me. Any time you wanted."

Thomas almost groaned. "You don't debate fairly."

"I want you to be happy." She sat up and continued working on his muscles. "I don't understand why you have become so important in my programming, overriding even my codes for self-preservation. Nevertheless, it seems to have happened."

Thomas put his hand over hers. "What are you going to do?"

"I don't know." She turned her hand over and curled it around his fingers. "In a few days, you will be well enough to fly the Winchester home."

"Yes, I think so." Two days might be pushing it. If he had trouble while he was alone in the jet, he could end up in the water. He doubted he could force himself to stay here any longer, though.

"Take that much time to decide," Alpha said.

His hand tensed around hers. "Decide?"

"If by the time you're well enough to fly the Winchester, I haven't convinced you to take option one, you can go home." Quietly she added, "We will each have our own life and we will never see each other again, unless your Air Force or NIA catches me, a possibility I will use all of Charon's resources to avoid."

He could well imagine. "It's my choice?"

"Yes."

Thomas let out a silent breath. "Thank you."

Her voice lightened. "I get two days to convince you."

Intrigued, he tilted his head back. "What did you have in mind?"

Alpha slid out from behind his chair, her body brushing his, her leather smooth on his skin. She came around in front of him. Taking both his hands, she tugged. "Come on."

Thomas stood up carefully. "Alpha . . ."

She regarded him like a sleepy black cat. "That's me."

"Last year, after my first heart attack—" He hesitated.

"Yes?"

"I didn't want to touch a woman for months."

"Why?"

"Well, at the time I thought it was the drugs."

"Is that how you feel now?"

"Right now," he murmured, "I am very glad to be alive." He put one of his hands behind her neck and kissed her, savoring it. Then he spoke softly. "I've wanted to do that all morning."

"Good," she murmured.

"I don't want you to expect more than I—"

She stopped him by putting two fingers against his lips. "Whatever you need, whatever you want, is fine. If you just want to lie together, fine. If you want more, that's fine, too."

She took his hand then, and drew him into the station.

Thomas stirred and rolled onto his side. He watched Alpha in the moonlight sifting through the window. She was so quiet, lying next to him with her eyes closed. He wasn't sure what she was doing, something about maintenance on her matrix, but it resembled sleeping.

It was so easy to forget she wasn't alive. Perhaps the problem was his definition of life. She could be soft or wicked, as gentle or as misbehaved a lover as he desired. She could make him feel twenty years younger at night and become his bodyguard during the day. She would never grow old, yet she didn't seem to care about his age. Was he crazy to give that up?

No, he wasn't crazy. She was one of the greatest threats he knew to the security of his country, possibly to the world. Her primary purpose wasn't as a pleasure toy, however much Charon had included that in her design. She was the prototype for a new generation of warriors, one that would change warfare forever. He had a responsibility to bring her back with him, and if that wasn't possible, he had to return with whatever information he could about Charon's plans, including the Winchester and its secrets.

Admit it. You want her to come with you. He hated giving her up. But could he protect her? He couldn't guarantee her political asylum even if she agreed to cooperate with the NIA and the Pentagon. He thought of contacting

Sunrise Alley. One of their purposes seemed to be advocacy and protection of formas. They had helped Pascal. They had let him into their shadowy realm, and Sam as well, and that led to the negotiations between the Alley and the Pentagon. Thomas didn't know where those discussions would lead, but if Alpha became a factor in them, it would be that much harder for anyone to take her apart.

They might refuse her. Charon had been the one threatening Pascal, and Alpha had worked for Charon. If the Alley *didn't* turn her away, it could precipitate a completely different problem. Who knew what might evolve if Sunrise Alley *added* Alpha to their EI mix?

He ran his hand over her side. Her curves were velvety and toned with muscle. She stretched next to him, long and languorous, and her eyes opened, sensual in the dark. When he reached for her, she pulled him close and her kiss blanketed his worries. Then she nudged him onto his back and got up to kneel over him. She sat back, straddling his hips, and slid her palms in a caress over his chest.

"Come back to D.C. with me," Thomas said.

"I can't."

"Listen." He caught her hands. "Ask for political asylum."

Her forehead furrowed. "What?"

"Crazy human leap of faith. Ask my people to give you asylum from Charon's people. In return, you'll tell mine about his organization."

"Crazy is right," Alpha said. "Political asylum applies to people from other countries. Two strikes against me. I'm neither people nor the citizen of a country."

"That's the point." Thomas released her hands and pushed up on his elbows. "If you ask for asylum, we will have to figure out what those concepts mean for biomech formas. As long as we're looking for answers, you're safe."

"And if they decide I'm neither? Then I'm just a prisoner. Again. How is that different from me hauling you off to Brazil?" She shook her head. "At least I'm offering you a good life. I'm not threatening to take apart your brain."

"I've no guarantees if I go with you, either," he pointed out. "This could all be a ploy to get information out of me."

"It's not." She leaned over him, bracing her weight with her hands on either side of his head. "In either case, one of us has to trust the other. But I have more to lose. If your people decide I deserve the rights of a human being, what then? Do I go on trial for kidnapping and almost killing a general?"

"No. Bargain with them."

"They might refuse. Or lie."

"I can't give you promises." He couldn't bring himself to lie about it, however much he wanted her to come with him. "But I have almost no doubt that they'll bargain and do it honestly."

"Your government will go after Charon's finances."

"Possibly. I take it they're rather extensive."

"Rather," she murmured. "Twenty billion."

Thomas stared at her. "Good Lord. He's worth that much?"

"It was more before he started building androids." She shifted her weight in a way that would have seemed unconsciously seductive had she been human. Could an android seduce without intent? It could be deliberate, but he didn't think so.

"Charon is dead," she said. "He has no known relatives."

"What happens to his money?"

"I control his finances." Her voice turned sultry. "Twenty billion dollars, Thomas. Ours."

That stunned him into silence. Theirs? *No.*

"Yours and mine," she said.

"I don't believe you." He couldn't believe it, because if he did, he didn't know if he could walk away from that temptation.

"Let me prove it to you," she murmured. "We can access his accounts from the Winchester."

"Alpha, no."

She slid her hand across his chest. "He was building himself another android. It isn't finished. It needs more work. It has no features. No fingerprints. No eyes. No teeth. But it has a matrix ready to accept neural patterns."

The room suddenly seemed cold. "Why are you telling me this?"

"It doesn't have to be him." Her voice was as dark as night. "It wouldn't need much modification to make it you instead. The perfect body. You would never worry about your health again. You would be young forever. You could make love all night long. You could take up the Banshee, pull twenty gees, crash it, and walk out alive." Her words were a seductive whisper. "With twenty billion dollars to spend. That's what I offer you."

He could barely find his voice. "It would be wrong."

"Why?"

"It isn't your money." That barely touched the surface of his objections, but he couldn't say what he really felt, that she offered a temptation almost beyond his ability to conceive. Almost. If he conceived it, he didn't know if he could resist it, and if he didn't resist, she would turn him into Charon.

"He gave me control of his money," Alpha said.

"He gave an AI that operated according to his instructions control. You've gone far beyond that."

"Maybe. But it's my responsibility. Would you rather his goons spent it to make mercenaries?"

"I'd rather the authorities decided what to do with it."

"No, you don't."

"I don't want to be an android." If he said it enough, he would believe it was true.

"Endless health, youth, and riches." Her voice was molasses. She raised her hips and slowly came down on him, taking him inside of her. He told himself he didn't want her, didn't want her intoxication, but his body was ready. She sheathed him with her heat and squeezed her muscles until he groaned. Bracing her hands on either side of his head, she drew her hips up and slid down again, slow and tantalizing. She was a siren, a temptress, a dark beauty driving him to madness, but such a sweet torment. He thrust against her, and she rocked against him, steady and mesmerizing. He moved with her and told himself he wouldn't think, only feel.

Thomas finally lost control. As pleasure burst over him, Alpha whispered against his ear. "I'll make you a king."

She offered paradise—and all she asked for was his soul.

XIV

A Curtain of Rain

The walk down the beach was the longest Thomas had ever taken, and it wasn't because of his splinted leg or how much he leaned on his cane. Neither he nor Alpha spoke. She didn't look at him. The Banshee waited, glittering in the sun, unbearably beautiful, and the Winchester stood beyond it. He wondered if they could take off with such a bad runway. Probably. Charon didn't stint on his aircraft.

In the past two days, Alpha had shown him plenty with the mesh onboard the Winchester. Her claims about Charon's wealth were true—and she had access to it all. The half-finished android existed. It could become Thomas. All he had to do was trust Alpha. He didn't, but what she offered was almost worth the risk.

Almost.

It felt wrong at a level that went deep within him. She essentially wanted him to become Charon. No matter how much he tried to convince himself he would be a benevolent emperor of those vast holdings, nothing would change the corrupt nature of what she offered. They would have to deal with the criminal side of Charon's far-flung realms. Alpha might claim they would live in idyllic peace in some Brazilian mansion, but it wouldn't be that easy.

And he might never see his family again. His children. His grandchildren. Everyone he loved.

Yet to have perfect health. An enhanced body. A lover who could be any woman he desired.

Eternal youth.

Endless wealth.

Every step toward the jets brought him closer to the moment he had to decide. He didn't know if he was even thinking coherently anymore. He had been Alpha's hostage for over two weeks. For days he had balanced on the edge of death. Then she saved his life and became his lover. If any scenario was bound to destroy his judgment, this was it. The prospect of never seeing her again was like a wound. His children had their own lives now. He thought of returning to his empty house and his failing health, and his life seemed too barren to contemplate.

They had reached the fighter. Alpha stopped, and Thomas stood with her. He remembered those moments after Charon's death, after Alpha went for the stretcher— the dark tunnel, the beautiful light at the end. *I'm not ready,* he had thought.

He had awoken in the weather station. Alive.

The tunnel and the light could have been hallucinations. His logical mind knew that. As close as he had come to dying, he had pulled through. But another part of him believed it had been his time and God had granted him another chance. His impressions might be no more than the fanciful notions of a dying man, but they felt real. And with that, his decision became clear.

Alpha was watching him. He cupped his hand around her cheek. "Good-bye."

She didn't seem surprised. Perhaps she was hiding whatever she felt. Her face didn't look neutral today; she wore the strained expression of someone trying to show no emotion. He had never realized until this moment how different that looked from someone with no emotion at all.

"Good-bye." She offered him a handheld control unit for the Winchester.

Thomas took it, but then he hesitated, awkward. He raised her hand and kissed her knuckles. When she didn't respond, he made himself let her go. Then he limped away, toward the Winchester.

"Thomas."

He turned around. She was still standing there.

"You can have the flight jacket in the closet on the jet," she said. "If you want."

"Thanks." He stepped toward her. "Alpha—"

"No." Her voice cracked. "*Go.*"

Go. Somehow he turned around and walked to the jet. He wanted so much to look at her, but if he did again, he wasn't certain he could ever leave.

When Thomas reached the Winchester, he did finally look back. Alpha was already in the cockpit of the Banshee. She couldn't take off until he did, and it wasn't going to be easy for either of them. Breathing deeply to steady himself, he checked the exterior of the Winchester as well as he could manage. Then he used the handheld to bring down the boarding stair from the door. Going up wasn't easy with a splinted leg, but after everything else that had happened on the island, this felt simple.

Inside, the Winchester was even more luxurious than he had expected. Carpeted floor, plush seats, entertainment center, gaming console—it was a rich man's toy. An open door at the back revealed a bedroom furnished in sumptuous red, crystal, and gold.

He found a leather flight jacket in the closet. Alpha's last gift to him. Her only one, since he had refused the others. In the cockpit, he strapped in and methodically went about his preflight checks. He had never piloted a Winchester, but it was enough like aircraft he knew that he could manage as long as he didn't encounter anything drastic, like another irate MiG.

If he kept busy enough, he wouldn't dwell on what he had just given up. *Who* he had given up.

Finally he was ready to go. He sat back, looked out the windshield—and froze.

Alpha was standing on the beach, blocking his way.

For a moment, he just stared. Then he unstrapped from his seat and limped out into the cabin. He hesitated at the door, unsure if he should go further. But he opened it anyway. Outside, Alpha had come around to stand below him on the beach.

"What are you doing?" he said. Had she changed her mind about letting him go? It was a bit late for that, given he was up here and ready to take off. She could chase him with the Banshee, though.

She didn't answer, and she was guarding her expression.

"Alpha?" he asked.

"Can you come down?" she said. "So I don't have to shout."

"No." If he went down there, he might never get back here.

"I won't break my word," she told him.

"I'm not sure I believe that."

"Thomas." She stepped closer. "Trust me."

If he went down, he would be risking everything. So foolish. If he didn't go down, he would spend the rest of his life wondering what she had wanted to say. Of course, if he took off, she could get angry and shoot him down with the Banshee. He didn't believe she would, though. Perhaps that was naïve, but he believed it anyway.

He tapped the handheld, and the Winchester's stairs unfolded. It took a while for him to come down, and he felt painfully exposed. Every step hurt. It wasn't his broken leg; that ache had receded. He hurt inside. It would have been better just to take off. Stretching out this goodbye made it that much harder to stick to his decision. But he couldn't tell her no.

At the bottom, he stood holding the stair rail with one hand while he regarded her. It would be so easy to pull her into his arms. He barely resisted the urge.

"What is it?" he asked.

She spoke in a low voice. "You can pilot the Banshee."

Good Lord. She was giving him Charon's superfighter?

"I'd like that." What a colossal understatement. "Have you ever flown the Winchester?"

Her gaze never wavered. "I'm not going in the Winchester."

Thomas took a moment to absorb that. He heard the words, but his mind couldn't process them. He was afraid to believe what he thought she meant, for he wanted it too much.

Finally he said, "You're not staying here, I take it."

"No."

"But you'll let me take the Banshee."

"Yes."

"Under duress?"

"You mean, will I coerce you to fly where I want?"

"Yes."

"What for?" she asked. "I could fly it myself and lock you out of the controls."

Thomas feared to hope. "Then I don't understand."

"You have infiltrated my mesh systems." She pushed her hand through her hair, mussing it around her shoulders. "The more my code evolves, the more it reproduces, propagates, and evolves sections pertaining to you. I can't get rid of them; I would have to delete far too much of myself in the process."

He didn't know what to say. "What are you trying to tell me?"

"With all this new code, I can't put you out of my life. I believe humans refer to this type of disturbance as 'devotion.'"

A smile was beginning inside of Thomas. "Is that an EI way of saying you're falling in love with me?"

"I don't know. However, that would be the logical conclusion."

"Very logical." He didn't see why such a blunt and

unromantic declaration felt so incredibly good, but it did. He finally did what he had wanted to since their first good-bye on the beach, which was pull her into his arms and kiss her, good and hard.

After several moments, when they paused, she smiled slightly. "I've a lot of coding about that, too."

"About kissing me?"

"And other things." She put her palms on his shoulders and pushed him away. "I'm changing the options."

He stiffened, suddenly wary. "How?"

"We go in the Banshee. You pilot. Lock me out if you don't trust me. I'll input the flight plan for Brazil. It's your choice: go there or go home. You won't have to decide right away. The Banshee can hide from your military's best detectors. You can make your choice practically up to the last moment: home or Brazil. Either way, I come with you."

Hell and damnation. Just when he thought he had resisted the temptation and could walk away, she changed the game. He had feared if he went back to say good-bye, he might never leave. Now she wanted him to spend hours in the Banshee with her, contemplating how easy it would be to change his plans and accept what she offered. He couldn't refuse to take her with him, not if he had the chance to bring her back to the Air Force. Regardless of their conflicted, confusing relationship, he should jump at the chance. But if he spent the next few hours with her, he didn't know if he would be strong enough, in the end, to resist the Faustian choice she offered.

He spoke softly. "You're killing me."

Her voice was strained. "If you aren't sure what you want, then let me off at the private airfield where we got the Banshee. You don't have to come with me today or tomorrow or next year. If you don't turn me in to your authorities, the android will still be there for you no matter when you decide to come to me."

He wanted to groan. "I can't let you go, not if it's within my power to bring you in. You're too important."

"I would rather be free." She set her palm against his chest. "As would you."

Thomas held her hand against his chest. "I can't choose."

"When the time comes to decide," she said, "you will."

Yes. He would. But it was no longer a clean choice. Letting her go and bringing her in were both wrong. Asylum had seemed like a good idea when he first thought of it, but the more he and Alpha had debated, the more he doubted it. If they decided to take her apart despite his protests, he couldn't stop them. If he let her go, he was freeing a potentially devastating threat. He wanted to believe she wouldn't seek harm with Charon's empire, but he didn't have the right to gamble on that. Either he had to sacrifice Alpha or he had to sacrifice the principles that defined his life.

No matter what he did, he would hate himself for it.

Rain pounded the Banshee as it arrowed through the darkness in the hours before dawn. Lightning cracked far too close to the jet, spectacular in its jagged brilliance. Thunder roared. Thomas had flown in bad weather before, but never like this. It demanded his attention; even an AI as advanced as the Banshee's couldn't make the decisions necessary to fly on instruments in weather this brutal.

The jet's stealth capability was every bit as good as

Alpha had claimed. He was approaching the Eastern Sea-board of North America, and no one had picked them up yet, neither a civilian nor military air command. He still didn't know what he would do: let Alpha off so she could disappear, bring her back with him, or return to Charon's secret airfield to refuel for a trip to Brazil.

They were precariously low on fuel; no matter what he decided, they had to land soon. It wouldn't be long before he entered the air defense interdiction area that protected Washington, D.C. If he kept this course, he had to contact the authorities soon; otherwise, he risked having his own people shoot him down.

He had to decide: divert or go home.

Alpha was in the backseat, a silent, unforgettable presence. She had hardly spoken throughout the flight. It left Thomas to wrestle with his thoughts, a more effective means of persuasion than if she had kept talking, trying to convince him to go with her.

"I have a duty to my country," he said suddenly, his voice almost lost in the rumble of the storm.

Silence.

He thought of his children and grandchildren. "I love my family."

"They all have their lives," Alpha said. "What do you have?"

"Them. And my work."

"You can't live vicariously through them. And you're past retirement age."

He didn't want to think about how he and Janice had planned for his retirement. Moisture threatened his eyes. Damn it, he wasn't going to get maudlin. He turned his concentration back to the storm.

After a few minutes, Alpha asked, "How do you feel?"

Such a simple question—with a world of temptation behind it. What could he say? *I feel like shit.* He wasn't breathing well. His leg ached with a constant pain that had worsened during his hours in the Banshee. Even if the doctors fixed his immediate problems, that wouldn't take away the effects of age on his body. Once he had felt as if he would live forever; now every day reminded him of his mortality. His diminished eyesight, his inability to sleep well at night, the struggle to stay fit with a body that tired far more easily than it had fifty, thirty, even ten years ago. Always, in the back of his mind was his fear of another heart attack. Bit by bit, day by day, he was dying of age and loneliness.

"It would hurt my family if I disappeared," he said.

Alpha spoke softly, with an incredible compassion that two weeks ago he wouldn't have believed possible. "It will devastate them when you die of a heart attack."

"No!" His hand jerked on the stick and he almost knocked the Banshee off course. Angry at himself, he focused on his flying.

When his pulse settled, he said, "I took an oath to my country."

"You've served your country for half a century. You've a record to be proud of, Thomas. But you deserve a life of your own."

He thought of all the times Thomas Jr. had told him exactly that, of all the times Leila had urged him to take a vacation, of Fletcher's teasing that Dad needed to get out more and have fun.

"Alpha, don't." He wasn't even sure what he was asking her not to do. *Stop making me see the paucity of my life.*

Silence.

Then she said, "How long were you married?"

"Forty-five years."

"Did you ever cheat on her?"

The damnable moisture gathered in his eyes again. "No."

"Never?" She sounded incredulous. "In forty-five years?"

"Never."

"Was she your childhood sweetheart?"

"Yes," he whispered.

She spoke with a longing that seemed almost tangible. "I would give anything to be loved that way."

Anything. Unlike most people who used that phrase so easily, never expecting to be called on it, Alpha meant her words. She could give him anything: youth, limitless wealth, perfect health, a body stronger and faster than any human, the incredible power of Charon's empire, an enhanced intellect, even immortality.

Love.

He thought of the flowers he often left on Janice's grave. A tear ran down his face. "Alpha, I—I don't know."

Softly she said, "I would love you."

And I think I could love you. He couldn't say it aloud. Such words had never come easy to him, and now they were impossible.

But he had a way to tell her without speaking. Intent on his instruments, Thomas slowly brought the Banshee around until they were headed in a southward direction. Toward South America.

Alpha had to know he had changed course; she would see it on her console. If she said anything, anything at all, he would change his mind and head back to Washington. But even in the short time they had known each other, she had learned to judge him well, to see that her silent presence worked better with him than words. Only one other woman had ever known him that well. Janice.

Suddenly another memory came to Thomas. *See my kitty, Grampy? Her name is Soupy.* He saw Jamie's face smudged with paint, her tousled gold curls, a cranky angel who needed a nap, a wide-eyed child hanging on his every word, a small girl who already showed signs of the formidable woman she would someday become.

"I'm sorry," he said softly.

"Thomas?" Alpha asked.

His voice caught. "Forgive me."

Then he changed course again.

They reached the airport at three in the morning, in a pounding storm that had closed facilities all along the Eastern Seaboard. In the end, with their fuel too low to offer any leeway, Thomas had to land at the Baltimore-Washington International Airport. After tense—and *fast*—negotiations between the port authorities and Thomas and the Pentagon, they let him land, though he was arriving in one of the deadliest fighters ever created, fully armed, with no ID anyone recognized, during the worst storm in decades.

They told him a doctor and ambulance were waiting. Thomas said he didn't need either. Maybe he was fooling himself, but no medical help could change how abysmal he felt.

After he landed, an airport crew wheeled a sleeve through the slashing rain, up to the jet. The sleeve was a mobile corridor that expanded and contracted like an accordion, and rose up to the height of the Banshee's canopy. It couldn't make a seal with the cockpit, so they brought a stair-bot to serve as a bridge. As Thomas clambered out of the jet and onto the bot, rain blasted across him. He got a good dousing in the few second it took for the stair-bot to swing him over to the sleeve.

Just inside the mobile corridor, he stopped. Too many people were crowded in here, at least five security guards and even more gate personnel. Two men in overalls stepped onto the stair-bot to cross to the Banshee. Normally a larger ground crew looked after a jet, but they couldn't follow the usual procedures. Although the port had a cadre of workers cleared to serve military craft, Thomas doubted they had ever expected a jet like this, especially at three in the morning. The Pentagon was in the process of rousing an Air Force team from their sleep and dispatching them to guard the fighter until they could refuel and move it to a base, but until then the Banshee would make do with an airport crew.

One of the security guards came forward, a man in black trousers, a white shirt, a dark tie, and a badge. "General, welcome to BWI." He motioned to a nearby wheelchair. "We have a chair-bot if you need it." In the same instant that he spoke, another man farther up the sleeve whistled, staring at the Banshee. "My God, that's gorgeous."

Distracted, Thomas spoke to the guard, "Thanks. But I don't need a chair."

A dark-haired woman was making her way forward. She wore what looked like a manager's badge on her blue suit, but Thomas couldn't see well enough to be certain.

Four guards and three other people blocked his view. The trio, two men and a woman, were trying to get past the guards as they called out questions to Thomas. The guards were apparently trying to verify their identities. Although the trio wore no press badges, they looked like reporters to Thomas. It made no sense. The Pentagon had insisted the port clear this area and beef up security. Thomas had landed only minutes after he broke radio silence, however, and it had left neither the night shift nor the military time to prepare. No one from the Air Force had yet arrived, and right now everything was confused. He was disoriented, worn out, and feeling guilty as hell. The tumult of so many people was too much. To escape, he turned toward the jet—in time to see Alpha climb out of the cockpit.

His pulse hammered in his chest. If an EI could hate—and he had no doubt she was an EI—she must loathe him. As the stair-bot swung her over, through the storm, she never took her gaze off him. The wind tossed her hair wildly, and her black eyes were filled with a dark, angry fire that no downpour could douse.

She stepped into the sleeve next to him. Rain had plastered her shirt to her skin, outlining her nipples, and he had a very primitive, very male urge to cover her up so no one would see what belonged to him. Except she belonged to no one—and he had given up any nebulous claim he might have had to her affections the moment he changed course back to Washington.

As Alpha looked past him to the crowd in the sleeve, her face shifted into a scowl, as if she were ready to crack them all over her knee for making noise. Despite the nerve-wracking situation, Thomas smiled, though he felt regret more than anything else, for he might never see that indomitable stare of hers again. She armored her vulnerability with her implacable mask, but he saw beyond it now to the struggling, incipient sentience within her.

Light flared behind him. With an angry start, he swung around, stumbling on his splinted leg. One of the damn reporters had swept out a hidden camera and was making images.

"General," the man called. "What is your fighter? An F-42?"

"Why is it armed?" the woman asked.

"Who is your backseater?" the other man asked, staring at Alpha with undisguised fascination. Thomas wanted to punch him. He looked for the manager, to insist she get rid of the reporters and ask why the blazes they were here. The manager was trying to reach him, but the four guards were inadvertently blocking her as they herded the reporters away from Thomas and Alpha.

The guard who had greeted Thomas said, "I'm sorry about the confusion. We were caught by surprise, I'm afraid."

"Where did those reporters come from?" Thomas asked.

"I'm not sure."

The guards were escorting the protesting trio away, back toward the gate. Thomas pressed his fingers against his temples. His head ached and he knew he needed the wheelchair, but his pride kept him on his feet. He didn't want to leave until the reporters were gone, but rain was gusting across the end of the sleeve and dampening his face. At least the flight jacket kept his torso dry. Alpha's gift. He felt like a cretin wearing it.

"Thomas," Alpha said.

He turned to her. "We'll go as soon as they clear the area."

She spoke in a low voice. "I need to talk to you."

The security guard spoke. "I can keep everyone back."

"Thank you," Thomas said to him. "If you hear anything—you didn't."

"I understand." The guard moved away a few steps and stopped the manager, who was approaching. She didn't look happy, but she stayed put, out of hearing range.

Thomas spoke softly to Alpha. "I'm sorry."

"This may be the last time I see you before they take me."

"I won't betray you," he said. But he had already done that.

She wiped her palm across her face, pushing wet hair out of her eyes. "Your General Chang might. Lie, get me to talk, then let the mech-techs take me apart."

"If they try that, they have to deal with me."

"And if they tell you to back off?"

Thomas knew what she was asking; how far would he go to protect her? "I won't do it."

"Listen, Thomas. On the island, Charon checked in with his people. He put a stop to the rumors of his death."

It didn't surprise him. "But now he's dead." *Again*.

She spoke with difficulty, as if she had to push her words past a barrier. "His corporations are legal."

The area was quieter now, and Thomas could no longer hear the reporters arguing with the security guards. The drumming of rain on the sleeve covered Alpha's voice, but several guards and the manager were still in the sleeve, standing back, waiting. Soon the military would arrive. He and Alpha couldn't stay here long.

"I don't understand what you're trying to say," he said.

"His corporate workers are legally employed," she replied.

"I know." The NIA had been investigating Charon's corporations ever since they had discovered he existed.

"His *human* employees."

She was struggling to tell him something, and he had a guess as to why she was having trouble: it probably required she go against Charon. She had killed him, the ultimate act of defiance, but she was still breaking the mental chains he had inflicted on her. As much as Thomas wanted to give her time, they were running out of it fast.

"You're trying to tell me he has more constructs," he said. "Androids? Robots?"

"Only the one android. But yes, many robots." She was finally showing emotion when she spoke of Charon—hatred and anger and perhaps even a sort of love—and her face and body reflected her battle to topple the barriers of her programming. "He has an EI that knows the criminal side of his empire."

"General Chang needs to know how to find it."

"If she gives me asylum," Alpha said flatly, "I'll tell her."

"It's a good bargaining tool, yes." He couldn't see why she was bringing it up now, though.

"Thomas—"

"Tell me," he said gently.

"I think Charon left his EI a message." She bit out the words. "If you show up alive, Charon must be dead."

A gust of wind splattered Thomas with rain, and he shivered. "It's a logical assumption, given the situation on the island."

Her face contorted with her effort to speak. "If the EI decides Charon is dead, it will take over his operations." She touched his cheek, the barest trace of her fingertip on his skin. "You know too much. I'm sure he told the EI to have you killed if you turn up alive, especially with me or the Banshee."

Thomas let out a long breath. "I see." It would be Charon's final vengeance against the man who had stolen the one thing Charon couldn't control, the "perfect" woman he had created, a warrior Galeta to his inhuman Pygmalion. He spoke quietly. "Thank you."

She folded her arms and rubbed her palms up and down them as if she were cold, though she could easily handle temperature extremes that debilitated humans. "For what? Saying you're going to die?"

"For warning me."

She took his arm gently. "Come on. Let's get this over with."

As he limped forward with Alpha, the manager came to meet them, a slim Asian woman of about thirty. "Hello, General Wharington."

Thomas nodded his greeting. "Thanks for getting rid of all the people."

She looked apologetic. "They were here for the arrival of a football team. The athletes only had a stopover, so we let the reporters come to the gate for interviews. The airplane was diverted because of weather, and then you showed up. We just had a skeleton crew and only minutes to clear the terminal. They slipped past us by posing as airport staff."

"Can you keep them here until my people arrive?" His voice rasped with fatigue. "We'd really rather they didn't print this story." To put it mildly.

"Security has them in custody." She was watching him closely. "Are you sure you don't want the wheelchair?"

"I'll be all right." His broken leg had gone numb during the flight, but the circulation was returning with a vengeance. Pins and needles prickled from his foot to his thigh. He felt woozy from lack of sleep and the sustained tension of the past few hours. But he had to keep moving. If he didn't, he would probably collapse, which he couldn't let himself do yet. He had too much to take care of first—like ensuring no one shot Alpha.

Thomas took a step. Pain stabbed through his leg and he stumbled, but at least it didn't buckle under him.

"Damn stubborn man," Alpha muttered. She put her arm around his waist. "Lean on me."

Thomas laid his arm across her shoulders and limped up the sleeve with her supporting over half his weight. The manager walked with them, her expression both curious and tense. He knew she wanted him to sit down. But he couldn't pause, or he feared he wouldn't start up again.

As they entered the gate, he saw a welcome sight: C.J. Matheson was striding down the concourse, accompanied by airport personnel, Air Force officers, and sec-techs. Thomas would have been even more relieved if doubts weren't plaguing him. He was no longer certain he trusted Matheson. He and C.J. had played football together, watched each other's children grow up, worked through crises large and small. He hated these doubts, but until he figured out who had helped Alpha, he couldn't trust anyone.

Alpha was watching the sec-techs. As she let go of Thomas, he took her shoulders and turned her to face him. "Trust me."

"Good-bye." Then she said, "Tell your granddaughter I'm sorry I scared her."

He lifted his hand to touch her face, but before he could, people surrounded them: C.J., staff, guards, sec-techs.

"Thomas!" Matheson took his arm. "Are you all right? We have an ambulance waiting." As he deftly separated Alpha from Thomas, the sec-techs surrounded her. She didn't protest, she just kept watching Thomas—while the officers locked her wrists behind her back with manacles that even an android couldn't break.

"Wait," Thomas said. But the sec-techs were already taking her away, down the concourse.

Alpha looked back once just before they turned a corner. Then she was gone.

XV

Home Fires

The moment the guards let Jamie into the house, she dashed into the living room. As Thomas got up from the couch, his granddaughter ran over and threw her small arms around him.

"Grampy!" She squealed when Thomas lifted her up into his arms.

"Hey, Moppet." He kissed her cheek. "It's good to see you."

Jamie hugged him around the neck with that unrestrained affection he had always loved about her. He held her close, looking over her shoulder, and saw Leila standing by the stairs with Sergeant Hernandez, one of Thomas's bodyguards. Leila was holding her ID, which

Sergeant Spaulding at the front door would have already checked, after scanning her. Thomas knew from her strained expression what she wanted to ask: if the danger was over, if his kidnapper was in custody, why was he confined to his house with bodyguards? She probably thought it had something to do with Alpha, and he had no choice but to let her believe that. His health would explain his confinement, but he couldn't tell her that he might be in danger from the obsessive machinations of a dead man.

Alpha was in the safe house under even more stringent security than before. Thomas had spent yesterday at the Bethesda National Medical Center while medics treated him and the Air Force debriefed him. Everyone had wanted him to stay overnight. Thomas had wanted to go home, but grumbling at his doctors never worked, so he did as they said, and today they let him come home.

Leila walked slowly into the front room. She didn't seem to know whether to smile or frown. She stopped by the table where he had one of his mesh consoles.

Bewildered, Thomas set Jamie down. He had expected more response from Leila. It was the first time he had seen her since his kidnapping. "Is something wrong?" he asked.

"No. Nothing." She indicated his right leg with its new cast, which came up to his knee. "Is it okay?"

"Great," he said, and heard how forced that sounded.

"That's good." Leila stood stiffly by the table.

"Mommy?" Jamie asked. "Aren't you happy to see Grampy?" She looked up at Thomas. "She cried a lot when you went away."

"Oh, honey, don't." Leila's voice caught.

Thomas went over to his daughter and spoke gently. "It's all right."

"We thought . . . I was afraid you were hurting or—or dying somewhere. I—I—" Tears gathered in Leila's eyes.

"Hey," he murmured, and pulled her into his arms. She hugged him hard, silent with her tears. She was a lot like him, this daughter of his, struggling to express her emotions.

"I'm just so glad you're all right," she whispered. She let go and laughed awkwardly. "Well."

Warmth spread through him at the sight of her, so much like her mother with her blue eyes and yellow hair. "It's good to see you."

Jamie had gone back over to Sergeant Hernandez. She gazed up at the sec-tech. "Do you protect Grampy?"

Hernandez blinked at her. "Grampy?"

Jamie pointed to Thomas. "Him."

"Yes, ma'am, I do."

"If you get scared, you can borrow my kitty." She showed him her stuffed cat. "She scares away bad guys."

Hernandez smiled. "Thank you, ma'am."

Leila called to her daughter. "Jamie, let the man alone." Her voice trembled and her face was wet with tears, but she was smiling.

Karl walked into the living room, holding his ID, and Jamie immediately dashed to her father, full of excitement. Thomas was glad she didn't understand the full import of his bodyguards. He caught Karl's gaze, and his son-in-law nodded, understanding; Jamie didn't need to know her grandfather was in danger. Karl scooped the small girl up into his arms and kissed her cheek as he carried her back to Leila and Thomas. For a disconcerting moment Thomas thought his son-in-law was going to hug him, too, even while holding Jamie.

Karl didn't, though. Watching Thomas's face, he just said, "Lord almighty, it's good to see you."

Thomas laughed, a bit unsteadily, and so did Leila. Then his son-in-law was shaking his hand, Leila was telling Thomas he should sit down, Jamie was giggling, and Thomas knew he would be all right. His worries about Karl were easing, too. From what Leila had said on the phone last night, Karl had been spending more time with his family since the first kidnapping.

He thought of Alpha's last words to him: *Tell your granddaughter I'm sorry I scared her.* He would find the right way to tell Jamie without upsetting her. He wanted to see Alpha, or at least know how she was doing, but no one would tell him anything. Given what had happened on the island, he doubted Chang would even let him near Alpha until the general was convinced his judgment hadn't been compromised.

"I want to sit with Grampy," Jamie announced. She started to kick, catching her father in the side.

"Hey!" Karl said, laughing. "Take it easy with your old man." He handed Jamie to her grandfather. "You win all the ladies' hearts, Thomas. The rest of us don't have a chance against you glamour boys."

Thomas smiled at Jamie. "Hello."

"You're awakier today," Jamie said.

Leila nudged Thomas's arm. "Dad, why don't you sit down? Karl and I will fix lunch."

He suspected Leila knew he was already tiring. "I guess I could."

Leila winked at her daughter. "Jamie will watch over you."

"Me and Soupy," Jamie said.

Thomas grinned. "I'm a lucky man." He knew what Leila wanted; Jamie needed the reassurance of seeing her grandpa was all right. A few minutes with him might do her good. Him, too.

While Leila and Karl went into the kitchen, Thomas settled on the couch and put Jamie next to him. "So how is your math?"

"It's fun. Mommy and Daddy got me tests."

So they had done it after all. He chucked her under the chin. "What did they say?"

She snuggled next to him. "The test lady was nice. She said for me to go to college in this many years." She held up five fingers.

He smiled. "I think she meant more years than that, Moppet."

"Maybe. Mommy cried."

"Cried?" That didn't sound right. "Why?"

"She said for me not to grow up too fast. Daddy took me to one of his classes."

Thomas gaped at his granddaughter. She'd gone to Karl's class? He was teaching calculus with analytic geometry this semester. "You understood all that?"

"Not much," she confided. "I liked the pictures, though. Lots of squiggly lines and how fast do they change."

"My God," Thomas said. That she even understood the concept of second derivative change stunned him. Was his granddaughter some sort a genius? It actually wasn't that surprising, given her parents, but even so.

"Grampy?" she asked, looking worried. "Are you still sick?"

He laughed softly. "Not at all. Just surprised."

She watched him with concern. "Mommy says you can't go to work."

"For a while." A thought came to him. "Jamie, do you remember the day you came to work with me?"

"I got a badge! And we went under the ghost arch."

"The Hughes arch, yes. Do you remember when you stayed with General Matheson?" C.J. had kept an eye on her while Thomas went to call Senator Bartley. Although Jamie had claimed she heard the call, security had never found any problems. Thomas had assumed she misunderstood something he said. But perhaps she understood better than he realized. He kept thinking about Matheson. Could C.J. have been eavesdropping and not have realized Jamie overheard? It seemed unlikely, and he didn't want to believe it of Matheson, but he couldn't think of a better explanation.

"I drew pictures," Jamie said.

"That's right." He thought back to what she had told him in the car. "You heard me talking. You were in one room and I was in another. Do you remember?"

"I didn't hear that," Jamie said.

Relief surged in him. *He* had misunderstood. "You didn't hear Senator Bartley?"

"He said I could call him Bart."

That stopped him cold. *Bart?* The only one he knew who used that name was the EI in Sunrise Alley. "You *talked* to him?"

Her eyes were wide like large blue buttons. "Was that bad?"

"No, Moppet, no." Thomas knew he had to keep his questions low-key. If she sensed he was upset, she might be afraid to answer. "I just didn't know you had met him."

"He came to my desk."

"But you were sitting at a box." He remembered the chair they had set up for her at a packing carton, like a miniature desk.

"It had a screen on it." She pointed to a stack of holoboards on his console-table. "Like those."

Thomas couldn't remember the specific carton, but many of them had holo-labels with packing information. It was conceivable that someone with a sophisticated enough mesh could transmit rudimentary images to such a label. But sending it to someone inside the NIA was a whole other story. For Bart to rove the NIA meshes, he had to break some of the toughest security in the world. If Sunrise Alley could crack the offices of the Director of Machine Intelligence, they could get in almost anywhere—

Including the safe house.

A chill went up Thomas's back. "What did Bart say to you?"

"He asked me about an Alpha. I said I didn't know that."

Thomas felt as if he were in quicksand. Had the Alley helped Alpha escape and capture him? To what damn purpose? Yes, they wanted the NIA to stop him from investigating them, but Thomas had already agreed to a moratorium, besides which, they had to know that eliminating him wouldn't stop any probes. He needed more than the words of a three-year-old to go on, though. Jamie could be mistaken or he might still be misunderstanding her.

"What else did Bart say?" Thomas asked.

"I don't remember." She beamed at him. "I can sing the alphabet backwards. Want to hear?"

The buzz of his mesh glove came from somewhere not too close. He looked around, but he couldn't remember where he had left it.

"Dad?" Leila came into the room, holding a spatula in one hand and a box of macaroni in the other. "Isn't that your comm?"

He started to lever up from the couch. "I left it upstairs."

Karl walked out of the kitchen. "Thomas, you relax. I'll get it."

"Thanks." Relieved, Thomas let himself back down on the couch.

As Karl went upstairs, Thomas turned back to Leila. "Is it true about Jamie, about the testing?"

"Yes. Dad, you were right!" Leila shook her head, as if she still had a hard time believing it. "She's even more advanced than we realized."

The melody of a comm page suddenly played in the kitchen.

"Hey!" Leila swung around, which sent macaroni flying out of the open box. "That's mine." She bustled back into the kitchen, leaving bent noodles scattered across the floor.

"Mommy made a mess," Jamie said.

Karl was coming down the stairs with Thomas's glove. He walked over with that subdued look he always got when something reminded him of Thomas's status in the military. He offered the glove. "It's General Chang."

Uneasy, Thomas pulled on the silvery-black glove and spoke into the comm. "Wharington, here."

Chang's brisk voice snapped out. "They put up a damn

blasted holo. By the time we found out, it was all over the mesh."

"A holo of what?" He was almost certain he knew, though. Then he realized she couldn't talk about the "what" over an unsecured line.

Leila came out of the kitchen wearing her own glove, a white mesh. She had a strange expression, as if Thomas had grown a second head.

"Go look," Chang said, and gave him a site name.

"I'm going to the console now," Thomas told the general. As pulled himself up off the couch, he gave Leila a questioning look.

"It's one of my girlfriends." Leila sounded bewildered. "She wants to know if you're really my father and are you single."

"What the hell?" Thomas said.

Karl offered his arm, but Thomas said, "I'm okay." It was just a few steps to the console and he could walk in the cast. At the table, he lowered himself into a chair in front of the screen. "United News Service," he said and gave it the site Chang had provided. The article came up immediately—and when Thomas saw the headline, he swore out loud.

Air Force General Brings Ultra-Fighter into Airport.

If Jamie and Leila hadn't been there, he would have cussed down the wall. The article included a holo that had been sharpened until the scene was clear, though the shot had been taken at night in the rain. It showed Thomas next to Alpha, his hands in the pockets of his flight jacket. He was *smiling*. The image didn't look doctored, but smiling was the last thing he had felt like doing last night. The Banshee was behind them, a wonder of modern aerodynamics. Alpha was as gorgeous and as deadly as the jet, her clothes plastered to her body, her dark eyes furious.

Then Thomas remembered; he had smiled when Alpha came out of the Banshee. Cameras had flashed. He looked more confident in the image than he remembered feeling, his legs planted wide, his wet hair tousled on his forehead. He had been standing that way to balance on his injured leg, but the splint was hidden by Alpha and the angle of his body.

"Good Lord," Leila said. She leaned over the table to see better. "Dad, who is that woman? And good grief, what are you doing, looking like *People Magazine's* choice for Sexiest Man of the Year? You're a grandfather!"

Karl came up on his other side, and Jamie squeezed in between him and Leila so she could see, too. "Grampy is happy," Jamie said. "The bad lady is mad."

"*That's* the woman who took you hostage?" Karl asked.

Thomas spoke into his comm. "General, I'm looking at the holo."

"I don't want you to leave your house," she said. "If the publicity gets bad, we may move you out to the safe house."

"I understand."

"Good. Stay home. No going out."

"I will."

After Chang ended the call, Leila said, "That woman in the holo—she's not some escaped nutcase, is she? This is something about your work and that jet."

Thomas knew she would see through any smoke screen he put up. He couldn't give her secured information, so he said only, "It's complicated."

Leila spoke to Jamie. "Moppet, could you get Grandpa's aspirin out of the bathroom?"

Jamie's eyes widened. "Grampy? Are you sick?"

Leave it to Leila to realize he had forgotten his aspirin. His daughter knew him too well. He was usually organized about his medicines, but his routine had fallen apart these past weeks.

He kissed Jamie's forehead. "I'm fine. Your mother worries about people she loves, like you and me. It's part of being a mom."

"I can help." Jamie ran off, earnest with the errand.

When she had gone, Thomas regarded Leila. "What didn't you want her to hear?"

"Doctor Enberg said you've had two heart attacks in the past week." Her voice had a ragged edge. "He thinks you almost died."

"I'll be all right." Thomas wished he could talk about it with her. With anyone. But he couldn't, unless he counted the shrink he would probably have to see after Chang finished going over the text of his debriefing.

"Leila and I are just a few miles away," Karl said. "If you need anything, we can be here in minutes."

"Thanks." Thomas tilted his head toward the sec-tech posted discreetly by the stairway near the entrance foyer. "I have Hernandez, here, and Spaulding out front, too."

Leila tried to look stern, but a smile played around her lips. "And quit the sex symbol stuff, okay?"

Thomas laughed softly. "Didn't know your old man had it in him eh?" Neither had he, actually.

Jamie came trotting into the living room with a bottle of aspirin and a glass of water. Belatedly, it occurred to

Thomas that she had never seen the bottle before. To find the aspirin, she had to have read the label.

"Here, Grampy." She gave him the bottle.

"Thank you," he said. With Jamie watching, her gaze solemn, he took two aspirins.

"All better?" she asked.

"Just great, Moppet."

"Well." Leila tried to look bright. "Shall we eat lunch?"

As they went to the dining room, Thomas thought of what Alpha had told him about Charon's EI. Could she have meant the Alley? He sincerely hoped not, because if Sunrise Alley was backing Charon, he doubted anything could stop them.

After his family left, the house felt empty to Thomas. Except for his guards. He appreciated their protection, but they didn't say much. The guards Alpha had knocked out had recovered, and the investigation cleared them of wrongdoing, but they were no longer assigned to Thomas. He had a total of four new ones, and they guarded him in shifts of two. Hernandez and Spaulding were large, muscular, and quiet, Hernandez with dark hair and Spaulding with yellow. They carried stasers on their belts and rifles over their shoulders. They were so discreet he could almost forget they were there. Almost.

He sat at his console and read the Banshee article. It didn't say much, just that low fuel had forced him to land at BWI. An Air Force spokesman had given out the story that an F-42 pilot had diverted due to the weather. Precedent existed for a general taking up a jet even three decades ago, when the Air Force Chief of Staff, General John P. Jumper, qualified in the F-22 Raptor. The article referred to Alpha as Thomas's backseater. Although few women had been fighter pilots in his youth, it happened enough now that she didn't raise too many questions. The rest of the article described how security cleared out the reporters and confiscated their cameras. Apparently the fellow who took this holo transmitted it to his girlfriend's glove before he lost his equipment. Nothing in the article, however, explained why a director from the NIA was up in an armed fighter at three in the morning.

Thomas moved his fingers through the holo. In it, he looked younger, brash, and full of life. That wasn't a tired, lonely old man. It wasn't him, either—but it could have been if he had accepted Alpha's offer.

He had done what he had to do. But part of him would always wonder what he had given up for the sake of his conscience.

XVI

The Spectral Code

On Thomas's first day home from the hospital, he visited with his family and slept. During his second day, he slept, called C.J., and did what work he could manage from home. The publicity died down quickly and Chang decided to let him stay in his house, with the understanding that his guards would remain with him at all times and he wouldn't even go for a walk unless he cleared it with security.

On the third day, Chang sent Major O'Reilly to see him. Thomas and the major sat in the family room, Thomas in an armchair and O'Reilly on the sofa. Acutely self-conscious, Thomas was tempted to make a dumb joke, asking O'Reilly if they should switch seats, given that

O'Reilly was on the couch instead of Thomas. He managed to restrain himself.

O'Reilly was also the psychiatrist assigned to Turner Pascal's case. On the basis of his reports and Thomas's recommendations, the Air Force had released Pascal into Sam Bryton's custody. Neither Sam nor Pascal had wanted to see O'Reilly, and now Thomas understood how they felt. He didn't want to discuss his private life, either. Unfortunately, he had to go through with this.

"You've had quite a ride," O'Reilly said.

That remark had far too many double meanings. Thomas said only, "Apparently so."

O'Reilly smiled slightly. "This is where I say, 'Do you want to talk about it?' Then you portray yourself in the best possible light, while wishing you were anywhere but here."

Thomas wondered if mind reading was included these days in medical degrees. "I'm ready to cooperate, Doctor."

O'Reilly settled back, his face friendly, his posture attentive but not tense. "Relax. You're not under investigation."

Thomas raised his eyebrows. "Sure I am. Alpha wants a status that requires we decide whether she is a person or a construct. I've recommended we grant it to her, that to do otherwise would amount to slavery. Obviously, my mental state in making that determination will come into question."

"Well, she did kidnap and nearly kill you."

"Yes."

"And slept with you," O'Reilly added.

At least he didn't beat around the bush. "Yeah," Thomas said. "And slept with me."

"Do you think we have reason to question your judgment?"

"Yes."

Surprise flickered on O'Reilly's face. He had probably expected Thomas to build his case for why his sleeping with Alpha didn't negate his judgment. Thomas knew he should do exactly that, but he couldn't make himself discuss something so private.

After a moment, O'Reilly said, "Why should we question it?"

Thomas had asked himself the same question many times since his return home. "First she was going to kill me. Then love me. Then kill me. Then love me. That would wreak havoc with anyone's mind. Erratic positive reinforcement is one of the most powerful coercive tools known."

"Do you feel coerced?"

"No."

"Why not?"

"She gave me a choice," Thomas said.

"It was a hell of a choice."

He let out a long breath. "Yes."

O'Reilly rubbed his chin. "Were you hoping, if you slept with her, that she would slip up in guarding you or give you information about Charon?"

"I'm not sure," Thomas admitted. "Maybe." He wanted to leave it at that, but he made himself go on. "The first time it just happened. After that, she wanted to convince me to go with her."

"Did you consider her offer?"

"Hell, yes."

"But you didn't go."

Thomas shrugged. "I have to live with myself."

"Did you try to get information out of her?"

"No. Yes." Thomas exhaled. "I wasn't trying to trick her, if that's what you mean. We talked a lot. I tried to find out how she escaped the safe house."

"A lot of people would like to know that," the major said dryly. "Your report says you think she had inside help."

"I see no other way she could have managed." He didn't suggest names because he had no evidence, but he had to report his suspicions to Chang. Realistically, the person who could have most helped Alpha was Matheson. Thomas considered himself a good judge of character, and his experiences over the years had borne out his judgments. He couldn't see Matheson committing treason. But that left what Jamie had told him, the word of a three-year-old, an unusually precocious one, yes, but still a small child. Could she really hold the key to one of the worst security breaks in history?

Thomas didn't know, but somehow he had to find out.

By the end of the week, Thomas was driving C.J. crazy with his calls. General Chang finally took pity on the beleaguered Matheson and allowed Thomas to come to work, with the agreement that he travel only to and from the base and nowhere else. He suspected she gave the order as much to prevent her restless lieutenant general from overdoing things as to protect him from a threat that might or might not exist.

In his office, with access to his secured files, Thomas could do a more extensive search for Sunrise Alley. He read everything he could find about the Baltimore Arms Resources Theater and Bart's evolution since its demise.

He sifted through obscure, hidden, or marginally legal mesh sites. He traced the call Bart had made to his office until he lost the trail at the University of Maryland. He checked every record of Bart's contacts with the Pentagon, and every one led to a dead end. He found no path to the Alley. How did you contact a disembodied entity that lived "out there" in the world meshes? He had no idea.

Finally, in frustration, Thomas went to the internal NIA page that had his picture, bio, and contact information within the agency. It was accessible only to someone on the NIA meshes, which meant it was surrounded by layers of their best security.

Jamie might be mistaken about Bart. Perhaps she heard Thomas discussing the Senator or the EI and confused that with the time she had spent in C.J.'s office. A hundred ways existed to explain the call she thought Bart had made to her.

Or it could be exactly what she had said.

Thomas added a short message at the bottom of his NIA mesh page:

Bart, call me.

General Chang met Thomas in the NIA café for lunch. A waiter-bot with a tray-top rolled over, took their order, and trundled off, lights blinking. Chang settled back at their table by the window. Outside, sunlight slanted across the buildings, lawns, and parking lots of the base. In the gilded autumn light, the four stars on Chang's shoulders gleamed. It bemused Thomas; he was old enough to recall when a female general, while not unheard of, was rare enough that he had never expected one as his CO. They were still rare, but less so now, and more and more women were coming up in the ranks.

"Jim turned in a report to me this morning," Chang said.

"Jim O'Reilly?" Thomas asked.

"That's right."

That could explain this lunch invitation. "He worked fast."

"Oh, he wants to keep seeing you. This is just an interim report." She leaned her elbow on the arm of her chair. "However, he doesn't expect his conclusions to change substantially."

Thomas wondered what she would do if he came out and asked how the doctor had evaluated him.

Chang was watching his face. "Interested in his results?"

"If you feel it would be appropriate, then yes." That was a major understatement, but she probably knew that.

"He thinks you're tired and disoriented."

"Oh."

"He's also concerned that you seem forgetful."

"I see."

"And he thinks you're lonely," she added.

Thomas winced. This was excruciating.

Chang smiled at his expression. "Doctor O'Reilly also says you're dealing well with everything, and that he has confidence in your assessments of your situation while you were a prisoner."

Thomas didn't realize how much he had tensed up until his shoulders relaxed. He didn't want to show too much reaction, though, so he just said, "Well. Good."

"He also says," she added firmly, "that if you have

problems with irritability or with your memory, or if you feel unusually tired, go see Doctor Enberg."

It was exactly what Daniel had told him. Thomas's latest attack had been less serious than the last, and the episode on the island might have been only an arrhythmia, or irregular beat. But it could have developed into cardiac arrest if he hadn't had nanos releasing medicine into his body.

"I'll be careful," Thomas said.

Chang seemed satisfied. "This business with Alpha is a mess."

"She'll talk when you give her asylum."

The general spoke dryly. "Asylum from what country?"

"From Charon's organization."

Chang exhaled, and the lines around her eyes showed more than usual. "Her cooperation would be invaluable. But we don't know if she'll try to trick us. If we take her apart, we may not get it all, but we can analyze everything we do get, and it won't be filtered through her own agenda."

Her comments chilled Thomas. "It would be murder."

"It could be murder. But *is* it?" Chang rubbed the bridge of her nose with her thumb and forefinger. "With Turner, it's more clear-cut. He was a man, a citizen. His body is his own, despite the replacements. It's easier to think of him as alive. Alpha doesn't even *try* to act human."

"She seems very human to me." That was what drew him so powerfully to Alpha; the woman he saw developing.

"Half the time she talks like a mesh system," Chang said. "She doesn't give a damn how we view her. She told one agent he 'annoyed her processor.' I think she does it on purpose."

A smile tugged his lips. "She's ornery as all hell."

"Yes, well, mesh systems raise my blood pressure enough even when they aren't trying to provoke me." Chang gave him one of her famous, or perhaps infamous, looks, as if she could turn him inside out with a glance. Even after working with her for years, he still found her sharp gaze unsettling.

"And now you think we ought to recognize Sunrise Alley as a sovereign nation?" she said. "Good Lord, Thomas."

"We have to do something." He thought of his talk with Jamie. "I've reservations, though. Alpha had to have help escaping from the safe house."

"You think it was Sunrise Alley?"

"Well, they help formas. And she's an android."

"So was Charon. The Alley claims they find him abhorrent."

"So they say."

"You have evidence otherwise?"

"Nothing concrete," Thomas admitted. "Bart may have accessed a holo-label on a crate in Matheson's office."

"We need the record."

"The crate was thrown out. I just have the witness." Wryly he added, "Unfortunately, she's only three."

Chang frowned at him. She already knew, from his debriefing after the first kidnap attempt, that he had brought Jamie into work. Although she hadn't reprimanded him, she obviously didn't like it. Taking care of Jamie had given him a window into what Leila dealt with every day. Perhaps that was why Chang didn't censure him; with three children, she had dealt with the same. To reach her position, she would have had to manage her family life without disruption at her job. She had come up through the ranks as one of the few women at her level, her every action under scrutiny. Sometimes that made a person harder on those in similar situations, but underneath her tough exterior, Chang had a flexibility she used well. She knew when to stand firm and when to give. She read people better than anyone else he knew, including himself, which was probably why she had four stars and he had three.

Today she said only, "It's not much to go on."

"I'll let you know if I find anything concrete."

"Good." She fell silent as the robot rolled over with their lunches in its tray.

"Your repast is prepared," it said, and gave them their food.

"Thanks," Chang told it. After the bot left, she laughed. " 'Repast'? Who programs those things?"

Thomas smiled. "Not a poet, I guess."

She lifted up a spoonful of her soup. "Look at this bowl."

Thomas saw nothing unusual. The surface resembled porcelain, but it was a composite woven with a rudimentary mesh that monitored the temperature of the soup and kept it warm. It wasn't any different than most modern synthetic materials.

"It looks fine," he said.

"It's a damn computer. Everything we use, everything we wear, every place we sit, stand, sleep—it's all woven with meshes. We can't escape them."

He knew what she was getting at. "Our ability to secure them has also developed with the technology." He had to believe that, because if he didn't, it would weaken the tight lid of control he had over his fear. Alpha believed he was in danger, but he had no idea what form that threat would take or even if it really existed.

Chang clunked her spoon back in the bowl. "Find out what the Alley is up to."

"Do you have a contact for them?" he asked.

"Sam Bryton. But I want her out of this. She empathizes too much with EIs."

It had been his thought, also. "I'll see what I can do."

She sat appraising him for a while, until he grew uncomfortable. Then she said, "I'll put through your clearance to see Alpha."

That was unexpected. Appreciated, yes, but she had to have ulterior motives. "I take it you want me to keep you informed of anything I learn."

"That's right. And Thomas—"

"Yes?"

Quietly she said, "Be careful."

By the time Thomas reached the safe house, night was settling over the mountains, with stars sharp in a cold sky. Major Edwards was driving, Hernandez sat in the passenger's seat, and Spaulding was in back with Thomas. The closer they came to the house, the more Thomas's agitation grew. He didn't know how he would react when he saw Alpha. What he had thought he felt before could have been brought on by his intense situation. He might see her tonight and feel completely different.

Alpha's room was dark when they entered. Edwards, Hernandez, and Spaulding came with him, and also two guards thinly disguised as orderlies. One of them brought up the lights, but just a bit, a simple kindness that left the room dim enough so someone's eyes could adjust. Someone human. For Alpha, it didn't matter.

She was lying on the bed, on top of a blue quilt, dressed in a blue jumpsuit, her eyes closed. Thomas sat on the bed, gazing at her face—and knew without doubt that his feelings hadn't changed. The same rush of desire came to him. No, desire was only part of it. He wanted to talk to her, laugh with her, tussle with her, all those things people did when they fell in love. It was ridiculous for a man his age, especially with a forma, but nevertheless, it was how he felt.

Alpha opened her eyes. "Hello, Thomas."

"Hello."

She sat up easily, with no sign of the stiffness people usually had when they awoke. She looked past him to his armed guards, then back at him. "You don't trust me."

"Actually, General Chang doesn't trust you."

"And you?"

She was so close, it was all he could do to keep from embracing her. He couldn't, though, with all these people in the room, no matter how discreet they made themselves.

He answered in a low voice. "Should I trust you?"

"Probably not." Her eyes smoldered. "Stay here too long, and I'll be tempted to haul you off to another island."

When she looked like that, he didn't care how many people were watching. He pulled her into his arms and held her, his head against hers, his eyes closed. She put her arms around his neck and molded against him. It stirred memories of the island, both fear and desire. It was useless, wanting her, because he couldn't have her, but his emotions had a vexing tendency to ignore his logic.

After a while, one of the orderlies shifted and his uniform crinkled. Thomas drew back, self-conscious again, and Alpha regarded him with a scorching gaze that made him glad he had guards, because otherwise he didn't know what she would have done with him. But ah, the pleasure of finding out.

"Your emotions are so easy to read," she said.

That was new. All his life, people had told him he needed to express more, not less. "What do you read?"

"I scare you."

"You don't." Or maybe it was a thrill of fear.

"Oh, I do," she said. "You like it."

"I think I frighten you, Alpha."

"No one frightens me."

"Not even Sunrise Alley?"

Her posture stiffened and she seemed to withdraw, though she hadn't actually moved. "They don't like me."

"Why?"

"I'm Charon's lackey."

"You're a forma," he said. "Ask for their protection. We're negotiating with them. If they make your safety a part of those talks, no one will touch you."

Her voice cooled. "You wouldn't tell me that unless you want something from me."

"I do." And he told her the truth. "I want you to live." He couldn't say, *I'm afraid I'm falling in love with you,* so instead he added, "Your well-being matters to me."

She let go of him and crossed her arms. "If that were true, you would never have brought me here."

He wished he knew how to make it all right. "I couldn't do what you wanted."

"Why not?" Her fists clenched in the cloth of her

sleeves. "All you had to do was let me go."

Quietly he said, "My country also matters to me."

"I won't contact Sunrise Alley."

He spoke in a deceptively soft voice. "Interesting."

"What?"

"You never asked *how* you would contact them. Do you already know?"

She only hesitated a moment, but that pause spoke volumes. "I didn't ask because it doesn't matter. I've no intention of contacting them."

"Why not try?"

Silence.

He didn't know how to judge her reaction. If an EI could act guilty, she was doing it. She had no reason to *simulate* guilt. In fact, he didn't believe she planned her emotions anywhere near as much as she claimed. Her mesh code was evolving on its own, without her specific direction.

"How long can you stay?" Alpha asked.

He touched her cheek. "You're avoiding the subject."

She pushed away his hand. "I don't want to talk about it."

He let it go. His analysts could tell him later if they thought she was experiencing guilt or faking it. He wasn't objective enough to judge.

"I can stay maybe an hour," he said.

She indicated his guards. "With them?"

"Afraid so." He wished they were gone, too. When she looked at him with that dark gaze, he wanted to stay with her all night. But he couldn't, not now, maybe never.

So instead he said, "Walk with me by the lake."

"It's dark." She tapped his temple. "You have no IR." Her finger lingered on his skin.

He folded his hand around hers. "I don't mind."

This time she didn't push him away. "All right."

So they went out into the woods on the grounds of the safe house. Edwards, the orderlies, and Thomas's bodyguards came with them as they strolled through the trees. Lampposts along the path lit their way like sentinels of yellow light.

Neither he nor Alpha mentioned Sunrise Alley again.

Thomas discovered the message at 2:56 a.m.

He couldn't sleep. He kept brooding on his visit with Alpha. Over and over, he castigated himself for his infatuation. Except it wasn't infatuation. He was old enough to recognize love. Why couldn't he want someone safe, a woman of his age and background? Alpha was off-limits, bad for his health, and not human.

Finally he got up, donned his robe, and took out his polished oak cane with the lion's head at the top, the present his sons had given him when they visited earlier this week. Then he made his way to his office downstairs. Hernandez and Spaulding were on the night shift, Hernandez in the front room and Spaulding pacing the house. Thomas missed his privacy.

His console was active twenty-four hours a day, with a fast mesh connection. It was similar to the setup in his office at the Pentagon, except he couldn't do secured work here. He had bought the best fortress-firewall protection available, though, and tonight he ran an extra check to verify his system was clean of invading programs.

Then he saw the message: *Here is your call.*

The words glowed in the lower left corner of the screen, along with an old-style Internet address, a string of numbers and periods, a protocol used before the advent of the mesh. Nor was that the only oddity. The message didn't appear in any screen. It was part of his console's background design. Whoever put it there had reached into the guts of his unit at a basic level, which meant either his security was a lot less effective than he thought or else his visitor was a mesh bandit on a level beyond just about anyone.

Thomas had left Bart the note at the base "to call" him so he could find out if the EI could access the NIA—and was willing to admit it. If this was Bart's response, that meant Sunrise Alley had infiltrated the base. That the message appeared here instead of at the NIA at least gave Thomas reason to hope the break hadn't gone far.

He had to admire the approach, though. Most people wouldn't recognize the IP address Bart had left because browsers no longer dealt with them. But Thomas had lived through the birth of the computer age and the rise of the world networks, from the days of ARPAnet, Bitnet, the Internet, and the World Wide Web, which had become just the web and finally the mesh.

It took a while to make his system recognize the old address. When he finally figured it out, an ancient grey web page came up on his screen, one so dull and dated, he wondered if that was a message itself, an oblique means the Alley used to say they wouldn't contact him. Then a swirl of speckled lines replaced the grey, and a holo about one foot high formed in front of the screen. It was a man, but not Bart, at least not the image he had used before. This man looked more mature, more seasoned, with darker hair. He had a sense of intelligent confidence possessed by few people Thomas knew.

The man nodded. "Good morning, General Wharington."

"Hello," Thomas said. He noticed Spaulding standing outside his office door. The guard gave him a questioning look. Thomas raised his hand to indicate he was fine, and the sec-tech withdrew.

"Are you Bart?" Thomas asked the holo.

"Not exactly," the man said. "Though I draw on part of his code. Call me Steve."

His excitement stirred. This must be another of the EIs in Sunrise Alley. "Did you send me that mesh address?"

"Yes. Can you come to Greenbelt State Park? Half an hour."

Thomas blinked. "At this hour? What for?"

"You'll find out when you come."

Sure. His cynicism kicked in. "You want me to come alone, right?"

"Bring your bodyguards."

"Can't you talk to me here?"

"Face to face is better security."

"Why should I trust you?"

Steve regarded him steadily. "No harm will come to you. But you may learn a great deal. For yourself and for Alpha."

His pulse leapt, but he suppressed his reaction. Supposedly Sunrise Alley didn't know about her, but he didn't believe it for a moment.

He said only, "Who is Alpha?"

"Half an hour." Steve vanished and the screen went grey.

"Hey." Thomas tried to bring back the holo, but nothing

worked. His screen just showed a grey mesh page. Finally he sat back, brooding. He had no desire to visit a deserted park in the middle of the night. If he showed up, the payoff could be great—or he could end up dead.

Thomas got up and went into his living room. Spaulding was sitting on the couch and Hernandez stood posted by the window across the room. Spaulding rose to his feet as Thomas entered. "Good evening, sir."

Thomas nodded self-consciously to both of them. He pushed his hand through his hair, which he still hadn't gotten around to cutting. "I have to go to Greenbelt."

Spaulding came over to him. "Now?"

"Afraid so."

"Sir." Spaulding shifted his weight. "General Chang advised us that you were to stay home this week."

"She didn't order me to." That was pushing their understanding, but she hadn't actually said he *couldn't* leave.

"Your heart condition, sir."

Thomas scowled at him. "I'm in recovery. Not dead. I won't keel over if I go talk to someone."

"Yes, sir," Spaulding said. Just when Thomas thought he was done, the officer cleared his throat. "Sir."

Thomas wanted to groan. They called him "sir" when they knew he didn't want to hear what they had to say.

"Go ahead," Thomas said.

"Doctor Enberg said for you to take it easy during the early morning. Particularly in cold weather."

"I am taking it easy. And it's not that cold."

"But, sir—"

"Spaulding!"

"My apologies. But, sir—" Spaulding paused. Hernandez had come closer and was listening intently.

Thomas made himself stop glaring at them. "Go on."

"This could be an ambush," Spaulding said.

"Yes, it could." Thomas spoke quietly. "I don't think it is. I can't give you proof; I only have my instincts. But if I don't go, I may lose information that could affect our country."

After a moment, Spaulding said, "Yes, sir." He didn't look happy, but at least neither he nor Hernandez offered more protests.

Thomas went upstairs to change into jeans, sweatshirt, and under it all, a flex-suit of body armor. He got his magnum out of his nightstand and put the gun into the pocket of his jacket.

The park gate was locked, but it was only a framework of orange pipes across the road. There wasn't even a fence; anyone could walk around the gate. Hernandez parked by the curb at the entrance. He got out and opened the back door for Thomas while Spaulding got out on the other side. They used no flashlights. Thomas's guards wore IR mesh-visors that allowed them to see the heat generated by an object, that tracked Thomas's position, and that let them talk by radio or communicate silently by blinking a code. Thomas had one, too, though for now he left it up on his forehead. The sky had only a few clouds, and the full moon cast a silvery light. After his eyes adjusted, he could see well enough.

In the distance, beyond the curve of the road, a vehicle hummed by on Greenbelt Road, probably headed to some job that started too early in the morning. The air smelled fresh, without pollution. Maybe some Saturday he would bring Jamie here and they could learn plants. It could be fun. If he didn't get his head bashed in this morning.

He pulled his jacket tighter against the cold, and his flex-suit chafed under his clothes. Limping in his cast, with his new cane, he stepped up on the curb with his bodyguards and walked past the gate.

Steve hadn't said where to go, and years had passed since Thomas's last visit here. He remembered the park as a huge grass field with some beautiful old trees and a playground. Woods bordered it and a road went around the perimeter. The road they were on now wound up to the one that circled the park.

They continued on, but no humans named Steve or anything else showed up. Their walk had an insulated feel, as if they were alone with the darkness and the brooding silence. The night seemed to be holding its breath.

It took about twenty minutes to reach the hover lot of the park. No vehicles were in sight, and if anyone was here, he wasn't showing himself. A huge grassy field stretched out beyond the lot. Silvered by the moonlight, it rolled down in a long slope until it faded into the shadows of a distant woods. On the left, the field extended out to a closer bulge of the forest, and a playground lay to the right. Chill breezes bit Thomas's cheeks and nose.

"We have company," Hernandez said, and stepped in front of him.

Thomas peered where Hernandez indicated, on the left, and saw a figure in dark clothes coming toward them from the woods. Spaulding moved closer to Thomas's side. Both men had drawn their guns, Spaulding with his staser and Hernandez with his revolver. Thomas put his hand in his pocket. His magnum felt cool and solid.

When Thomas pulled down his visor, the figure became

a red blur in the shape of a man. A message from Hernandez appeared on the lower edge of Thomas's visor screen: *no weapons found.* Probes in the visor could detect materials, signals, even bumps in clothes that suggested weapons. It wasn't foolproof, but the person approaching them also had none of the tics or mannerisms Thomas had come to associate with a potential threat. The man made no attempt to conceal himself, and he walked with his hands in the open.

Thomas blinked in a code the visor translated as words. His response replaced the message from Hernandez, as it would also be doing in the visors of his guards: *Don't shoot.*

Yes, sir, Hernandez answered. Neither he nor Spaulding put away their guns, however.

Thomas felt exposed even with all these precautions. It was fortunate their visitor came alone; he doubted his sec-techs would have let more than one person near him.

The figure resolved into a leanly built man, tall, with dark hair. Thomas pushed up his visor so he could get a more natural view of his face. "Steve?" he asked, startled.

The man stopped a few yards away. "Hello, General."

Thomas nudged Hernandez, who was in front of him. "I'd like to talk to him."

"Yes, sir." Although the sec-tech stepped aside, he kept his gun trained on the man.

"How did you get out of the computer?" Thomas asked.

Steve smiled slightly. "It's more, 'How did I get in?' The EI you met used to match my neural patterns."

"You mapped your own brain?"

"Something like that."

Thomas had wondered about the origins of the other

EIs in Sunrise Alley, but he had never expected one to be human. Nor could he figure out why Steve looked familiar.

"Are the other EIs in the Alley like you?" Thomas asked. "Copies of a person?"

"We're all unique."

That was vague. He wondered if Steve would tell him anything. And Thomas *recognized* him. What was it . . .

A chill went through him. He *had* seen images of this man. On the mesh. But Steve looked no older than pictures that were thirty years old.

"God Almighty," Thomas said. "You're Steve Hughes."

The man inclined his head. "Pleased to meet you."

Thomas stared at him, the namesake of the Hughes arch and numerous other innovations. No one had seen the reclusive genius in decades. Many questioned whether he even existed. "You're a forma," he said slowly. "Sunrise Alley designed an android and downloaded one of its EIs into it. Into you. That's why no one has ever seen you. Your forma self couldn't exist until technology reached its current levels." He hesitated. "Though your EI must have evolved along with the tales."

Hughes's face was shadowed. "Those tales started over thirty years ago. EIs didn't exist then."

"The rudiments did."

"Barely." His smile was a ghost of white in the dark. "A fanciful idea, General."

"Is it a true idea?"

"Truth is relative."

Relative, indeed. Thomas hoped he didn't end up dead because of it. But his roller coaster life these past few weeks was worth it for these incredible meetings with . . . with what? People or formas? Alpha, Bart, Turner and now Hughes: in combining both human and synthetic aspects, did they become more than their sum?

"You wanted to see me in person," Thomas said.

Hughes indicated the dark field. "This is more private than any mesh, no matter how secured."

And less safe. "You want privacy." Thomas could guess the rest. No guards.

"It's up to you," Hughes said.

Thomas thought of Charon's relentless, vindictive ambition. If the Alley had helped Alpha, they could be involved with Charon.

"I can't send my guards away," Thomas said.

"Then I cannot speak."

Thomas wanted to hear out this enigma who might or might not be human. In the past, he had assumed the stories were tall tales. It would be fitting if the legend were actually an EI in Sunrise Alley. But Hughes had a point. An EI couldn't have existed when those legends took root. Maybe the myths had come first, and the Alley created Hughes based on them. Maybe Hughes had once been human. Or maybe he had been a rogue EI that redefined itself from the legends.

Hernandez still had his gun trained on Hughes. Thomas spoke to the sec-tech, "Stay with me, but move out of earshot."

"Sir—" Hernandez clearly wasn't happy. "We can't risk your safety. General Chang would skin us alive."

"I won't let Chang skin you. And I'll be fine."

Spaulding cleared his throat. "Sir."

Sir again. It didn't bode well. "Yes?"

"You say this a lot, that you'll be fine. Then you get kidnapped and nearly die."

Thomas smiled wryly. "I'm not asking you to leave. Just step away."

"We can't go more than ten yards," Hernandez said.

Thomas doubted they would give more than that. So he said, "All right." If Hughes wouldn't talk under those conditions, he would be pushing Thomas's trust too far anyway.

His bodyguards withdrew until they were dark figures, far enough away to hear only if he shouted or used his visor.

Hughes glanced at the mesh glove Thomas wore on his left hand. After considering him, Thomas brushed his finger over the mesh. It took only seconds to deactivate. His glove would make no further record of this meeting.

Hughes lifted his hand toward the field. "Shall we walk?"

Thomas kept his hand on the magnum in his jacket. "All right."

So they went. Hughes took it slow so Thomas could manage with his cane and cast, and Hernandez and Spaulding kept pace. The moon gave enough light so Thomas could see without his visor, but the park was full of darkness.

"We expected Alpha to come to us," Hughes said.

Cold fingers walked up Thomas's spine. *Us.* Not *they.* Hughes considered himself part of the Alley. He almost said, *You helped her escape,* but he held back. Better to see what he could learn first.

"To the Alley?" Thomas asked.

"Yes. We shelter formas."

"How would she know about you?"

"We told her."

Thomas clenched the gun. "You did help her." *They* were the ones who had set him up. "How did you get into the safe house?"

Hughes spoke carefully. "Some of our EIs are former military codes."

Thomas had considered the possibility. "Too old, too limited. I don't believe they could crack our security."

"They didn't."

"Then how did Bart know what I posted at the NIA?"

"Your granddaughter."

Thomas stiffened. If the Alley had interfered with Jamie, they were declaring war against him. "Leave her out of this."

"She contacted us," Hughes said. "With an NIA mailing label."

That got Thomas's attention. "Go on."

"Apparently she was playing with a mesh-controlled label. She didn't realize she had opened a backdoor that could be used to access the NIA post office. Bart told her how to close it." Hughes regarded him with a sphinxlike gaze. "We were not aware children her age were capable of such."

"Neither were we," Thomas said dryly. Inside, he felt a rush of pride. Smart kid, his granddaughter. He had to be careful, though. "I take it Bart helped her close the door with himself inside the NIA."

"Only a small portion."

Thomas didn't care how small, it was still unacceptable. "How far has he spread into our internal systems?"

"Just through the post office mesh," Steve said.

Thomas didn't believe him, but at least he knew where to start. "How does that piece of Bart talk with the Alley?"

"He sends bits of himself out on the labels of unsecured mail."

It made sense. Sooner or later, after the package left the base, someone outside would link to one of those labels. Bart could jump through their system to the world mesh. Even if he really had accessed only the post office, security had been compromised. The mesh gurus would have to check *every* NIA system. It would be one hell of a job. At least it helped get Matheson off the hook. If anything, it pointed suspicion at Thomas; he was the one who had given Jamie the crate. Who would have thought a three-year-old could open a backdoor with a post office label? The officer who gave Jamie her badge had explained how to behave on the base, but it hadn't occurred to anyone that Jamie could manage something so sophisticated or arcane. Thomas wasn't certain he could have done it, at least not that quickly.

"If I hadn't checked out what happened with Jamie," he asked, "would the Alley have come clean?"

"I don't know," Steve said, his voice shadowed.

Thomas didn't like his answer. "Even if this is all true, the NIA post office has no links to the safe house." They had isolated the house from other meshes, even more so since Alpha's break out.

"We accessed the safe house through Alpha."

"You got into Alpha's internal mesh?"

"Yes."

Despite the cool air, sweat gathered on Thomas's palms. If the Alley could do so much, and had links to Charon, they could probably kill him even with his sec-techs here.

He had taken a risk coming to this meeting, but he needed to know what Hughes had to say.

"How did you get in her mesh?" Thomas asked.

"It happened after she took you and Sam Bryton hostage the first time," Hughes said. "When the Air Force moved to rescue you, they weakened Charon's security. It gave Bart a chance to punch a hole and jump into Alpha's internal mesh."

"Why Alpha instead of Charon?"

Hughes's voice went flat. "We find Charon vile."

So do I. If Bart had stashed part of himself inside Alpha, the analysts working on her might have found him, but his chances of hiding while piggybacked on her mesh were better than those of his breaking into the safe house on his own. And it meant he hadn't cracked the place from outside, which Thomas had believed impossible. Given the trouble Bart had caused, it didn't surprise Thomas that the Alley had sent a different EI to talk with him. He would have been tempted to give any physical manifestation of Bart a hard right hook to the jaw.

"Why would the Alley set me up?" Thomas asked, his hand gripped on his magnum.

Hughes stopped in the middle of the field. "We didn't."

"Alpha came straight to my house."

"We expected her to come to us. Our agreement was this: in exchange for our protection, she would tell us everything she knew about Charon."

It was reassuring to know the Alley hadn't so pervaded human civilization that they knew everything and went anywhere.

"She reneged," Thomas said.

"Yes. After she deleted Bart from her mesh."

Thomas's voice cooled. "His decision to help her escape could be considered a hostile act against this country."

Hughes's eyes were dark. "His first loyalty is the Alley."

"So why should I trust him? Or you?"

"We could just as easily ask the reverse."

Thomas remembered his last conversation with Bart, when the EI called for a moratorium on attempts to "control and abduct" the Alley. Trust had to work both ways. "If Bart was in Alpha's mesh, he must have known what she would do to me."

"He had only limited access. She isolated him in her matrix."

"So that's why she says the Alley won't help her."

"I imagine so."

"Is she right?"

Hughes met his gaze. "Yes."

Thomas felt that strange sense of dislocation that came when he spoke of Alpha, as if she were a part of his life confined to a box, desired and forbidden, edged in gold and danger. It would have been ironic if he had asked the Alley to help her and it turned out they sought to further Charon's purposes. They claimed otherwise, and Hughes had warned him about a major security break at the NIA. That counted for nothing, however, if Thomas never made it back to tell anyone.

His unease grew. "I should get home."

"All right."

As they were walking toward the parking lot, however, Hughes said, "I have one other thing to discuss."

Thomas tensed again, still holding his hidden gun. "What?"

Hughes let out a slow breath. Once Thomas would have

assumed that meant he was human, since androids didn't need to breathe. He was no longer certain. People communicated with many types of nonverbal cues. Androids designed to seem human might as well.

Hughes spoke quietly. "Our intervention with Alpha nearly caused your death."

Thomas wished he could wipe his sweating palms on his jacket. It would reveal his fear, though. "And?"

"Sunrise Alley has a debt to you."

Thomas thought of Alpha's dark promises of wealth. "I don't want your blood money."

"Not money. An exchange. A new lease offered for an old one."

What the blazes? "You want to rent me a house?"

"A life."

"I already have one." He intended to keep it.

"We can give you more."

Suddenly Thomas understood. It was the same offer Alpha had made. "I'd rather be human. Not a forma." But even as he spoke, he hesitated. How would he feel in ten years? Twenty? When old age left him stooped and wrinkled, when it took his acuity and strength—if he survived that long?

Hughes was watching his face. "Think about it. Take as long as you need. Weeks or years. Decades."

Thomas still didn't trust him. "I don't take bribes."

"Nothing is expected in return."

"You say that now."

"Once you have a biomechanical body and matrix, we cannot take them back," Hughes said. "We would have nothing to bargain with."

"I don't know if I trust your motives."

"Find out yourself." They were crossing the parking lot. "Become part of us."

Join the Alley? He didn't know whether to be tempted or put off. The idea tantalized. He wanted to ask if he would have the choice no matter how long he waited, but he couldn't say the words. It wasn't only the problem of trust. He had yet to reconcile the concept of becoming a forma with his sense of himself as human, with his religion, or with his family. He might never find that accommodation. Some people knew exactly how they felt: they either embraced the new technologies or turned away without doubt. For Thomas, it wasn't clear. Perhaps he was too set in his ways. He didn't know. But he wasn't ready to make that leap.

"I will think on it," he said. "But thank you."

Hughes inclined his head. "You are welcome."

They had reached the road that circled the park. Hughes left then, headed in the opposite direction Thomas would go to reach his car. The man's lean figure faded into the night until nothing remained except the legends of his existence.

XVII

The Missed Exit

At 3:55 in the morning, few cars were out on Kennilworth Avenue in Greenbelt, Maryland. It was one of the only times the county could do substantial road work without causing a traffic jam. The area was all roads and overpasses, a multilane highway surrounded by other highways, with little beyond them but an industrial park. Bathed in the harsh light of a few lamps, a crew in down jackets and hard hats were working on the on-ramp to Interstate 95, which would take Thomas to the Beltway and his home just north of Washington, D.C.

"Damn," Thomas muttered. He wanted to get home and sleep. His exhaustion had caught up with him. If the ramp was closed, it would take that much longer to find an alternate route.

Hernandez slowed down, making it clear he wanted

to use the ramp, and a husky man on the crew glanced up. As Hernandez let the car settle on the pavement, the fellow headed over to them. Spaulding reached unobtrusively into his jacket to his shoulder holster, and Thomas took hold of his magnum. The other three men on the crew glanced up, their faces shadowed under their hard hats.

The husky man knocked on the driver's window. Then he waited, rubbing his eyes as if he weren't sure he had woken up. Hernandez lowered the window, then rested his hand on a lever below eyesight that could bring armored plates slamming down. If the man reached into the car, the plates would chop off his arm. Thomas felt a little foolish with all the precautions, but better to feel silly than take chances. At the same time, they didn't want to cause any civilian injuries or deaths.

The man bent to the window. "There's an exit back toward NASA," he said. "Take a left on Greenbelt and you'll see it pretty quick."

Hernandez nodded with the impassive expression he wore for everyone except Jamie. "Thanks." Even his casual response sounded military.

Spaulding suddenly said, "Comm is out!" He hit a lever, and the transparent polycarbonate armor snapped down, a grade of bulletproof "glass" that could withstand even grenade explosions. As Hernandez revved up the turbo fans and lifted the car into the air, the man in the hard hat stumbled back. Thomas's safety harness snapped around him, tight against his flex-suit. He didn't know why they had gone into defensive mode, but if someone had isolated them from outside communication, they were in trouble, and not only from the implied threat. It took a high level of interference to cut them off.

Hernandez swung around in an arc tighter than most cars could manage, until they were pointed southward—in time to see another car humming up the highway toward them, dark and sleek, an armored Hover-Shadow 16. Thomas knew the type; this car he rode in, for all that it appeared mundane, had a similar design. It was faster than the Hover-Shadow, which was why the Air Force called it a Cheetah.

Hernandez swore and kept steering the Cheetah around until they faced north again. A second Hover-Shadow was coming from that direction, and beyond it, on the otherwise empty highway, a third was on the approach.

"Hell," Thomas said and pulled out his magnum.

Hernandez continued swerving in a circle, so tight it pushed Thomas against the armored door. Spaulding had all three Shadows on his mesh screen. It didn't look as if anyone was driving them; they were robot cars controlled by AI brains.

In the few seconds it took Hernandez to get the Cheetah facing south again, the first Hover-Shadow had almost reached them. Spaulding was speaking to the Cheetah's AI: "Fire guns A-three and A-four."

Machine gun fire burst from forward ports on the Cheetah. The approaching car swerved and skidded on the road. As it careened past Thomas's car, it fired a stinger, one of the two miniature rockets carried by a Shadow. The Cheetah immediately released chaff and flares, but it was already too late—the stinger detonated under them.

The explosion threw the Cheetah sideways. Thomas groaned when his head hit the window. The blast didn't destroy the car's armor, but they skipped along the road like a rock skimming a lake, except unlike water, the asphalt was scraping the blazes out of the car. Its underside was reinforced, as was the Kevlar skirt along its lower edge that held the cushion of air, but they couldn't withstand a beating this rough without damage. It all happened too fast; Thomas's mind couldn't absorb the full import. After everything he had survived, he couldn't believe he would die here.

The men in the supposed work crew were running toward the Cheetah in military-like formation. Hernandez managed to get the Cheetah into the air, its engines groaning with the strain of moving too much weight too fast. The first Shadow, the one Spaulding had fired at, swung into their path, and the Cheetah barreled into it with a screech of armored composites smashing together. It threw Thomas forward, and his body yanked his harness. He prayed the tight band of pressure on his chest came only from his flex-suit.

Both the Cheetah and the Shadow slammed down on the asphalt. Hernandez shoved his foot on the pedal, and for a moment the Cheetah surged drunkenly back into the air. Then it dropped again. A grind came from under its body as Hernandez tried to unfold the wheels, and the car tilted crazily to one side. Thomas hung on to the door, his pulse thrumming too fast.

The other two Shadows from the north were almost on them. They pounded the Cheetah with gunfire, and Spaulding returned it, the AI implementing his instructions faster than he could have himself. None of the shots penetrated the armor of the cars, neither for the Cheetah nor the Shadows. The men in hard hats stayed clear, crouched behind concrete dividers, which probably had far more reinforcement than they would have ever needed if they had only been for construction. No other vehicles appeared, which was strange even this early in the morning. The crew must have blocked off the area, maybe even accessed the county grids that controlled traffic and cameras. Even if someone reported the tumult, it would take time for the police to arrive, especially if they had to get past a roadblock—and far too much could happen in a few minutes.

Spaulding spoke urgently to the AI. "Fire rockets."

Two flares of light burst from the Cheetah and hurtled toward the Shadows north of them. The first hit the hood of the leading car and exploded with a muffled boom. That Shadow careened into the path of the second rocket, which also exploded on the hood and finally penetrated the weakened armor. The car's fuel tanks detonated with a plume of fatally beautiful orange flame shot through with the silver of liquefied metal. The damaged Shadow spun in a whirl of ragged parts and crashed into the third Shadow, which had veered to avoid the wreckage.

The rattling of gunfire suddenly became louder and more violent. In the same instant that Spaulding shouted, "Breach!" something hard slammed the seat next to Thomas. Blasted, burnt leather flew through the car, and he threw himself to the side, against the door. His chest felt as if it would burst. Debris pummeled him, ripped his clothes, and could have torn him apart if he hadn't been wearing flex-armor. He instinctively raised his arms to cover his head, as if that useless gesture could protect him against projectile bullets.

"Breach sealed!" Spaulding said. He took an audible breath. "General Wharington?"

"I'm fine." Thomas lowered his arms. Nothing separated him from Spaulding; the sec-tech was still at his weapons console, but he had nothing at his back. The gunfire had destroyed the upright portion of the passenger seat. Spaulding must have thrown himself out of its path; otherwise he would have been smeared all over the car. Bile rose in Thomas's throat, and he forced it down.

Hernandez finally got the Cheetah's wheels deployed, and he took off with a screech. The third Shadow was trying to pull away from the sizzling wreckage of the second, and as Hernandez raced down the street, the first Shadow leapt in pursuit.

Intent on his console, Spaulding swore. "Their fog is killing my bees."

Thomas knew the trick. The Cheetah could send beebots to track and target the enemy vehicles, but the Shadow could release a fog of bomblets that destroyed the bees.

"Can you reverse the nav-chip in your bots?" Thomas asked.

Spaulding looked back. "Sir?"

"Have the bees fly backward. Bomblets have no AIs, just chips to direct pursuit. If the bees leave, the bomblets will follow. When the fog clears the Shadow, send in more bees."

"We don't have many left," Spaulding said.

The car's AI spoke. "Sixteen bees remain."

Hernandez suddenly cursed and slammed on the brakes. Thomas jerked forward, but his harness kept him from thudding into Spaulding. The sec-tech wasn't so lucky; the projectiles that had destroyed his seat had also shredded the supports of his harness, and he slammed into the dashboard.

Swearing fast and low, Spaulding pulled himself upright. The impact of his body had jumbled his controls, and he had lost the signal from the bees. Up ahead, a wall of dividers blocked the street, backed up by concrete mixers and dump trucks. Hernandez was working to get the Cheetah into the air, but Thomas doubted they could make it over the dividers. Even an undamaged hover vehicle would have trouble navigating that barrier. The Cheetah growled like a cat warning of its intent to attack, but it wouldn't lift off the ground.

The Shadow chasing them fired a stinger, then swerved around and took off down the road. The rocket exploded against the back of the Cheetah and the car slammed back and forth. Thomas groaned as his cast knocked the door and pain shot up his leg. He felt as if he were trapped in a crazy-house ride at a carnival. He thought a siren wailed in the distance, but it could have been the ringing of his ears from the detonation.

The Cheetah's AI spoke. "This vehicle is unlikely to survive another hit."

Hernandez quit trying to go over the barrier and brought the car around to face south, the way they had come. "Those Shadows have used all their rockets except one," he said.

"We have none left," Spaulding said grimly.

Thomas craned his neck to see Spaulding's screen. The first Shadow, the one that had just fired at them, was far down the road now, past the remains of the second Shadow that Spaulding had destroyed with rockets. The third had foundered in the rubble and wasn't going anywhere. Its

AI brain didn't seem able to handle its own damage with the added confusion of other wreckage. It was the Cheetah's one advantage in this three-against-one combat; with mesh brains instead of human drivers, the Shadows were less versatile opponents.

The first Shadow, however, was operating fine—and coming back at them.

"Spaulding, can you send the bees that way?" Thomas pointed eastward. He didn't know enough about the Cheetah's mesh or AI to give the full commands it needed. "Wait five seconds, blast our bomblet fog at that first Shadow, and then hit their fuel with whatever ammo we have left."

Spaulding spoke rapidly to the AI, incorporating Thomas's ideas in his commands. Bee-bots swarmed out of the car. The silvery fog hanging around the approaching Shadow leaked after them, leaving behind no more than a metallic shimmer. Thomas held his breath as the Cheetah and Shadow hurtled toward each other. Then a cloud of bomblets billowed out of the Cheetah's ports and poured into the Shadow's gun ports like a gleeful, living fog. Gunfire from the Cheetah hammered its armor.

Time became thick. The Shadow seemed to swoop by in slow motion, its sides pocked by bullets. With majestic slowness, its armor buckled into the fuel tanks that Spaulding had targeted. For a second that lasted an eternity, the Shadow seemed fine—and that was when it fired its last rocket. Then its tanks exploded in a blur of flames and shrapnel.

The rocket from the Shadow blew off the trunk of Thomas's car. With a protest of metal like a scream of pain, the Cheetah flipped onto its roof. Thomas felt as if a huge hand yanked him against his harness. He groaned and hung upside down while his heart slammed in his chest. Someone shouted, but with his ears ringing, he couldn't decipher the words. The Cheetah creaked as it labored to support the vehicle's weight. Even the reinforced armor couldn't withstand such continual stress after all the battering of rockets and gunfire. Spaulding was sprawled below Thomas, either unconscious or dead.

Thomas clawed at his harness, desperately trying to free himself before the car crumpled down and crushed them. Hernandez got free first and dropped next to Spaulding. Then Thomas's harness gave way and he fell onto the roof of the upside-down car. As his cast hit the floor, he gasped with pain. The Cheetah shuddered, and a plate on the driver's side buckled.

Working together, Thomas and Hernandez wrestled open the door on the passenger's side and crawled out, dragging Spaulding with them. The air smelled of smoke and electrical discharges. The early morning chill hit them like a punch, and Spaulding groaned. They helped him stand, but not all the way; they had to stay behind the car, which was their only protection then from the wrecked Shadows and their machine guns. Spaulding recovered fast, greatly relieving Thomas, though it was also a sobering reminder of his own age, for he could no longer snap back that way.

Suddenly, Hernandez grabbed Thomas and shoved him *back* on the ground, behind the door they had so painstakingly pushed open. Thomas had a crazily tilting view of the street; then his guards were crammed around him, both firing at the dividers that bordered the supposed on-ramp construction. The careening paths of their cars, racing up the highway and back again, had returned them to where they had started.

Then Thomas saw it: the top of a hard hat behind a divider. He could guess why the hat showed; its tip had equipment that could target them. Hernandez and Spaulding were both firing, battering the divider with bullets. The concrete cracked and turned to dust, but that only revealed the darker surface of a harder, stronger composite underneath.

Thomas sighted on the hat. His magnum couldn't compare with the projectile guns, but he didn't need much to destroy that small control tower. As he fired, the hat disappeared, though it wasn't clear if his shot hit it or its wearer had withdrawn. Behind them, the car groaned, on the verge of collapse. They had to get out of the way, but if they ran out of cover, they would be easy targets.

Suddenly a deluge of shots came from the left, farther up the street. With dismay, Thomas realized someone must have ridden in the Shadows after all. They were out and shooting, and he and his guards were trapped here, in a car about to crush them.

Except the shots weren't coming at the Cheetah, they were raining over the dividers, even going behind the barriers. A man jumped out from behind a divider and ran straight for the Cheetah, firing a machine gun. Thomas whipped around his magnum, fired—and the man went down, sprawling on the street. More shots rattled from the left, hammering the dividers as if they would split the night in pieces.

With a screech, the Cheetah began its collapse. Thomas's guards scrambled to their feet and grabbed his arms, hauling him up fast. Then they *ran*. He lurched across the street, half carried by his bodyguards, his broken leg dragging on the asphalt. The cold air shocked his sweating body. He glimpsed police cars to their left, red and blue lights rotating in the night. It was the *police* who had fired, without warning, striking before the hard hats could kill Thomas and his guards, but how they had known where to fire, Thomas had no idea. They could have ended up killing him and the sec-techs—

Pain exploded in his chest.

It was agonizing. *Unbearable.* Behind him, the world screamed as the Cheetah smashed down in a shriek of armor and reinforced glass. Thomas crumpled and dragged down his guards. His teeth hurt, they hurt so much, such agony, it was killing him, and the damnable pain in his *teeth* would be his final thought.

He was aware of his knees hitting the ground, of his guards crouched next to him, of running feet and shouting people. Most of all, he knew *pain*—in his chest, arms, shoulders, neck, and teeth.

Then he knew no more.

XVIII
Vigil

Fractured, blurred images.
General Chang, her face strained.
Leila crying, her eyes huge and hollowed.
His taciturn, impassive sons. Crying.
Daniel Enberg.
C.J. Matheson and Major Edwards.
Hernandez and Spaulding.
Doctors, nurses, orderlies.
Fragments of talk:
Too soon after his last attacks . . .
Hard hats staked out his home . . .
Planned to blow up his house . . .
Someone, somewhere, said, *Full cardiopulmonary arrest.*

Someone said, *Coma*.

Someone said, *Never wake up again* . . .

Someone said, *I'm so terribly, terribly sorry*.

He wanted to say he wasn't dead. But he couldn't speak. He was slipping further and further away. Janice was here, beckoning . . .

XIX

Beyond the Lake

A face slowly resolved before him—into Daniel Enberg. Not Janice, beautiful, ethereal Janice, but instead it was Thomas's cantankerous, balding doctor, checking monitors by a bed. Hospital bed. Unable to move or talk, Thomas just watched.

After ages, or perhaps moments, Daniel straightened up, turned toward the bed—and froze.

"Thomas?" he asked.

"Hi." His answer was almost inaudible.

"*Thomas?*" Daniel shouted the word.

Thomas winced. "Yes?"

"Oh my God. *My God.* I can't believe it!"

"Too loud . . ."

"I'm sorry." Daniel gave an unsteady laugh. "Good Lord, you're back!"

Thomas managed a smile. "I'm a tough old bird."

"You sure as hell are." Daniel's eyes had a glossy look. If Thomas hadn't known better, he would have thought his curmudgeonly doctor was about to shed tears.

Daniel told him what happened after Thomas had collapsed. A helicopter had brought Thomas to the hospital. Doctors operated for hours. Twice they believed they had lost him, and twice his beleaguered heart had begun to beat again. But afterward, Thomas had lapsed into a coma. That had been eleven days ago.

Somewhere during all that, Daniel buzzed for the nurse. She brought in Tom, Leila, and Fletcher, who had been sleeping in the waiting room. Groggy and still half asleep, with tears in their eyes, his children hugged him, and admonished him, and cried some more. Hernandez and Spaulding stood back, as discreet as always, but they smiled slightly, a great show of emotion for them.

His children told him more about what had happened. Apparently someone had seen the cars fighting and called the police. The story hit the local papers first, then the national press. The Air Force spokesman said a multinational cartel dealing in illegal weapons and robotics had tried to kill Thomas after he learned too much about their operations, resisted their coercion and bribery, and nearly died bringing in their superfighter. The public loved it. Thomas, it seemed, was a hero. He didn't feel heroic. But he was alive, and with his family, and that was what mattered.

❈   ❈   ❈

Thomas spent another week in the hospital. When he got restless and started to call Matheson, General Chang showed up. She told him that if he insisted on working, he should write his report on Hughes. Thomas suspected she knew that it stressed him more to do nothing than to work, and she probably figured this way he wouldn't get up and go into his office.

He wrote the report on his laptop film and sent it over a special line to the Pentagon. Then he waited, dozing or browsing the mesh. Sure enough, Chang showed up that afternoon, secured his room with tangle-comm beetles, and grilled him on his report.

Chang also told him the rest. They had finally determined that the robot cars belonged to a corporation owned by Charon, though tracing the elusive connection had been difficult. Around four a.m. that morning, a man claiming to be Steve Hughes had called the police and Pentagon about an emergency near Greenbelt Park. The police thought it was a prank at first, but the Pentagon listened, for Hughes identified Thomas, Hernandez, and Spaulding by name. The police knew whom to go after because they had descriptions of the cars. Shooting first and asking questions later was a risk, but less of one than hoping the Cheetah didn't crush Thomas and his bodyguards while the police resolved the situation.

Was the Alley involved? Although no hard evidence existed that they had abetted Charon's plans and lured Thomas out for the attack, the circumstantial evidence convinced everyone.

Except Thomas.

He didn't claim to understand the Alley. He didn't trust them. But he didn't believe they wanted to kill him. He was convinced they wanted to be rid of Charon just as much as their human counterparts did. He reiterated to General Chang his recommendation to deal with them as a sovereign country or in a manner that acknowledged their status as sentient beings.

It helped that Hughes had confessed the Alley's infiltration into the NIA. As it turned out, Bart had already cracked several other agency meshes. The mesh gurus cleaned him out of the NIA systems. To Thomas's relief, C.J. Matheson came up clean, and even received a commendation.

General Chang didn't like his recommendations about Sunrise Alley, but she listened. He knew her well enough to know she would take them into account when she wrote her report for the President.

Thomas arrived at the safe house with Leila and Jamie. Ironically, it had been harder to clear Jamie for this visit than Leila. Jamie was to touch nothing and stay with Leila at all times. The small girl walked with her mother and looked around the forest, wide-eyed and alert. Thomas went with them, slowly, leaning on his cane. Major Edwards came as well, and two orderlies.

They found Alpha by the lake, standing at the water's edge where only grass came to the shore and no trees. Today she wore low-slung jeans and a white top. Small waves lapped over her tennis shoes. Thomas wished he could take her out of here. He couldn't, of course. What would she want with him anyway? If the Pentagon ever let her go, she could have a man as young and healthy as she desired, someone who was less conflicted than Thomas about her being a forma.

She was staring out at the water, but she turned as they came up to her. Jamie stopped several yards away and hung back, holding her mother's hand. Edwards waited a few steps behind them while the orderlies arranged themselves around the group. Leila watched Alpha with a cold, hard gaze unlike anything Thomas had ever seen from his daughter. Perhaps this was the notorious attorney that defense lawyers faced in the courtroom.

Thomas crouched next to Jamie, bringing his eyes level with hers. It was difficult in his cast, but he managed. This was too important to let a broken leg interfere.

"It's all right," he assured her. "Alpha just wants to tell you something."

"Will she hurt us?" Jamie's voice trembled.

He put a hand on her small shoulder. "Not a chance."

As Thomas stood up, Alpha came toward them, but she stopped as soon as Jamie moved back against her mother.

Alpha regarded Leila. "You are Thomas's daughter."

"That's right." Leila's voice could have chilled ice.

"I'm pleased to meet you." Alpha was so stiff, Thomas was surprised she even got the words out. He had never heard her be this polite. Leila just barely nodded.

This time when Alpha stepped forward, Jamie watched her with wide eyes, but she didn't back away. Alpha crouched in front of the girl. "I'm sorry I scared you that night."

"You hurt Grampy's leg," Jamie said.

"I didn't mean to."

"Are you still mad?"

"No," Alpha said. "I was sick before. I'm getting better now."

"I had the flu once," Jamie said. "I felt bad and I yelled at Mommy."

Alpha smiled. "It was something like that."

"You must have been *really* sick," Jamie said.

Alpha gave a startled laugh. "I guess."

"Are you and Grampy friends now?"

Good question, Thomas thought. Alpha had many reasons to hate him.

Alpha looked up at him, her face unreadable. Then she turned back to Jamie. "We'll see."

Jamie hesitated. "Can you ever leave this place?"

"Maybe someday."

"Oh." Jamie looked out at the lake. "It's pretty."

Alpha's face gentled, an expression unlike any Thomas had ever seen her show before. In that moment, she was more beautiful to him than in all their sultry nights together.

"So it is," Alpha said. She stood up and shifted her gaze to Leila. Alpha didn't seem to know what to say. Neither did Leila. Although Leila's face still showed no welcome, at least some of her chill had thawed.

Edwards chose that moment to come forward. "We can't stay long."

Leila started at his voice. "Yes. Of course." She turned to Thomas. "We'll see you tonight."

"Thank you for coming," he said.

Leila nodded, his lawyer daughter atypically without words. Then she and Jamie left with Major Edwards.

When she and Thomas were alone, Alpha went to stand by the lake again. Thomas joined her, aware of the orderlies taking up positions on either side of them.

"Nice kid, your granddaughter," Alpha said.

"Yes." That barely touched the surface of what he felt.

"Your daughter loathes me," Alpha added.

"Give her time."

"I suppose." Alpha glanced at him. "You look good. Rested."

"Too rested," he grumbled. "My doctors won't let up on me."

She hesitated. "General Chang came to see me this morning."

The day suddenly seemed to go silent. *Waiting.* "And?"

No reply. But then she said, "They're going to give me asylum."

"I knew it!" He wanted to shout to the sky. "I knew Chang would come through."

"Don't get so excited," Alpha said dourly. "I'm still a prisoner." She didn't look displeased, though.

"I asked Chang to release you into my custody. She said they probably would if they gave you asylum. It will be some time before things are settled, though." He wanted to take her hand, but the presence of the orderlies constrained him. So instead he said, "It's a beautiful day."

Alpha looked exasperated. "Are we going to discuss the blasted weather? Why do humans always do that? It is truly boring."

Thomas laughed softly. "Come on." He set off along the shore, using his cane. Alpha walked at his side and took hold of his free hand with none of his self-conscious hesitation.

The hairs on Thomas's neck prickled. He stopped and looked back. The orderlies were coming with them.

"You can wait here," he told them. "We're just going to walk around the lake."

The two men hesitated. Then one said, "Yes, sir."

As the two men stopped, the first one said, "We have you on our trackers. If you need help, we'll know. You can also contact us with your mesh glove from anywhere on the grounds."

"I understand," Thomas said.

After he and Alpha set off again, she spoke in a low voice. "Wish I could get rid of them that easily."

He smiled. "Rank does have a few advantages."

It wasn't long before they were in the forest. The trees were losing the last of their foliage, and red and gold leaves drifted around them, lazy on the air, or crunched under their feet.

Thomas drew her to a stop. "I've wanted to do this ever since we got back." Then he kissed her soundly, good and long.

It was a while before they separated. Then she drew back and gave him one of her smoldering gazes, full of sultry promise.

Eventually they resumed their walk, until they found a bench near the lake, under the trees, where they could sit and hold each other. Thomas felt like a kid in high school having to take his girl to the park to misbehave.

"So what do your military shrinks say?" Alpha asked, leaning against him. He had his arm around her shoulders. "They think you're crazy?"

"Not crazy." Wryly he added, "Odd, yes. But stable."

"Do they want you to retire?"

"I don't think so."

"Do you want to?"

I don't know. But maybe he just didn't want to admit it. "I'd like a rest."

"What would you do if you left the Air Force?"

"Consult, probably."

"Good."

"Alpha—when this is over, however long it takes . . ."

She waited. "Yes?"

"Will you come with me?"

"Come with you where?"

"Anywhere."

She blinked—she the forma, who never needed to blink. "As your companion?"

"Yes."

"Your family wouldn't like that."

Thomas knew it wasn't going to be easy. But given enough time maybe they would accept Alpha, or at least tolerate her. "No matter how much I love them, I can't live my life to please them."

"You're sure this is what you want?"

His gaze never wavered. "Certain."

A smile came to her, one slow and somehow amazed. "Then yes. I would like to go with you."

"Good." That one word held a world of emotions he couldn't express. She had said yes. She, who could have had any man.

"Yes, well, Thomas, we have to do something about these people hanging around all the time." She motioned in the direction where they had left the orderlies. "Guards, everywhere. As long as I'm stuck here, you have to stay some nights, too, without fake orderlies wearing those I'm-going-to-rip-out-your-insides guns."

He had been having similar thoughts. "I'll see what I can do." He paused. "Alpha—"

"You have that look again."

"What look?"

"As if you're about to fall off a cliff. You never get it when you should, like if you really are about to go over the edge of something. It only comes at the strangest times, like when you want to ask how I feel about something."

Thomas felt his face heating. That had, in fact, been exactly what he had intended to ask. He ran his knuckles down her cheek. "I'll be seventy-three in two weeks."

"So?"

"It doesn't bother you that I won't take a forma body?"

"Of course it bothers me." She glowered at him. "So go on. Die. Leave me by myself after I go through all this trouble so I can be with you."

His face was doing that gentling thing again. "I'm not planning on dying for a long time."

"I'll hold you to that." Her voice softened. "Your age matters to me, Thomas, only in that it means I won't have you for long. But even if you changed your mind, it's too late. Your Air Force knows about the android. They'll have it soon."

He hadn't told her about the Alley's offer. He hadn't told anyone, not even Chang. "Then you'll take me as I am?"

"As long as you take me as I am."

He grinned at her. "Deal. Just remember, I break more easily than you."

"I won't forget." Darkly, she added, "I'll be a lot better bodyguard for you than those phony orderlies."

He took her hands. "You won't be here forever. Only until we clean up the mess Charon left."

She interlaced her fingers with his. "Thomas—"

"Yes."

"I'm glad you came today."

"Me, too."

He didn't know if he would ever come to terms with the idea that he could become like her. What mattered most was that she wanted him as he was. He could live out his limited human life or he could rethink his decision in the future, but she would stay regardless, not for his youth or strength, but for him.

To Thomas, that made her human.

Epilogue

In November 2032, Alpha received political asylum.

In May 2034, the Supreme Court ruled that Turner Pascal was an American citizen. They sidestepped the question of his humanity by reinterpreting one word in the Constitution. Just as historically "man" had often been used for both men and women, so the justices extended the word "person" in the Constitution to include someone like Pascal, who had been a citizen before becoming an EI and who passed every Turing test he was given. It didn't solve the more complex problem of how humanity would draw the line between human and machine, but it established a precedent that set debates raging, for it gave someone with an EI brain the rights of a human being.

In July 2034, the NIA contained Charon's last EI in a fully independent mesh and ended his illegal operations.

In September 2034, Sam Bryton and Turner Pascal

were married at a chapel in the Blue Ridge Mountains of Virginia.

In February 2035, the Air Force released Alpha into the custody of Lieutenant General Thomas Wharington.

In April 2036, Thomas retired from the Air Force.

In August 2036, the United States government granted Sunrise Alley a status equivalent to a sovereign nation. The question of how to define a forma, however, remained unanswered.

In December 2037, at the age of eight, Jamie Harrows completed her first class at the University of Maryland at Baltimore County. She received an A in Principles of Biomechanical Theory.

In June 2038, Thomas and Alpha moved to rural Virginia. No one knew Thomas well enough to notice how healthy and young he appeared compared to six years previous, when he had nearly lost his life to cardiopulmonary arrest.

Had anyone asked, he would have simply said that love made a man younger.

The following is an excerpt from:

The Ruby Dice

by

Catherine Asaro

Available from Baen Books

January 2008

hardcover

I

Hall of Circles

The Highton language was rife with allusions to the Carnelian Throne that symbolized the reign of the Eubian Emperor, phrases such as "He commanded with magnificence from the throne" or "His glorious Highness sat on the esteemed Throne of Carnelians" or "Only a fool would put a half-grown boy on the damn throne." None of those phrases referred to the emperor actually sitting on a chair, of course. Unfortunately, however, the Carnelian Throne did exist. And it was about as comfortable as a rock.

Jaibriol sat in the throne, leaning to one side, his elbow resting on its stone arm. He was alone in the Hall of Circles except for his guards. The room was like ice. Its white walls sparkled, designed from a composite of diamond and snow-marble. Rows of high-backed benches ringed the chamber, all snow-diamond and set with red cushions like drops of blood on frost. A white dais supported his throne, and red gems glinted in the chair, as hard and cold as the Hightons who sat atop the empire's power hierarchy.

His bodyguards were posted around the walls, three mammoths where he could see them and four others behind him. They wore the midnight uniforms of Razers, the secret police who served the emperor, their dark clothes jarring against the brilliant white walls. These Razers had so much biomech augmentation, they were considered constructs rather than human beings. Their thoughts lurked at the edges of his mind, mechanical, not quite human.

The captain of his guards waited by the dais, alert and still, his feet apart, his arms by his sides. Although his face remained as impassive as always, Jaibriol never felt ill-at-ease with him. He had selected these men over time, choosing those with no Aristo heritage.

It disturbed Jaibriol that the Aristos identified their Razers only by serial numbers. His guards seemed more human to him than the supposedly exalted Aristos. He had named the captain Vitar, because the guard resembled Jaibriol's younger brother. But he had come to think that wasn't right, either; he should have asked the Razer what he wanted to call himself.

A chime came from his wrist comm. Jaibriol lifted his arm and spoke into the mesh. "Yes?"

The voice of his personal aide, Robert Muzeson, came out of the comm. "Your joint commanders are here, Your Highness."

"Send them in," Jaibriol said. His pulse ratcheted up, and he took a breath, schooling himself to calm. He had summoned them to this frozen place rather than to his office because the presence of the throne accented his authority.

The towering doors across the hall swung open like cracks widening in ice. Vitar's biomech arm flashed as he communicated with the other Razers, and they moved into position, flanking the entrance. A retinue of military types swept into the hall, a general and an admiral, with six other officers in a crisp formation. The Razers fell in around the retinue and accompanied them down the central aisle.

General Barthol Iquar strode at the front of the group. He was Tarquine's nephew, a powerfully built man in a dark uniform. Admiral Erix Muze, a leaner man in cobalt blue, walked with him. Both commanders were Hightons, members of the highest Aristo caste, which ran the military and government. They topped the hierarchy of ESComm; together, they commanded the Eubian military.

Jaibriol remained relaxed on his throne while they came to him. He allowed neither his posture nor expression to reveal his discomfort. Their minds were great weights pressing on his, smothering him; as they came nearer, his perception shifted and they seemed like chasms that could pull him into darkness and pain and swallow his sanity. He shored up his mental shields, both protecting himself and hiding his mind, for he could never let them suspect he was a psion. He carried out this farce that defined his life, every day of every year, until he felt as if he were walking down an infinite corridor of frost.

Seeing their alabaster faces, it was hard for Jaibriol to remember they existed because of an attempt to protect empaths. That well-meant research had produced a monstrous result. The geneticists tried to mute the painful emotions empaths sensed, but instead they created a race of anti-empaths. Aristos. When an Aristo's brain detected the pain of a psion, it shunted the signals to its pleasure centers. The stronger the psion's agony, the greater the effect. Aristos considered the resulting explosion of ecstasy they experienced the greatest elevation a human being could experience. They named it "transcendence" and called the psions they tortured to make it possible "providers."

In their brutally warped logic, the Aristos believed their ability to transcend raised them into a superior form of life, and that the agony of their providers elevated them. If the Aristos ever suspected their emperor was a Ruby psion—the ultimate provider—his life would become a hell almost beyond his ability to imagine.

Almost.

Watching the approach of his commanders, Jaibriol fought to maintain his mask of indifference. Robert, his personal aide, came in after the retinue. His presence both calmed Jaibriol and stirred his guilt. Robert's unusual name came from Earth. Eubian merchants had "liberated" Robert's father from his ship. Of course they weren't merchants and they hadn't liberated anyone, but that sounded so much more palatable than saying pirates had kidnapped him and sold him into slavery. Jaibriol couldn't undo the sins of every Aristo, but he had managed to bring Robert's father to the palace and reunite him with his son after decades of unwanted separation.

The retinue stopped at the dais, and Barthol and Erix bowed to Jaibriol. None of the aides were full Aristos, so they all went down on one knee. Jaibriol had to stop himself from shifting his weight. He had never liked having people kneel to him. His parents had raised their children in secret on a world with no other people, so they never bothered with court protocols. He wasn't certain which disturbed him more, that Eubians believed all human beings except Aristos should kneel to their emperor or that he was becoming accustomed to that treatment.

He didn't immediately tell them to rise, not because he had any desire to see people kneel, but because to do otherwise would be viewed by Hightons as a weakening of his authority. Early on in his reign, he had learned the hard way: behave as expected or deepen the risk of assassination.

A memory jumped into his mind of the day ESComm had found his father and taken him away. Jaibriol had been fourteen. ESComm had wrested his father from his world of refuge without knowing the man they found had a family. After that shattering day, Jaibriol's mother had hidden her children on Earth with one of the few people she trusted, Admiral Seth Rockworth. Then she had started the Radiance War. Almost no one knew she had done it to reclaim her husband. Jaibriol had ascended to his throne with the foolish hope that he could end the hostilities between the empires of his parents, but after ten years among the Aristos, he despaired that he would ever make headway.

Finally he moved his hand, palm down, permitting the aides to stand. Although their gazes were downcast, they caught his gesture. After they rose to their feet, he stood up and descended the dais, taking his time, studying the general and admiral. Both were tall, especially Erix Muze, who stood nearly eye to eye with Jaibriol when the emperor stopped in front of them.

"I am pleased," Jaibriol said. He wasn't; he liked neither of his arrogant joint commanders. But even if they loathed him, especially Barthol, at least they were more loyal than the previous two, who had kept trying to murder him.

Jaibriol motioned toward the closest bench. He didn't invite them to sit; such a direct comment from one Aristo to another would be a profound insult.

As soon as Robert saw Jaibriol lift his hand, he spoke with deference. "General Iquar and Admiral Muze, it would please the emperor if you would join him."

The three of them took their seats on the bench, Jaibriol on one end and his commanders in its middle. It was an awkward arrangement for a conference, but he had no intention of making this easy. He was tired of their delaying tactics. If he had to spend time in their mind-torturing presence, he wanted them off balance. He had discovered that the more uncomfortable he made the Aristos around him, the less likely they were to notice his discomfort, or his "penchant" for treating non-Aristos as if they were human.

Captain Vitar stationed himself next to Jaibriol, a stark reminder of the power wielded by the emperor, that he could command ESComm's billion-credit Razers as his private bodyguards. Vitar wore the face of a mechanical killing machine with no emotions. He didn't fool Jaibriol. His guards loved, hated, laughed, and wept like other humans. He sometimes had the odd sense that Vitar enjoyed intimidating Aristos he knew Jaibriol didn't like. The Razer would of course never do anything to suggest he harbored such inappropriate sentiments, so Jaibriol could never be sure. He had difficulty picking up moods from his guards because the extensive biomech augmentation to their brains changed their brain waves.

Barthol Iquar spoke the requisite formal phrases. "You honor the Line of Iquar with your presence, Esteemed Highness."

Erix spoke. "You honor the Line of Muze, Esteemed Highness."

Jaibriol inclined his head. In the convoluted Highton language, it meant he accepted their words without rancor, but without any particular encouragement, either. To Barthol, he said, "I understand you have acquired a new corporation."

"Indeed," Barthol said, cautious. "A good business. Furniture."

Good business, indeed. The general was leaving him no openings. No matter. Jaibriol had expected this. "Perhaps I might look at your inventory. I understand you have an excellent selection of tables."

Although neither commander showed a reaction, they knew what he meant. The peace table. Their negotiations with the Imperialate. He felt the spark of their anger even with his mental barriers up. They would have to live with it. The negotiations had been stalled for years, and he was heartily sick of their maneuvers to avoid the talks.

"I will have an inventory sent to you," Barthol said smoothly.

Jaibriol just sat, letting the silence lengthen. The tactic sometimes prodded Aristos to speak, as if they couldn't bear a hole in the convoluted webs of discourse they wove. These two were too well versed in Highton to show discomfort, but their moods trickled over Jaibriol: unease and anger. Neither had any desire for peace with the Skolians. Barthol also thought him a callow youth with peculiarities that bordered on intolerable.

After several moments, Jaibriol said, "I'm sure you know best what inventory would suit my interests. Perhaps the most knowledgeable person can assist my review."

The general's eyes were hard and clear, like the gems in the Carnelian Throne. "Of course, Sire."

"I would particularly like to see any unusual pieces." Jaibriol didn't say *Skolian*, but they knew. He intended to reopen the talks, if he could convince the Skolians, and he expected at least one of his joint commanders in attendance. Barthol had a close relation to Tarquine, as her nephew, but he harbored a greater antagonism toward Jaibriol than Admiral Muze.

"We are always happy to seek the betterment of the empire," Erix Muze said.

"It pleases me to know." Jaibriol didn't doubt he meant it. He also had no doubt that "betterment of the empire" didn't include negotiations with Skolians.

He dismissed the commanders with body language, a slight shifting of his weight, a glance to the side. Suddenly Robert was there, escorting the officers away. He had developed his ability to read Jaibriol's Highton gestures to an art.

Captain Vitar directed the other bodyguards using commands Jaibriol couldn't see, except for the lights flickering on his biomech arm and those of the other Razers. The captain had biomech limbs, nodes in his spine, bioelectrodes throughout his brain, and threads and high-pressure hydraulics networking his body. Yet when Jaibriol looked into his face, he saw a man.

After his commanders were gone, Jaibriol stood up and beckoned to Vitar. The guard came over, looming above even Jaibriol, and bowed. The conduits on his dark uniform glinted. Although protocol demanded that everyone except other Aristos kneel to the emperor, Jaibriol shared one trait in common with his predecessors on the throne: he preferred his guards on their feet and ready to defend his person.

"Vitar, do you like your name?" Jaibriol asked.

"Most certainly, Sire. It is an honor." Disappointment flashed in his gaze, though he quickly hid the emotion. "But if you wish to withdraw it, I will be honored to obey your wishes."

"No, I didn't mean that." Jaibriol rubbed his chin. "I just thought you might like to choose your own."

The Razer paused only a moment, but for someone with a brain as much biomech as human, it was a long time. Then he said, "I would never presume to such. But it is a most esteemed offer."

"It's not a presumption," Jaibriol said. "If you could pick any name, what would you choose?"

Vitar thought for a moment. "Hidaka. Sam Hidaka."

"All right. If you would like, I will call you Hidaka."

For one of the few times in the years Jaibriol had known him, the captain grinned in an all-out smile. "Thank you, Sire! You are most generous."

Jaibriol didn't feel generous, he felt like a cretin. He should have asked Vitar years ago what name he preferred. No, not Vitar. Hidaka. He would have to remember.

He regarded the Razer curiously. "It's an unusual name. Did you make it up?"

The captain shook his head. "It is the name of the founder and chief executive of the most successful coffee business on Earth." Then he added, "Coffee is one of the Earth people's greatest achievements."

Startled, Jaibriol smiled. He wondered what other Aristos would say if they knew his Razers admired or even knew about any aspects of cultures outside the euphemistically named Eubian Concord, which as far as Jaibriol could see had achieved "concord" only in the Aristos' united desire to subjugate the rest of humanity.

"Well, Hidaka, you have an excellent name," Jaibriol said. "Your men may choose names as well, if they wish."

The captain bowed. "You honor us."

Jaibriol couldn't answer. It wasn't an honor, it was appalling it had taken this long for him to offer the choice.

They left the hall then, and as Jaibriol walked through the black marble halls of his palace, he brooded. He wished his joint commanders were as straightforward to deal with as his guards. He doubted he would ever convince Barthol Iquar or Erix Muze to endorse his wish for peace. And without support of the military, he didn't see how any talks with the Skolian Imperialate could even succeed.

"Jeremiah Coltman," Dehya said.

Kelric looked up from the console where he was scanning files on army deployments. He and Dehya were in a room paneled in gold and copper hues. It was one of many offices that honeycombed the hull of the Skolian Orbiter space station used as a command center by the Imperialate.

"Jeremiad what?" he asked.

Dehya regarded him from her console, a slender woman with long hair, sleek and black, streaked with white, as if frost tipped the tendrils curling around her face. Translucent sunset colors overlaid her green eyes, the only trace she had of her father's inner eyelid. Kelric didn't have the inner lid either, but he had his grandfather's metallic gold eyes, skin, and hair, modifications designed to adapt humans to a too-bright world.

"Jeremiah Coltman," she repeated. "Do you remember?"

"I've no idea," he said, rubbing his shoulder to ease his stiff muscles. He had many aches these days; he hardly recalled the years when he had been bursting with energy and youth.

"That boy from Earth," Dehya said. "About a year ago we had trouble with the Allied Worlds over him."

Kelric searched his memory, but nothing came. **Bolt,** he thought, accessing his spinal node. **You have anything on him?**

His node answered via bioelectrodes in his brain that fired his neurons in a manner he interpreted as thought. **Jeremiah Coltman was detained on a Skolian world. I'm afraid my records are spotty.**

Kelric remembered then. It had come up the day Jeejon died. He recalled little from that time, and he had recorded nothing well in the long days that followed. Even now, nearly a year later, he avoided the memories. They hurt too much.

"I thought the man they locked up was an adult," Kelric said. "A professor."

"An anthropology graduate student." Dehya was reading from her console. "He spent three years on one of our worlds while he wrote his dissertation. Huh. Listen to this. They didn't throw him in prison. They like him so much, they won't let him go home."

Kelric turned back to his work. "Can't somebody's embassy take care of it?" It surprised him that she would spend time on it. Dehya served as Assembly Key, the liaison between the Assembly and the vast information meshes that networked the Imperialate in space-time—and in Kyle space. Physics had no meaning in the Kyle; proximity was determined by similarity of thought rather than position. Two people having a conversation were "next" to each other no matter how many light-years separated them in real space. It allowed instant communication across interstellar distances and tied the Imperialate into a coherent civilization. But only those few people with a nearly extinct mutation in their neural structures could power the Kyle web. Like Dehya. As Assembly Key, she had far more pressing matters to attend than a minor incident from a year ago.

"Ah, but Kelric," she said. "It's such an interesting incident."

Damn! He had to guard his thoughts better. He fortified his mental shields. "Stop eavesdropping," he grumbled.

She smiled in that ethereally strange way of hers, as if she were only partly in the real universe. "He won a prize."

"Who won a prize?"

"Jeremiah Coltman. Something called the Goldstone." She glanced at her console. "It's quite prestigious among anthropologists. But his hosts won't let him go home to receive it. That caused a stir, enough to toggle my news monitors."

Kelric felt a pang of longing. Had he been free to pursue any career, he would have chosen the academic life and become a mathematician. He and Dehya were alike that way. Those extra neural structures that adapted their brains to Kyle space also gave them an enhanced ability for abstract thought.

"Why won't they let him go?" Kelric said. "Where is he?"

"Never heard of the place." She squinted at her screen. "Planet called Coba."

He felt as if a freighter slammed into him. Jeejon's words rushed back from that moment before she died: *You never told anyone where you were those eighteen years.*

"Kelric?" Dehya was watching him. "What's wrong?"

Mercifully, his mental shields were in place. He didn't think she could pick up anything from him, but he never knew for certain with Dehya; she had a finesse unlike anyone else. So he told the truth, as best he could. "It reminded me of Jeejon."

Sympathy softened her sculpted features. "Good memories, I hope."

He just nodded. His family believed he had been a prisoner during those eighteen years he vanished. He let them assume the Eubians had captured and enslaved him, and that he didn't want to speak of it. That was even true for the final months. But he didn't think Dehya ever fully believed it. If she suspected he was reacting to the name Coba, she would pursue the lead.

He had to escape before she sensed that his disquiet went beyond his memories of Jeejon. Dehya's ability to read his moods depended on how well the fields of her brain interacted with his. The Coulomb forces that determined those fields dropped off quickly with distance; even a few meters could affect whether or not she picked up his emotions.

He rose to his feet. "I think I'll take a break."

She spoke softly. "I'm sorry I reminded you."

His face gentled, as could happen around Dehya. She

was one of the few people who seemed untroubled by his silences and reclusive nature. "It's all right."

He left the chamber then, his stride long and slow in the lower gravity, which was forgiving to his huge size. Alone, he headed back to his large, empty house.

—end excerpt—

from *The Ruby Dice*
available in hardcover,
January 2008, from Baen Books

MERCEDES LACKEY:
MISTRESS OF FANTASY

BARDIC VOICES
The Lark and the Wren
The Robin and the Kestrel
The Eagle and the Nightingales
The Free Bards
Four & Twenty Blackbirds
Bardic Choices: A Cast of Corbies (with Josepha Sherman)

URBAN FANTASIES WITH ROSEMARY EDGHILL
Beyond World's End
Spirits White as Lightning
Mad Maudlin
Bedlam's Edge(ed.)
Music to My Sorrow

This Scepter'd Isle (with Roberta Gellis)
Ill Met by Moonlight (with Roberta Gellis)
Bedlam's Bard (with Ellen Guon)
Born to Run (with Larry Dixon)
Wheels of Fire (with Mark Shepherd)
Chrome Circle (with Larry Dixon)
The Chrome Borne (with Larry Dixon)
The Otherworld (with Larry Dixon & Mark Shepherd)

AND MORE!
Werehunter
Fiddler Fair
The Fire Rose
The Wizard of Karres (with Eric Flint & Dave Freer)
The Shadow of the Lion (with Eric Flint & Dave Freer)
This Rough Magic (with Eric Flint & Dave Freer)
Brain Ships (with Anne McCaffrey & Margaret Ball)
The Sword of Knowledge (with C.J. Cherryh Leslie Fish,
& Nancy Asire)

Available in bookstores everywhere.
Or order online at our secure, easy to use website:
www.baen.com
If not available through your local bookstore send this coupon and a check
or money order for the cover price(s) + $1.75 s/h to Baen Books, Dept. BA,
P.O. Box 1403, Riverdale, NY 10471. Be sure to include full name &
address for shipping. Delivery can take up to eight weeks.

IF YOU LIKE...
YOU SHOULD TRY...

DAVID DRAKE
David Weber

DAVID WEBER
John Ringo

JOHN RINGO
Michael Z. Williamson
Tom Kratman

ANNE MCCAFFREY
Mercedes Lackey

MERCEDES LACKEY
Wen Spencer, Andre Norton
Andre Norton
James H. Schmitz

LARRY NIVEN
James P. Hogan
Travis S. Taylor

ROBERT A. HEINLEIN
Jerry Pournelle
Lois McMaster Bujold
Michael Z. Williamson

HEINLEIN'S "JUVENILES"
Rats, Bats & Vats series by Eric Flint & Dave Freer

HORATIO HORNBLOWER OR PATRICK O'BRIAN
David Weber's Honor Harrington series
David Drake's RCN series

HARRY POTTER
Mercedes Lackey's Urban Fantasy series

THE LORD OF THE RINGS
Elizabeth Moon's *The Deed of Paksenarrion*

H.P. LOVECRAFT
Princess of Wands by John Ringo

GEORGETTE HEYER
Lois McMaster Bujold
Catherine Asaro

GREEK MYTHOLOGY
Pyramid Scheme by Eric Flint & Dave Freer
Forge of the Titans by Steve White
Blood of the Heroes by Steve White

NORSE MYTHOLOGY
Northworld Trilogy by David Drake
A Mankind Witch by Dave Freer

ARTHURIAN LEGEND

Steve White's "Legacy" series
The Dragon Lord by David Drake

SCA/HISTORICAL REENACTMENT

John Ringo's "After the Fall" series
Harald by David D. Friedman

SCIENCE FACT

Kicking the Sacred Cow by James P. Hogan

CATS

Larry Niven's Man-Kzin Wars series

PUNS

Rick Cook
Spider Robinson
Wm. Mark Simmons

VAMPIRES

Wm. Mark Simmons